Delicate

stories of light and desire

D0962883

Other books by Mary Sojourner—

Sisters of the Dream
DreamWeaving
Sister Raven, Brother Hare

Delicate

stories of light and desire

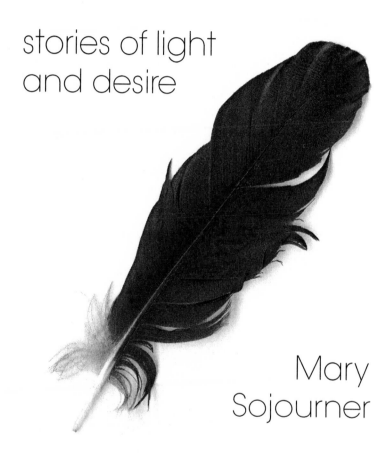

Mary
Sojourner

Nevermore Press
Flagstaff, Arizona
2001

NEVERMORE PRESS
HC30 #14
Flagstaff, Arizona 86001

First Edition
Limited to 500 copies
01 02 03 04 5 4 3 2 1

Printed in the
United States of America
ISBN 0-9709084-7-4
Library of Congress Control Number: 2001116681

Book design: Fretwater

Some of the stories reproduced here were
originally published, some in different form,
in *Story, Nimrod, Heresies, Northern Lights,
Chicago Tribune, the Sun, New Times, City,*
and the anthologies *Walking the Twilight I & II*

Dedicated to All
that make up these stories—
light,
sandstone and basalt,
desert rivers,
mountains,
honor,
vengeance,
and beloved friends.

Contents

 Bear House

I'M LIKE A TEENAGER when the phone rings. Generation Duh, ever hopeful, stomach lurching, heart racing, all of which would make sense under other circumstances. For instance, if I truly was fifteen and there was a potential boyfriend, or if I was actually writing enough to engender massive public approval. None of those circumstances is true, so when the phone rings and I jump, having not had the self-discipline to turn off the tone so I can get in some hard time at the computer, I feel guilty. Worse yet, I feel reprieved.

"Sheila," this husky voice says, "Sheila?"

There are no more words, just sobs, and the sound of somebody choking and coming up for air.

"Who is this?" I ask.

There is silence.

"It's me," somebody whispers and I know it's Rae.

"God," I say, "what is it?"

"Just a second," she says. "I have to get some tissues. I didn't think I'd lose it like this."

"It's your dime," I say, "you want to call me back?"

There's no reply. I hear her snuffling and cussing in the other room. I can picture her, big and fierce and truly blonde, I can see the room, lush plants and perfect hand-thrown pots shining like agate and anywhere from five to seven cats lounging in the late morning sun. I imagine her big, splayed fingers, the nails never quite free from clay and I see her gaze, intent as a hawk's, if a hawk had ice-blue eyes. She picks up the phone. I put the computer to sleep.

"I'm positive," she says.

"You've never been positive a day in your life," I say.

She is the most cynical woman I know. Something else occurs to me.

"What do you mean? You're fifty-seven. You had a hysterectomy when you were forty. No way you're pregnant."

"No," she says, "the other." She's off again, in a flash-flood of hard wet noises.

"Wait," I say. "No."

"Yes."

We are both quiet.

"Come on," I say, "you can't be. You've had the sex-life of a marble."

"No," she says. "I am. One charming old guy. And me going, 'oh well, that doesn't happen to grandmothers.' That's all it took."

I am furious. Death always makes me furious. And in my book, what Rae is telling me is she's dying.

"Okay," I say. "Just positive, or Kaposi's, or that lung crap, or what?"

"*Just positive.* Oh yeah, no big deal, just positive."

I cry. I go from icily furious to head down on the computer keyboard, phone clutched to my ear, what I can't shape in words howling into the keys.

"Oh great," Rae says. "My friend, the former mental health professional."

"Shut up," I say. "Just shut up."

We eat a couple bucks worth of long-distance silence, her hiccuping, me trying to make myself breathe. The only other time I cried like this was when Daniel, my one true love, took off and it was Rae walked me through that one.

"Okay," I say, "what do you need?"

We are both part of the great sisterhood of single aging women. Most of us have learned to rely on A: ourselves, and Z: one another and A to Z, combinations of those options depending on the severity of the crisis. Crises for single aging women range from the fuzzy spot on the mammogram, to five years since the last time you slept with another human being, to one MBA or one electronic gadget being hired to replace you and two other employees, the difference between the MBA and the gadget being negligible.

"What I need," Rae says, "is to hear the lab tech was drunk and made a mistake."

"Well?"

"No luck, got a second opinion. This is it."

"So."

"So. I need sun. I need you. I need to see places I've never seen, eat a ton of good Mexican food, see light that makes me want to fool around with shapes and glazes when I get home. I need to dance around those See-dough-now woo-woo circles, try anything anybody tells me will hold this thing off."

This last is a shock. She visited me four years ago. We wandered around the little New Age town south of here. She named it See-dough-now, as in the Nouvelle California ladies with perfect nails, and power pyramids in their shops see you, see dough, and want it now. Rae's final word on it had been, "The Town That Tee Shirts Made."

"Are you nuts?" I ask.

"Maybe," she says. "I do not want to die. I most especially do not want to die with my brain turning to blue jello. If anything can stop that, I'll try it."

"Come out," I say. "Tomorrow."

"No," she says, "I've got Charlevoix this summer and that big show in Maryland. I won't be free 'til September. I'll come then."

"Rae," I say patiently, "what are you going to need money for?"

"I don't," she says, "I just need to keep doing what I do."

She's a potter, not artsy-fartsy, but steady, centered as the bowls and cups and lamps she turns out on her wheel, winter after winter, spring after spring, when it's cool enough up North to fire the kiln without succumbing to heat stroke, when it's cold enough that the lady lawyers and people with terminally great hair won't come out to a craft show, no matter how much they need the perfect piece for the summer place.

"I know," I say. "I understand."

Single aging women earn their own livings. Most of us have for years. We know just enough about vehicles to bully garage guys. We can make minor electrical repairs. We, very likely, raised our kids by ourselves and, in addition to being gourmet cooks, make the best love you ever went cross-eyed over. We are good at many things, and great at a few. What we hate is the glitch, the moment when everything stops, when the house is abruptly quiet and nobody needs us and what we've got is what we see, our beautiful solitude, our lives alone.

"Sheila," Rae says.

"Yeah?"

"This is between you and me. Get it?"

"I don't know," I say. "I can't do this alone."

"You're not," she says, "I am."

"Fine."

"Hey," she says, "when it's all over, you can write about it. But, not 'til then."

"Lovely," I say.

"I'll sign a release form," she says. "In September. On your back porch."

RAE TAKES the train. "I want to see the glorious width and breadth of this great country of ours," she tells me.

I've taken the train. I know that what she really wants to do is sit in the club car and flirt. She tells me that the diagnosis has removed her from the front lines, but that, in no way, is she going to give up being an operative. Her one and only husband served a half tour in Nam, got sent back with one of those Million Dollar leg-wounds and got sympathy-laid for the next twenty-five years. When he's lonely, which is usually about six months after he marries the next wonderful woman, he heads out to a little Thai restaurant and makes quiet references to The Tunnels. It's never failed him. Did *he* get this nasty, creepy, fatal disease? No. Tell me God isn't a man.

Rae picked up that Nam lingo from him, which he still uses as abundantly as any other wannabe Platoonik, except for the term, Rear Echelon Mother which he was, his $1,000,000 wound caused by his own gun. Though he, that marriage, and that war are twenty-five years cold, she still talks like an Army wife.

"I guess he's still my skinny grunt with the perpetual hard-on," she'll say. Most of her friends are no longer kind enough to not point out that he is still just that, and that his gun is aimed in other than her direction.

I drive into town to pick her up. Our sixteen square blocks of neon shimmer against the dark mountains. The moon is in Venus, a frail crescent riding above the northernmost peak. I've rolled down the window and the rosemary scent of Ponderosa pine forest rushes past me. I feel brutally healthy, grateful—and guilty. Why her? Why not me, who's had the sex life of a boy mink and the dating skills of an amoeba. Bump me, I'm yours.

The train is miraculously on time. I stand on the platform, three green chile enchiladas in a take-out bag in my right hand, nothing in my left but the hug I wrap around her as soon as she is within range. She looks great. She's wearing the big-lady uniform, dark tights, a bulky sweater, suede high-heeled boots. She's taller than me by a couple inches. In the boots she can rest her chin on my head. Which she does.

"I love it here," she says. "There were two young cowboys who got off in Winslow. They told me the West was made for women like me."

I pull away and grin at her.

"You've never looked better," I say. "When did you start wearing make-up?"

"Around Raton," she says. "when those sweet boys got on. Bartender loaned me hers."

We wrap our arms around each other. I bump her with the enchilada box.

"Food," I say, "real Mexizona food."

"What I want to do," she says, "is pick up a couple bottles of Dos Equis, a lime, a pint of mocha ice cream, and have a picnic in that little park in front of City Hall."

"You *want?*" I say. "The Great Mother of Us All *wants* something?"

"This diagnosis is an awful miracle," she says. "A late-for-it, stupid, terrifying miracle."

"It's clear," I say, "that the epiphanies have started early."

"Easy," she says, "I'm not in pain. I can think. I am not exhausted by the effort to take a breath. I've been reading. I've been going to the weekly Positive Opportunities support group. And for once in my life, I've been listening."

"So?"

"I figure I better do the good part now."

She begins to cry.

"Oh shit," I say. "God damn it."

I take her big hand in mine.

"I know," she says between sniffles, "you don't know how to do this."

"I don't."

"Keep it simple," she says. "Ice cream. *Cerveza.* "

"There's a brewery-pub-espresso-over-priced deli on the corner of the next street."

"This is wonderful," she says. "I had killer sales at Charlevoix and Gaithersburg. I will be able to afford the simple charms of this unspoiled western town."

The park is pure emerald under the new Victorian street lights. The moon hangs fat and glorious in the southeast. Couples are everywhere, sitting on the new antique benches, lying beneath the pines, huddled together on the hillock that rises to the war memorial pylon.

"Boocoo boom-boom tonight," Rae says pensively.

"Rae," I say and hand her the enchiladas. "Eat. That war is over."

"Yeah," she says, "just tell me the part again about how numb-nuts and Nam are long ago and far-away."

"Nam is the place to be seen this vacation season," I say. "Besides, are you sure he was there?

"I am," she says. "There's a gay guy, Eddie, in my group. He was over there. He keeps talking about how it is to walk with death. They dragged him over there in '69, up near Lang Vei, him and a bunch of other Friggin' New Guys. He says this is like that. Death all-the-time on your ass, not knowing where it's coming from, can't tell a cold from the Big One, just like they couldn't tell a nice old lady with melons in her basket, from VC."

"Plus," I say, "you just might make it through for a while and then what?"

"Thanks," she says and takes a bite of enchilada. "Listen. I think we've got to be careful that we don't spend this whole trip talking about nothing but what I've got."

"Right," I say. For the life of me, I can't, at that moment, figure how we're going to talk about anything else. "You bet."

She opens a Dos Eq, rubs the lip of the bottle with lime. "Yes. This is perfect."

"So," I say, "tell me about the kids."

"Jerree is pregnant again." Rae looks at me over the top of the bottle.

"Nifty," I say. She snorts.

"J. Ellen made one hundred, seventy-six thousand, eight hundred and fifty-three dollars last year. Jen is regularly attending Love Your Child Within meetings and thinks I need to confront my eating disorder. Judy fell in love with a guy ten years younger than she is who is a professional scooter designer." She takes a big bite of enchilada. "And yours?"

"Steve is working sixty-five hours a week in corporate headquarters in Bangkok. Max is in Nepal teaching Tibetan refugees English. Ceily is raising Mollie twenty-two hundred miles east of here. Cal is too far east to write or call."

I shrug.

"Well, I told them I needed space."

We look at each other. In the green light, Rae looks like a hologram of her probable future. I know I'm not supposed to be thinking that way.

"So," I say and I can't think of one appropriate thing to follow. I am sitting on a historically accurate park bench with pale globe lights like perfect little moons in the heart of the most wonderful place I've ever lived. It is my second-favorite month of the year and I am with one of my best friends in my whole life and I can only pick up an enchilada, which I do not want, and take a bite out of it.

"They are very busy," Rae says. "My four. In some ways, they might as well be in Bangkok."

This information is a shock. Rae and her tribe have performed *Mother Courage* for years, going forward, husbandless, fatherless, through want and weird clothes, into a future of matriarchal solidarity. Christmases together, Easters, Fourth of July, Friday nights in front of the fire with Rolling Rock beer and pizza and a rating system for the girls' suitors. When Jerree got married, Mom and *Les* Girls held a bachelorette party that drew down two town cop cars and the discovery of Rae's private basement mushroom plot next to the pickled peaches.

"What are you telling me?" I ask.

"Things change," she says.

"Why?"

"I'm not sure."

"Is it because—" I stop. How do you say it? In those circles where it is common, how do people talk about it? It occurs to me that I'll have to go to the town's alternative bookstore and read up on this.

"You're thinking you better read about this, aren't you?" Rae says. "Sheila, this isn't quite like being a woman who loves too much or a fudge-junkie or whatever is currently the national diagnosis."

"…you told them you're positive?" I finish.

"No," she says. "I didn't tell them."

"So," I say, "you're going to just soldier on 'til something shows up and let them have their young womanhoods, right?"

"Right," she says.

"Hey," I say, "it's exactly what I would do."

"Besides," Rae mumbles.

We say it in unison.

"I don't want anybody to feel sorry for me."

SHE WON'T stay with me. I live in a cabin with an outhouse and she is of Germanic origins.

"I need a shower," she says, "and a bathroom where nobody sees me hike up to it in my baby dolls."

She rents a room in a old turquoise adobe motel in the heart of town. The flamingo neon of the Indian restaurant next door lights up her evenings, she tells me, and, at dawn, she can sit on the stoop, drink her coffee, and know that she's had one more day. I begin to realize that she is here not only to see me, but to see what she sees when she is out on that stoop, watching early morning traffic, studying how the light moves on the mountains in new patterns. The aspen begin to go pure yellow. Most mornings, a wreath of vapor circles the tallest peaks. Snow dusts the blue-black rock and is gone. She tells me all of that and she says that glazes and bowls and goblets are taking form in her mind.

She borrows my truck, takes off for hours. When she returns, we sit in the sun on my back porch. We drink coffee. She is quieter than I have known her. She doesn't tell me where she goes, but she brings me dried seed-pods, tiny geodes, feathers, a couple of perfect black-on-white pottery sherds which we agree neither of us will remember that she picked up. One fine afternoon, she brings home a grease-spotted paper bag and pulls out two slabs of Navajo fry bread.

"I'm getting used to you being here," I say.

We are sitting on my backporch, eating fry bread and honey. Rae is perched on the top porch-step. We face south where we can watch the bird-feeder stuck in the two-trunked pine. My cat, Vicious, chitters at the Steller's jays. They scream and dive-bomb the food and drop peanut shells on her head. She is furious, her tail switching back and forth. I think of Bette Davis playing Queen Elizabeth I.

"Has it ever occurred to you," Rae says, "that there is something faintly peculiar about loving birds and setting up this avian claymore?"

"Claymore?"

"Land-mine," she says. "Directional."

"Cats eat birds," I say. "And, in Vicious' case, play ping-pong with them. She does it whether I feed them or not."

"In all honesty," Rae says, "it reminds me of your youthful dating style."

"In all honesty" I say, "youthful appears to have been my *only* dating style."

We both sigh.

"Daniel," I say, "loved my dating style. Fabulous meals and then mutual pouncing. He can play ping-pong with me whenever he wants."

"That was fifteen years ago," Rae says.

I dip my frybread in my coffee. Nothing dies quicker than frybread and nothing brings it back to life like coffee.

"Christ, this is great," I say. We're both quiet for a minute.

"So how is Daniel?" I ask. One of us has to get this obligatory Q & A over with.

"He's happy. I see him maybe twice a year. He's got rentals and a cellular phone and he still looks like a pirate."

"What else?" I look down into my coffee. I remember to breathe.

"She's older than he is. Three kids, nearly grown. They're all living in that old place on Barkin Street."

"Thank you," I say. "That's enough." Rae tears off a corner of frybread, scatters it in my fire-pit. The Steller's jays begin a long, involved analysis of her gesture.

"You haven't ever let go," she says, "our Positive Opportunities facilitator says we can't move on 'til we let go. She says that at every meeting and somebody always reminds her that, in our situations, we don't exactly want to move on."

"There it is," I say.

"What happened to Wiley?" she asks. "The last time we talked, you said he'd moved into town."

"Well," I said, "the ol' wildcat himself is marrying my former dear friend, Rolynne. He, who believed it was suffocating to a man's free spirit to own property, bought a nice house up on the hill, and, when last seen, was following Rolynne into the local Santa-Fe-tasteful furniture store. I suspect that if I ever have the heart to drive by their place, there will be a polymer resin coyote in the front yard next to their Greenpeace banner."

"Letting-go," Rae says, "never your strong suit."

"I'm over it," I say. "It's weird. I didn't feel much about this one. Almost three years together, me and Wiley, a personal best for me since Daniel, and the most I feel is irritated."

"Well," she says. "Well."

The light begins to cool. My neighbor Jake pokes his head around the corner of the cabin.

"You guys want company?" he asks. "It's beautiful out here and I can't read another page."

Jake is a wiry little guy who rows the Big Colorado in the summer and hates college the rest of the year. He's thirty-nine, a sophomore. He's never been married and he rides a stripped-down Kawasaki. I love his hair. It's black and shining as the raven feathers that drift down from the pines. He's pulled it back in a pony-tail and on him, that's not a cliché. When he wears tank tops, which he does 'til mid-October, you can see what appear to be skinny claws emerging from his shoulder-blade. It's a tattoo. He got it when he had ninety days without cocaine.

"The monkey on my back is me," he tells anybody who asks. "All I have to do is look in the mirror to scare myself shitless. Scared shitless is the only way I won't do it again."

"Sit down," I say. "Rae brought fry bread. You want coffee?"

"Oh no," he says, "not me."

We laugh. He drinks maybe fifteen cups of coffee a day. His P.O. tells him he's lucky it's legal. He tells her he knows it. I fix him up a cup with brown sugar and half 'n' half. He pulls off a piece of frybread and dunks it. Rae watches him. She is grinning. This evening, the tank-top is fuschia and against it, in this soft, moonstone light, Jake's dark skin looks better than the coffee he's drinking.

"Rae," he says, "you can't go back."

"I know," she says. "But I've got to."

"Why?"

"My work," she says. "You can't just disappear from the craft circuit. You're gone one year, you're dead."

"Same with the Riv," Jake says. "All those young hunks are lined up waiting for an old geezer like me to falter."

"You come live with me," Rae says. "We'll split the rent." We all grin at each other.

"You and your friends," Jake says to me, "are the kind of women men ought to sell their souls for."

"And you," I say, "should set up basic training for guys over fifty."

Jake stands up, kisses the top of my head.

"Thanks, Sheila," he says. "I gotta get back to Piaget and those Swiss babies. You never know when it's going to come in handy."

Jake met a bunch of Rez kids in rehab. They all snuck out to share a joint. They told him how much they hated school. Nothin' but *Belecana* history. No old Navajo stories. No decent thrasher tunes. Nothin' for a bro to do. Jake, being the kind of guy who ran Class 10 Crystal Rapid on 'shrooms, got fire in his eye and told them he'd get his fuckin' degree and come up there to teach. They could count on it. Cause he'd show.

"Whoa," he spins on his heel, "I forgot to ask you. My Archeo prof is taking us down to Honanki next weekend. Do some clean-up. Some touron sprayed the petroglyphs. He asked us to bring volunteers." He grins and he is five years old. "I spaced it. Could you guys help me out?"

"What's Honanki?" Rae asks. "What's a touron?"

"Touron. Tourist-moron. Honanki. House of the Bear. Beautiful. In a cliff. You look out over a valley. This time of year it's like pure gold."

"A ruin?" Rae asks. She is hot for ruins.

"Sinagua," Jake says. "Eleventh century. So beautiful." He looks at me. "Right?"

I nod. I remember an April full moon night, Wiley and me and Rolynne and her husband, Mark. Mark had put Copland's *Appalachian Spring* on the truck stereo and opened both doors. The sun was going molten in the west, the moon already flooding Honanki's red walls with silver. Wiley and Rolynne and Mark had been pounding beers all day. I can't anymore, so I fled up into the rocks, following the clear call of an owl. The sunset was behind me and then, the sound of a man crying. When I finally turned, the sky was the color of ripe cantaloupe. Wiley was patting Mark on the shoulder. Mark waved me down.

When I reached the two of them, the light had begun to cool and Mark said to Wiley, "Do you know the words to this?"

He waved hugely at the music drifting around us. I remember thinking that it was as if we were held in a great scarlet bowl, the four of us and the music…sweet evening pouring in, filling the moment to overflowing.

"Ohmygod," Mark said, "you guys are my best friends ever in my whole life. You gotta know the words."

He put his arm around my shoulders and pulled Wiley and me into a three-way hug. Wiley looked over Mark's shoulder. His eyes were focussed on something I couldn't see. I leaned my head on his big chest.

"*Tis a gift to be simple*," Mark sang and, drunk as he was, his voice was beautiful, "*tis a gift to be free.*"

What overflowed in my heart was soft and blue as the light around us.

"Mark," I said. "Wiley." And then, I could not stay there in that beery embrace. My breath twisted. I wanted to feel what they were feeling and I knew I couldn't. I stepped back. Mark looked at me.

"Damn it, Sheila," he said, "where are you? I want you here."

I remember tapping the side of his beer can.

"Not here," I said, "not anymore," and when I looked up, Wiley was walking away. Moonlight poured over the perfect walls of Honanki. The world was silver. And I was all alone.

JAKE TOUCHES my arm. "You okay?"

"Yes," I say. "I got lost for a minute. Honanki is perfect. Not Sinagua though. Early Hopi. Parrot clan, maybe."

Jake puts his hands together in front of him and bows.

"So sorry," he says.

He knows how I feel about anthro-archeo-academics. Figuring out history, making up names when all they have to do is ask the Hopi, shut up, and listen.

"Sheila," Rae says, "you can be such a pain in the ass. Once a Catholic, always a Catholic."

"There's wrong," I say, "and there's right. Making up stories about people who have perfectly good truth about themselves is wrong."

Rae looks at me. I shiver. If anybody makes up stories, it's Modern Romance me.

"You'll go." Jake says. "How could you not?"

"There it is," I say.

He kisses us both on the cheek and walks away through the mint growing at the side of the cabin. The scent floods the air, wild and green.

"Do you really want to go?" Rae asks.

"Sure," I say. "Why?"

"You looked funny," she says and looks up into my face.

"I need to go," I say. "I haven't been there since…I mean…I think they had already started up. I think Wiley was staring off to where he thought Rolynne was."

"Excuse me," Rae says gently, "Maybe you could tell me the whole story."

So I do.

Rae spends the night. Jake tells us we have to be ready to leave at 5 A.M. because as the light shifts, the petroglyphs change. The desert bighorn that leaps out at dawn disappears at noon. The Snake priests striding across the red-rock at 3 P.M. are nowhere in sight by early morning. *Masau'u*, He Who Watches, the silent Lord of Life and Death, is gone through the day. Only at twilight, when the aqua light falls cool and fading, does he stare out at you, his mouth a great O, his eyes staring at you and seeing that which feeds him.

"Masau'u," Rae says sleepily. She's lying on my therma-pad on my floor. I've thrown a quilt over her and, with her sun-burnt cheeks and half-closed eyes she could be a kid on a camping trip. "You said he eats people?"

"No," I say. "That's just what I say when I pray." I stop. I'm embarrassed. The last thing Rae and I would have ever discussed was prayer.

"When you pray you say something to Masau'u about eating people?" she whispers, and giggles.

"No." I can't believe I'm going to tell her this. "I turn to the west…actually, I turn to the west after I face east and south. I'm outdoors usually." I stop.

She is quiet. I wonder if she is asleep.

"Are you asleep?" I whisper.

"No," she says, "keep going."

"Well, I face east and I say some kind of prayer, and then south, and then in the west…I talk to whatever eats that which is no longer necessary." I pause. "And then I face north, which if I'm here, is toward the mountains, and I ask for help getting older."

"What a good idea," Rae says.

I wait for her to say more. She is silent. I realize she is asleep.

The alarm buzzes at 4 A.M. I whack it. It falls on the floor.

"Sheila?"

"It's time to get up."

"I'm freezing."

I pull on my sweatshirt and socks and stumble into the dark living-room. I light the morning candle.

"Where are the lights?" Rae asks.

"I light a candle first," I say. She fumbles under her pillow, pulls out her flashlight, and shines it on my face.

"Why?"

"I told you," I say. "It makes me feel good."

"Shei-la?" she says, "Hon-ey? This isn't like you."

"I know." I say. "I can't talk about it now. Let me get some coffee. It's no big deal."

"It's okay," Rae says. "Just promise me one thing?"

"What." I step out of the flashlight's beam. I know Rae's mind. I know she's going to say something like, Warn me if you're going to start speaking in tongues.

"If you know anything that can help me," she says, "you'll tell me."

She huddles down deeper into the quilt.

"Rank," she says. "Mornings."

"What I do with the candle," I say, "is I light it and then I feel slightly encouraged and I agree that I'll consider what appears before me during the day."

Rae sits up.

"I can do that much," she says. She wraps the quilt around her and stands in front of the candle.

"Would you go in the kitchen?" she says.

I know how she feels. I have known for a while, and I suspect it's why the Hopi have closed their dances to outsiders. I go into the kitchen. I feed the cats, which on this particular morning, requires a lot of noise. I slam cans and doors. I talk to Vicious and Bad and Jaco. They don't look up. When Rae comes into the kitchen, they are head down in their bowls. She could probably drop dead right there and they'd go on eating.

"Well," she says, "I did it."

I nod. I realize I am going about this as delicately as I once would have listened to a woman talk about sex.

"I held the candle and I couldn't figure out the directions, so I just talked to all of it at once. I told the guy in the west that I am not ready to be eaten." She snorts. "And that is the first time in my life I ever said that to any man."

I grin.

"Apparently you're still necessary," I say. "Here's your coffee. Kona. The real thing. Here's to the simple life."

She lifts the cup to her wide, beautiful mouth.

"I don't want to die alone," she says. We stare at each other.

"If you need me..."

She doesn't let me finish.

"No," she says, "not you, because I want to die at home and you can't just take off for as long as it might take."

"That's true," I say. I almost wish I was married to a nice, safe, rich man so I could do just that. "But I'll figure out how to be there...whenever."

"I know," she says. "Let's sit in the living-room, drink this here cowgirl cawfee, look at the holy candle, and talk trash."

JAKE PULLS up in the Department's navy-blue van. We are the last people to be collected. I look around. Judgement rises in me as though I had the right. Thirteen charming, middle-aged people in Patagonia and REI and Grammici hiking gear, the requisite November–May couple, eight single women, two gay guys, and Dr. Chuck Collum.

Rae catches my scan, catches the stifled disappointment in my eyes.

"We never stop hoping, do we?" she whispers in my ear.

"Never," I say.

"Who's the guy with all the pockets and flaps on his jacket?"

"Dr. Collum."

"Chuck," Jake says, "you want me to go Route 17 or down the canyon?"

"Chuck?" Rae whispers.

"Not to you," I say. "Jake is the only one who calls him that. To you, he's Dr. Collum."

"It's 1994," Rae says, "that went out with Nehru suits."

"This is Arizona," I say. She nods.

"Route 17," Collum says.

May, of the November–May couple, raises her hand. She is slender, almost ferret-faced. She's outfitted herself at the local hip earth-wear shop, black tights, lilac ragg socks, purple-and-gray hiking boots. She's pulled her slightly altered blonde hair back in a pony-tail and she's wearing the requisite cool baseball cap. The logo says *Earth First!* I doubt it.

"Dr. Collum," she says, "I read an article in *Archeology Today* that suggested we could do more harm than good if we try to clean off the graffiti."

She sounds just like Rolynne. I hate her immediately. November, a fat guy with a beard and about a thousand bucks' worth of L.L. Bean boots, vest, shirt, shorts, pack, sunglasses and Tilley hat, stares out the window. You can't tell if he is uneasy with her amateur archeologyitis, or just hung-over. He reminds me of Wiley. I figure either the morning prayers didn't work or I am a little nuts.

"Yes," Collum says, "I read that piece. We're trying something different here. A different approach. No solution, just water. But thank you for the input."

She smiles primly and sits down. November keeps looking out the window. She flushes. I see her pick something off his fleece sleeve. He grunts. Wiley, for sure.

"Ya know," Rae says, "there are those moments when my solitude shimmers before my eyes like a Mo-nay waterlily."

"Yes," I say. I am briefly grateful.

Collum smiles at us. "Are there any other questions?" he asks.

"Who, on earth, bought you that jacket?" Rae hisses in my ear.

"Excuse me?" he says.

"My friend was asking me," I say, "do we need a special outfit for this? You know. Decontaminated, or something?"

Collum considers this. "Oh no," he says, "all we're going to do is take plain water and cotton rags and gently, gently wash away what we can."

"Oh good," Rae says, "I don't do windows."

Collum looks puzzled. "No," he says, "there are no windows at Bear House."

May pipes up. "These were built," she says authoritatively, "in the *early* 1100s. Anasazi. Before windows as we know them."

"Now Anasazi," Rae says, and she has suddenly acquired a vague, but brightly curious look, "that's like Hopi, right?"

Jake's neck goes red. Collum rears back a little on his heels. May leans forward in her seat.

"Anasazi is a period," Collum says. He looks hard at Rae. "I'll be briefing all of you once we're at the site." He turns and sits down.

May leans over and taps her arm.

"Technically," she says, "Anasazi represents a period in pre-history. The people were here, then gone. Poof, like that. Nobody knows what happened."

Rae wrinkles her brow. "Didn't they disappear about 1100? I think I read that in a *National Geographic*."

The truth is we spent one intensely caffeinated night arguing this with

Jake while he broiled us steaks and told us how much he loved arguing with smart women.

"Yes," May says. November has fallen asleep. He is snoring.

"Well," Rae says, "since that one village up at Hopi was settled sometime in 1100, don't you think they might have just headed up there?" She smiles.

"Oh no," May says, "I took a docents' course at the museum and they told us emphatically that the ruins and carbon dating show that we just don't know where they went." I hear Rollyne, knowing the last word on everything, good girl getting it right. I want to go home.

"Hmmmmm," Rae says. I've heard her say the same thing when some couple tells her that the glaze on the big pot doesn't quite go with the paint in the front hall.

"You know," Rae says, "I have so often felt that way myself."

May looks blank.

"Just didn't know where I went."

"Oh?" May says. "I'm afraid I don't follow you." She smiles sweetly, flips down her dark glasses and snuggles in against November's thick side.

"Don't you just love it," Rae whispers to me, "when these nice older men take their young friends out on excursions. I bet he's a professor and she's a little student."

Dr. Collum stands up again. He starts to tell us interesting facts about the settling of the valley. He says "these simple but wise people," a lot. I count the flaps on his L.L. Bean jacket. There are ten. I wonder if I could sleep 'til we get where it is we're going.

"This is a little tricky," I say.

"What?" Rae asks.

"Being here. I didn't think I would feel anything. But I do."

Jake has parked us in the same place Wiley and I parked the day of the night of the beginning of the end. I look around at juniper and agave and the dull green blades of yucca. I remember staring at a blooming cactus to try to clear my mind for what I was going to say. I remember telling Wiley that Rolynne had told me I was too good to him. I remember the strange way he looked at me. The silence. And then, how he had pointed to the cactus flowers and said, this guy whose conversational themes were limited to beer, beer, boats, duct tape, and beer, "Look, honey, aren't those...I mean I don't mean to change the subject, but aren't those flowers pretty?" I remember looking at him and knowing. Not knowing anything specific, but feeling that skipped beat in the air.

Rae and I are sitting in the van alone. Everyone else has cheerfully soldiered on, Jansport daypacks and calibrated water bottles and purple fanny-packs bouncing behind them. I watch them climb the trail to the ledge. May has charged ahead and is chatting brightly with Jake. November is sitting on a boulder at the foot of the slope. He is smoking a cigarette and he is sweating hard. Collum walks up to him and points to the cigarette. I can't hear anything, but I see November stub the smoke out on his heel and field-strip it. He waits 'til Collum is climbing the trail, flips him the bird and lights another cigarette.

"I don't think November is a professor," Rae says mildly.

"You can't tell anymore," I say. "There's a bunch of them at the college who ride Harleys. I find it personally embarrassing...you know how if you see somebody our age acting all girlie?"

"I do," she says. She looks at me. I'm wearing plaid flannel shorts, black high-tops and a hooded flannel shirt.

"Hey," I say, "I've always dressed this way."

She pats my hand. "It's true. I figured that was why Daniel loved you. You were the only other human being who dressed so he looked good."

I burst into tears. They are the first romantic ones I've cried since Wiley sat up in bed at 1:21 A.M. on April Fool's Day, 1993 and said, "I have to leave. I feel trapped. I'm not romantically involved with you anymore." And, I said, "Is there someone else?" And, he said, "No, I swear it."

"I hate this," I say. Rae puts her arm around me. I bury my face in her warm neck and I let loose.

"Hang on," I say. "This is supposed to be the other way around."

"I don't think so," she says. "Not right now."

"Duh," I say. I am crying so hard I'm scared I'll have a stroke.

"Is it Daniel?" she says. "Still? After fourteen years?"

"Yes," I say, "and no. It's all of it. From Daniel to Wiley and everyone in between. And I'm fifty-four and I'm scared to death there won't be anymore. Ever."

Rae holds me. I keep thinking I'm supposed to be the one comforting her. This trip is for her. She's supposed to be out there looking at those nine-hundred-year-old Desert Big-horns and priests and killer Gods of Life and she's supposed to be learning something, something that will grant her the grace to stay truly alive long enough to die.

"Sheila," I hear her say. She sounds a little stern.

"What." I say. No question, just flat, just WHAT DO YOU WANT FROM ME. I admit I'm a mess, I admit I have the friendship capabilities of a liver fluke.

"We don't have to get out of this bus," she says. "We can stay here if you want."

"I love you," I say. "Rae, I really love you."

"Thanks," she says. We sit quietly. I look out. Collum and his drones are moving up over the rocks. May has stripped off her jacket. She's wearing a tank-top. Her skin is skim milk pale against the burgundy rock face. She moves well. I see Rolynne. I remember her grace. I wish *she* was the one dying. I don't care if that is precisely the kind of thought that will cause the God of my childhood to strike me dead.

"Rae," I say. "Why you?"

She shakes her head. "I thought maybe when I came here I'd answer that. I've been to every power spot on the fifteen dollar See-Dough-Now Power Web map. I've laid face down in the holy vortex, drunk spring water that's probably going to kill me before this frigging virus does. I've had crystals laid on my chakras, drunk fermented Siberian mushroom tea—"

She starts to laugh. She's laughing and I'm crying and then, she says the thing that I will think of every day from then on.

"Sheila," she says, "I was careless. There it is. But, I've got to say this. This romance shit is what's going to kill *you*. It's as bad as what I've got."

My tears stop dead.

"When's the last time you wrote?" she says fiercely. "Anything more than some card to some guy?"

"Before you got here. A little. Not much, but steady."

"Don't stop," Rae says. I nod.

"That woman," I say, "she isn't Rolynne."

Rae looks puzzled.

"That woman that was telling you about the Anasazi? May? She's not Rolynne."

"Oh yeah," Rae says. "Did you think she was?" She looks worried.

"I'm okay," I say. "I'm not nuts."

"But?"

"But, every time I see a guy about Wiley's age and a younger woman I want to puke."

"I know," Rae says.

Collum sticks his head in the door. "Ladies," he says, "we need you. We've got two empty spots left on the grid."

THE STORY in my head is that Rae will be assigned to clean Masau'u and I will work next to May, who will turn out to actually be November's daughter. We will find sisterhood in our honor for the early people. Rae, by virtue of cleaning *Dean 'n' Kristi 4-ever* from Masau'u's great brow, will be instantly cured. Dr. Collum will have to admit the old Hopi grandmas and grandpas are right, and Jake and I, despite the great barrier of our ages and the fact that I outweigh him by forty pounds, will find the ancient priestess-consort connection together.

None of that happens. Rae works on a two foot-by-two foot block of wall that holds half a spiral and the tip of a big-horn's tail. May and November work side by side. I overhear them. He is helping her correct her errors in cleaning away what appears to be a charcoal drawing of a crystal. She has to bend over to do it. He spends most of his volunteer time studying her butt. Collum crouches at my side and tells me the details of a grant proposal he's writing. He's heard I'm a part-time writer and he's wondering if I'd like to line-edit it his seminal paper as part of my contribution to the cause. I don't say anything. What I love about male professors is that you don't really *ever* have to say anything.

Jake will tell me later that he fell in love that day. A little after four, when the light was going amethyst, he came around the corner of the room where Masau'u lives. He heard someone talking. He stopped. He slowed his breath. He could hear his heart pounding in his ears. The wind changed. The sharp, medicine scent of juniper drifted up around him. He looked down at his hands and he saw that for the first time in months, they were not shaking.

Rae crawled through the little doorway. She sat next to Jake. He says she touched the claws on his shoulder.

"Where should I put mine?" she said.

He watched her tears fall into the red dust. She touched the spots with her fingers. "Like stars," she said, "at sunset. What happens," she whispered, "when I really don't make sense anymore?"

He says he took her hand in his and told her he loved her. "No more jokes," he said. "You are truly beautiful to me."

"And," she said, "if I wasn't dying?"

"The same."

He told her to come back next summer. He said that he would take her places filled with blue shadows and garnet rock and seeps dripping with columbine. He told her to come back, year after year. He would be here and if it got so she couldn't carry much, he would sherpa for her.

"I understand," she said. He kissed her on the lips.

"It wasn't romantic," he tells me. "But it was personal."

And then, he made her promise something. He made her promise that she would tell her kids the truth as soon as she got home.

He doesn't tell me that last part. She does. It's the day before she leaves. Bear House is ours. And Montezuma's Well. The perfect one-room tower at Mesa Verde and the ancient juniper that rises by its broken wall. The October wind hissing in the ancient ball-court at Wupatki, persistent, inescapable, so you think of what was played there and what the winners lost. We have stood in all those places and in each of them, we have lit a candle. We have turned north, then east, then south, then west. We have heard each other pray. We have sometimes said the words together.

"Why us?" we have said.

Then, with the candle flame near-invisible in the bright Southwestern sun, my friend Rae and I have said, "Thank you." Those moments, I know, will some day burn in my memory, the after-image of light so terrible and beautiful it cannot be borne for longer than a breath.

Absolute Proof of the Cosmos in Life

M Y HUSBAND is possessed. We're driving Old Route 66 past a rumpled khaki landscape, somewhere between Ash Fork and Seligman, Arizona. Richard whipped off I-40 onto this stretch of nothing about 10 A.M. It's called Crookton Road and it's rapidly returning to earth, which I wish it had done years ago, thereby sparing me this part of our X-miss trip. X-miss, as in "Let's miss Christmas—please."

"Check the guide, honey," Richard says. "Read me the highlights again."

"Whatever," I say, which is more the way our kids would respond. They are not with us. P.J. is snow-boarding with friends in the Adirondacks, Sara house-sitting our place near Hoboken, doubtless doing exactly what she always does, which is to smoke, watch VH-1, and complain listlessly to whatever clone is slumped next to her smoking, watching VH-1, and going, "Totally. Whatever. Totally."

"Snow Cap Diner," I read. "Grand Canyon Caverns, which is for sale, god forbid you want to buy it, Peach Springs, Truxton, Valentine, Hackberry."

"And the mountains," he says.

"Hualapai, Magic, Peacock, Black, Jesus, Richard, who cares?"

"The Jesus Richard Mountains?" he says gleefully. "That's where we'll stop."

I hunker down in my seat. We have been on this road for what seems like a month, and we've seen two living things: a large brown bird, a red-tailed hawk according to my husband, who is now suddenly an expert on the Southwest, and a buzzard, who was bearded and wearing a truck hat and driving an old pick-up, which Richard instantly coveted. It seems *years* since we flew into Albuquerque, rented a car, and headed out on

Route 66. "*Old* Route 66," Richard said, "wherever we can find it. It'll be a blast from the past, and we'll escape X-miss."

Escape is one-tenth of this. I think we are really taking this trip so that Richard can recover from his grief at the death of Carl Sagan. Richard is a psych professor, not shrink, but mapper of neurons in the brain, not your average brain, but your Alzheimer's brain. Richard believes that Sagan was the genius of our time, a guy who went far beyond asking if there was absolute proof of life in the cosmos, a guy who, like Richard, understood the connections between the brain and galaxies and computers, all of which makes Richard sound like a manic-depressive. Believe me, he's not. Richard is as level as the flat-line on a dead person's EKG, which is my area of expertise. I am a hospice worker, have been for fifteen years. I am tired of death and I am driving through what appears to be the original Land of Dead Things.

Speaking of Dead Things, I came on this trip mostly because I thought an adventure might revive Richard's Dead Thing. We've had sex once in the last five years. There's something wrong with that. And there's something weird about a guy who swears every five minutes that he loves his wife and family more than anything and makes it home for dinner about two nights out of seven. And there are all the mystery withdrawals from our joint mutual fund. I'd think there was a mistress except for this: when Richard heard that Carl Sagan died, he locked himself in his home-office all day and when his mom departed, he didn't take time off to go to her funeral. This is not about a woman.

Maybe this is about once being an eleven-year-old science nerd who hid his handsome little face in books, and won a Science Fair prize with a demonstration of how the human brain is actually a machine.

"HONEY," Richard says, "we're here."

He pulls our cute rental Neon up in front of a white adobe shack, plastered with day-glo signs and X-miss lights.

"Where are we?" I say, "I am not eating here."

"Then don't. *This* is the original Snow Cap."

An old, spanking-clean white convertible, festooned with all-white X-miss lights, sits outside. There's a ramada, I think that's what they call the things, equally festive.

Richard drops his brand new Old Route 66 baseball cap on one of the benches. He pats my back, a gesture he's done a lot in the last five years, a gesture he tells me maturely loving people do.

"We'll be in Kingman in an hour or so," he says. "It's a more urban place.

You can probably get a salad or something. I'm going in." He heads for the door, turns and comes back. "By the way, that's a 1936 Chevy Silver Streak over there. Check it out."

"Richard, it's me. Remember. I take busses to work. I hate cars."

Who's he talking to? Is this some Click 'n' Clack equivalent of hubby waking in the night, screwing your brains out, and at the crucial moment, murmuring a name that's not yours?

I slam down on the bench. I stare across the street at an abandoned garage and miles of nothing stretching endlessly beyond a molting adobe house. I think of Hoboken, and I realize I am thoroughly homesick. My client's voices come back to me, rasping, cracked, barely audible—everyone of them says at some point the same thing, "I want to go home," and they are not talking about a hypothetical heavenly home, they are talking about Duluth and Brooklyn 1926 and Nova Scotia and somewhere that has, for the good of the neighborhood, been razed and gentrified.

Sitting on this bogus picnic bench, in the middle of Planet Nothing, I want to go home.

"Annie," Richard barrels out of the Snow Cap. My husband, Dr. Lo-fat, has two trays of food— burgers, hot dogs, milk shakes, *and* a huge pile of french fried onion rings. Mustard and ketchup bottles protrude from the pockets of the expedition-weight anorak he bought for this journey.

"I have returned," he sits across from me.

"I said I wasn't hungry." I shade my eyes and look at him. He smiles.

"Here, just try this. They're beef hots. They might even be kosher."

It's an old joke. He's Jewish, not religious, but raised by second generation Russians, whose only holy song was *The Internationale*. What he learned about *latkes* and *dreidels* and *Why is this night different from all other nights?* he learned from his gramma. I was raised terminal Catholic and gave it up for making-out. We met on that latter common ground, at a Manhattan Earth Day meeting. Six hours after we nine earnest college kids, two tired Nam vets, and one probable Mohawk finally achieved consensus, he and I were kneeling in front of each other on his twin-bed mattress. We were naked, grinning, we looked each other up and down, and he said, "It's okay. It's kosher." That was five centuries ago.

"Richard," I say. "You just made a sexual joke. Are you alright?"

He flinches. For an instant, his smile fades. Then, he shrugs and holds out a hot dog. "Here, you like mustard. Let me serve you."

I open the bun. He reaches across the table, squeezes the mustard, and it shoots straight at me. I jump and drop the hot-dog.

"For chrissake," I say. "What is wrong with you?"

His head is down. His shoulders are shaking. *Alright,* I think, *he's finally having some feelings about his mom.*

"Honey," I say. "It's okay. I know what you're feeling. It's okay. Everybody does it, you know, denial, anger, grief, whatever. You miss your mom."

"What?" He looks up. Tears run down his face. "No. Look." He holds out the mustard bottle. A thick yellow plastic thread droops from its tip. "It's a joke." He wipes his eyes.

"A joke?"

He presses on the bottom of the mustard. The yellow thread retracts. I pick up the hot dog. It's covered with grit from the table-top.

I look at it. I look at Richard.

"It's a joke," he says. "Annie, like the old days. Like Milton Berle, Sid Caesar, remember those guys? This Snow Cap guy's got fake ketchup stains and rubber french fries, and he says, 'Half a straw,' and that's what he gives you, a box of straws cut in half."

"Yee ha," I say. "I'm sorry. I'm just homesick. Whatever."

He pats my hand. "Come on, I'll take this stuff back and we'll head down the road." He carries the mustard into the Snow Cap. I hear laughter. I take the food out to the Neon. I watch him come out the western door and wander over to the Silver Streak. He walks around the car. He sets his palm on the fender as though he were touching the Torah—or *The Stereoscopic Atlas for the Human Brain.*

When he walks toward me, tall and lanky, what Sara calls his crazy professor hair wild in the desert wind, I suddenly want him. He unlocks the car-door, reaches across the seat, and lets me in.

"Actually," I say, "I *am* hungry."

The french fries are greasy. I eat them all, every luke-warm one. I think of penance. I'm not sure which commandment I have broken.

I WANT TO like this. We're in Kingman, Arizona. Richard just found a pen with a tiny road-runner suspended in violently blue liquid inside the barrel. He tilts the pen to the light. The bird runs forward and back against a desert backdrop. *Back,* I think, *yes, back.* I consider telling my husband to take me to the bus station. I know how to do that, how to go across country by bus. I did it twenty-two years ago, from Rochester to San Francisco, owning nothing but a suitcase and a blanket and my young body hungry for my Richard's touch.

"*This,*" Richard says, "would be perfect for Sara."

"Hello," I say, a perfect wan imitation of our daughter, "did you forget,

Absolute Proof of the Cosmos in Life

Daddy, that I'm like seventeen years old?"

"No, but she'll like it, and the blue's the same color as her hair."

"Right." I pick a Tanya Tucker tape out of the display. "And, this for P.J., or maybe one of those cute tee shirts that say *My folks went to Kingman and all they brought me was this tee shirt.*"

Richard buys the pen. I look at stamped copper earrings and bandanas with flaming Harleys on them and a package of instant rattlesnake eggs, which carries a warning *DANGER!!* and when you pick it up, it buzzes, god help me.

"You thirsty?" he says.

"Actually, what I want more than anything is a relaxing shower, a decent cup of coffee, and NPR."

"You bet." I have never heard Richard say *You bet* in all the time I have known him. He winks. The salesperson, a slender young man with a garnet in his nose, also winks. I am incorporating all of this when Richard puts his arm around me and says, "I've got a surprise for you. We're taking a detour."

"What about X-miss in Santa Barbara?" I say. "What about Dean and Susan and great food and later, we'll go to the ocean and it'll be just like old times?"

"Trust me. Come on. Get in the car, close your eyes 'til I tell you to open them and trust me."

I KNOW WE are on the road. I smell diesel fumes. I hear Richard slip a CD into the player.

"Just a second," he says.

Suddenly Boz Scaggs is singing *Drowning in a Sea of Love.*

"Okay," Richard says, "open your eyes."

I do. "Yes! I get it, Richard," I say calmly. "You have joined the mafia and you have brought me to the desert to kill me." I look north. I look south. No matter which direction I turn, I see nothing but sand and winter light, not ugly certainly, and acre after acre of trailers and suburban houses, ugly, pure UG-LEE. "Okay. You don't have to kill me. Go ahead. Leave me. Marry her. It's okay. I have my work. I have the kids. I still have great legs. I'll be fine."

"Annie," Richard says, "be patient. Look at those mountains."

I look up. The mountains do not look like mountains. I think of my beloved Adirondacks, black rock, black water, Mt. Marcy fierce against a fragile gray sky. These mountains look like the results of a huge act of arson, charred, shattered, rising up like burned-out tenements from the western horizon. The sun is setting. Suddenly, everything around us is copper, rose, shimmering with a beauty I don't recognize. And do. I've seen this light in the windows of Manhattan's old office buildings at sunset.

"Okay," I say, "I can live with this." I wonder if he is going to say anything about my saying "Go ahead. Leave me. Marry her." I wonder if he even heard me.

"Annie," he says. "I've been thinking about Sagan."

"No. You're kidding." That much for Hospice skills.

I look north. There's a barbecue and a biker shop and a trading post that seems to be collapsing back into the desert. I consider the weird suburbs metastasizing into the far nothing and I am cheerful. Everything will go back into the sand. I hope. I hope we will not need hospice for a dying planet. You can take the girl out of Earth Day, but you can't take Earth Day out of the girl.

"Yes," he says. He's using his precise scientist voice, the one that causes girl graduate students to decide to pursue a career in Neuroromance. "I think Sagan was about a lot more than space. I think he was about risk—and probability."

We begin a long, slow ascent into the mountains. Cactus and weird spiky trees twist skeletal against the persimmon light. Their thorns shimmer. I am being seduced.

"For instance," Richard says, "he left his marriage for one of his colleagues who he truly loved."

Aha. Here it comes. I rest my hands on my thighs, palms up. I breathe. I bring my attention away from the hectic light outside our windows, away from a quick glance at Richard's perfect, if slightly aging, profile. I concentrate only on the dry air moving into my throat, and out. *When you are beginning to panic,* I tell my clients, *you always have your breath. Slow your breathing. Pay attention. Let yourself feel your fear. Your anger. And, perhaps, some joy at the breath moving in you.* It works for everybody but lung cancer patients. I sit perfectly still in this bright red and ordinary Neon. I study the alien light. I listen for my husband to go on. And I wonder if I am dying.

Richard sighs.

I can't stand the silence. "Fancy that." It's an old Monty Python joke.

"I don't fancy that at all." He is perfectly on cue. "Seriously, I don't believe in that kind of risk." He pats my up-turned hand. "You're enough challenge for me."

I turn away. Tears blur my sight. The rock looks molten. When I look at one of the cactuses, it seems to be burning, last light a divine halo around the tips of its branches.

"I love you," I say.

Richard is quiet. He re-sets the CD player. Boz sings—*Goin' down one time—goin' down two times—I'm drownin'...*

WE'RE HOLDING hands by the time we cruise down a long, long hill toward what?—a blood-orange river, a power plant volcanic in the dying light, a kaleidoscope of cut glass, fake emerald, zirconia and rhinestone.

"Laughlin," Richard says. "Turn right at the Colorado River. I suspect this is not like anything we've ever experienced. X-*miss* in Laughlin, Nevada."

He laughs. He circles my wrist with his hand and presses his thumb against my pulse. "Risk—and probability."

I realize he is talking about love. I think he is talking about a hotel room, a shower in which we do anything but relax, a huge bed, the curtains open to last desert light. I run my hand up his thigh.

"Risk," I answer, "and probability."

RICHARD STANDS in front of me, blocking my access to huge cedar doors. He has his lap-top case in his right hand, his blue work-out duffle in his left. He will not let me pass. I shift my day-pack on my shoulder. I grin. A few minutes earlier, I grabbed a never-worn silk nightgown from my suitcase and shoved it in the pack. Richard hadn't seen me. He'd stood at the western edge of the parking lot and raised his arms to the sun's last shot.

Now he looks into my eyes. "Say 'Open Sesame.'"

"Open Sesame."

He steps aside. A valet opens the door. Richard walks in. I follow. I am in a jungle. Acid-blue water gurgles over polymer boulders. Parrots shriek in vinyl trees. For a moment, I see little. The path under my feet is invisible. I hear water and birds and my heart pounding in my ears. And then, the metallic rill of coins spilling. Laughter. Screams. I look through the trees toward pure glitter.

We move forward. A woman emerges from the smoky light. She wears a turquoise jogging suit appliquéed with gold feathers, and a plastic mask strapped to her face, oxygen pouring through clear tubing from a cylinder clipped to her walker. She carries a plastic bucket of coins.

She nods. I smile. I guess she is seventy-five, eighty, maybe fifty desiccated by what chokes her. Richard and I walk toward her.

We meet on the wooden foot-bridge over the tiny, pink-spot-lit stream.

I move aside. She stops, leans on her walker and pulls the mask away.

"Good luck, honey," she rasps. "Wild Rose was good to me."

Our room is perfect, queen-sized bed, huge bathtub, thick towels, tiny bottles of good shampoo and lotion, toilet paper to steal, all for twenty dollars. Bonus, there are no Christmas decorations anywhere, and the music weaving through the casino din is not *Silent Night*.

"You closet hippie," Richard says. He is holding me. We are looking at ourselves in the big bathroom mirror. I have just picked up the free stuff and said,

"Look at this."

"I still can't believe," I say, "that they just give you these. You're used to it. All those conventions and conferences."

He tightens his arms around my waist. "Right, and all I do, when I'm in those fancy rooms, is miss you."

I turn to him. He kisses my forehead, takes me by the shoulders and propels me into the bedroom. We go to the windows, pull the curtains wide. Below us, a river, gleaming soft as pewter, catches casino lights on its surface…red and green and gold.

"Can't escape X-miss," Richard says. I turn to him. He kisses me softly on the mouth. I stretch up against his body. He hugs me briefly.

"We've got plenty of time," he says. "Let's go see the sights, get something to eat, risk a few nickels."

I turn back to the river. "Look, there's a boardwalk down there."

Together, magically, we say, "Atlantic City."

Richard turns me to face him. He hold out his right hand, sets his left fore-finger against his lips. I remember. We link little fingers, press our thumbs together.

"What goes up the chimney?" he says.

"Smoke."

Together, we repeat the goofy magic charm, "May your wish never be broke."

We tug until our fingers move apart. That's when you wish, while your touch is holding. I wish. I wonder if he does. The wishes come true only if you don't tell.

They're busting their asses to convince us that this is the Old West— the Pioneer, Colorado Belle, the Golden Nugget, a cowboy two stories high waves at you, and you open the door to your room with a computerized plastic card. Richard and I stroll the Riverwalk, arm in arm, the air soft as an upstate August night. I can smell the river. Richard tells me it's tamarisk. I lace my fingers through his. In these moments, I love him fiercely. I am twenty-three and he is a passionate kid, a guy who burns for everything, a guy who would have read up on every aspect of this trip long before we embarked.

"I love that," I say.

He kisses the top of my head. "What?"

"That you know why the river smells like that. You're my scholar of joy."

He's quiet. We head away from the river, toward the front of the Colorado Belle. There is a moat and instructions. *Do Not Throw Coins.* Richard tosses a quarter in. "May you come back a hundred-fold."

"Do you believe in magic?" I say. "I feel so young."

He laughs. "You are. Look around."

I suddenly see that almost everyone around us is some degree between sprightly late-middle-aged, leaning toward kitty appliquéed sweatshirts, to ancient, leaning on just about anything.

"My god," I say. "It's a big shiny nursing home."

My husband steers me out into the huge parking lot packed with trailers and RVs. Couples sit in patio chairs in front of their places, under the hard glow of mercury lights. I hear muted television sounds in every direction. "My god, look at that," I say. "No, don't look. It's an elephant dying ground. My god, don't they need privacy?"

I look straight ahead.

Richard laughs. "They don't mind. Look. Those people are waving." He turns, tows me after him. *Where is my shy husband? Where is the guy who hasn't gone to a party in years?*

The couple is sitting in lawn chairs on bright green Astroturf in the middle of an ocean of asphalt. Chili pepper lights sparkle along the awning that shields them from stars made invisible by casino sparkle. A sign on their front door reads: *Welcome! This is our children's inheritance.* The woman waves us over. Her face is as hard and pure as what this desert must once have been.

"Have a seat," she says. "Will, get these folks a couple of chairs."

Richard shakes her hand. Will tugs chairs from the back of their immaculate pick-up. "There you go. Make yourself comfortable, 'course unless you're in a hurry to get in there and self-destruct."

I shrug. The woman reaches out her hand. "I'm Betty. Don't mind him."

"Annie," I say. "Actually, we're not here to gamble."

She laughs.

Richard sits down. "Table play the best?"

I look at him.

"Oh yeah," Will says, "but they got a nickel Progressive there at the Belle that's due to pop. Five hundred, thirty-three thousand plus change. Wouldn't that do the trick?"

"Early retirement," Richard says. He grins. "We'll see."

"You folks come here often?" Betty says to me.

Before I can answer, Will cuts in. "Sound like New Yorkers," he laughs. "Escaping the hellidays. Betcha five bucks."

"No bet," Richard says. "New Jersey. Hoboken."

"Isn't that where that comedian is from?" Betty says. "That Jewish fellow."

I stiffen. Richard laughs. "Could be, actually, Hoboken's just a small town at heart."

I think of my favorite cafe and Grazie's, where you can get elegant white pizza, of Fred and Nguyen's florist shop, the Korean vegetable guy and *Thad's*, home of the best jazz in New Jersey. Richard murmurs something to Will.

"Seinfeld?" I ask Betty.

"No," she says, "Youngman, something Youngman, wasn't he always making jokes about Hoboken?"

"I think so," I say. "But mostly about his wife."

She nods. "Just like a man."

"Are you on vacation?" I say.

"You bet," she laughs, "the long one. The casinos let you park in their lots free for a month. We go right down the line, one after the other, from November 'til it gets too hot, then we run over to Arizona and play the Indian casinos."

"Do you gamble a lot?"

"What else? This is the most fun I've had in years. Will plays black-jack. I play that Game King. We eat in the buffets. Let somebody else cook and clean up. I did it for sixty years. We go into those mountains, too. We're rock-hounds. Find the most beautiful crystals and what-not, run over to Quartzite with them in February."

She grins at me. "We're just stubborn old desert rats."

I nod.

Suddenly, she fixes me with her gaze. I feel uneasy.

"You understand," she says, "we worked hard all our lives. This is our pay-off."

I look at the plywood river boat sparkling against the washed-out sky. Betty touches my hand. "You have good luck. Black Rhino's been pretty good to me. Nickels. Let your husband play the big stuff."

I DON'T PLAY Black Rhino. Instead, I sit next to Richard at the nickel Progressive. This one's two hundred, sixty-eight thousand dollars and change. All you have to do is hit four Nevada Nickels. I like the colors of Nevada Nickels. Green and gold and a muted purple. Tasteful as one of Fred and Nguyen's displays, rare as orchids. Richard pokes my arm.

"Look," he says, "a cherry." Four nickels mount on the Credit screen.

"That's great, honey."

I'm not really playing. I tried for a while, didn't hit anything. I'm bored, and bloated from the buffet. What I really want to do is go outside, walk off the gray meat and bland lasagna. I want to walk back to the Edgewater and watch the feral cats play along the river. More than any of that I want to be back in our room, with Richard kissing me. I want him to say, "Hello, my friend, my love," the words I haven't heard for five years.

What Richard wants to do is play here for a while, then go over to the Hurricane Zone, where every half hour or so, fake puffy clouds swirl above you, lights flash, thunder crashes, and you can double, triple, quadruple, whatever you are winning during the mildly raging storm. I figure they don't want what they describe as "a new total sensory trip" to jolt geriatric players into heart attacks. What's happening here on Nevada Nickels isn't exciting enough to even raise your pulse.

"I'm sleepy," I say. "Plus, you've sunk about thirty dollars in that machine."

"Okay," he says. "The Hurricane Zone. Then we go."

Six storms later, Richard is down three-hundred forty dollars and my butt is numb. I watch him. I don't play. The middle-aged lady Zone attendant eyes me suspiciously every time she makes her rounds. I smile. She doesn't. I realize it's not personal. She's circled us fifty times. I bet her feet hurt. Richard hits the Change button and the attendant hands him a rack of dollars.

"How much is that?" I ask.

"A hundred," he says. "Look, I'll just play these out. With luck, I win. Without, I'm down an even five hundred and I can quit."

"What do you mean an even five hundred?"

"You know how I am." His face is flushed. He's run his hands through his hair over and over again, so he looks like a tousled kid. "Type-A. I don't like things messy. Five hundred is a nice, neat number."

I turn away. A cheerful old woman waves a hundred dollar bill in the air. A gutty guy in a silk cowboy shirt is playing three machines at a time.

Richard hands me five dollars. "Come on. We're on vacation."

I play a buck on Wild Rose. It looks like somebody's idea of a woman's slot machine, all fuschia and sparkly. Thunder rumbles above us. Lights flash wildly. Next to me, Richard is laughing. "Look, Annie. Look at your machine."

I see two purple sevens. While I watch a violently pink Wild Rose drops into the third space.

"You did it," my quiet husband shouts.

The old lady lifts her head and grins at me. She has no teeth.

10, the credits flash, 20, 60, 80, 120—and, then, while the clouds spin above us and Hurricane Lucky shakes the floor beneath my stool, the credits jump to 180, 240, and stop. For an instant, I believe the machine loves me.

The storm dies down. Richard glares at his machine. "Okay. I'm done. Cash out, babe, and we'll get some sleep."

He hands me the empty rack. I need another. The attendant brings one and pats my shoulder.

"You were a little slow getting started, honey," she says. "Now you hang on to some of that."

I cash in my money. $244. The cashier gives me two hundred dollar bills, two twenties, and four ones.

"Play those," Richard says. "The little ones."

"I'm set." I hand him the ones.

He slides them into a quarter machine and turns to me. "Hey. I've got an idea. You go on up to the room, take your shower, put on NPR and nothing else. I'll play these out and come up and surprise my very best friend."

"Okay," I say. "Just those quarters? Right?"

"You got it." He kisses me gently, turns me around and pats my butt. I walk toward the elevators. My head aches. My eyes burn. I hold my sleeve to my nose, and when I breathe, all I can smell is cigarette smoke.

THE TUB is huge. I turn on NPR. Mozart, of course, the announcer's voice as warm as the water into which I sink my body. No coffee, but I've carried a glass of surprisingly good Chardonnay up to the room. I've set candles on the sink-top for good luck. The room is rosy-gold, a soft desert light inside this huge jingling X-miss ornament where I hope I'll relax and my husband is taking a long time to come to our room. I have dutifully tried to call Sara. An electronic voice has told me that because of the pressure of holiday calls, my call cannot be completed.

I let my arms float in the chin-high water. I've always liked bathtubs better than hot tubs. No chemicals, no frantic waters, no possibility that a stranger will pad toward you and settle their unknown body into a bogus intimacy. I close my eyes. *Breathe,* I whisper to myself. I think of my most recent client.

He was a big man. Once. Now he lies on a rental hospital bed in his vast atrium living-room. There is a fireplace the length of one wall. The man faces the fire. He can no longer turn his head. He looks into the flames, and up at a dozen Waterford goblets on the mantel.

"They can hold the firelight," he has told me. "And the moon."

His wife answers the door and I know she does not want me there. "Is it you, Annie?" he says, his words separated by hard slow breath. "It is," I say.

The wife takes my coat, offers coffee, and leads me to his bed. Later, when the morphine is dreaming in his blood, she beckons me into the kitchen. "He adores me," she says. "He tells me he doesn't want to go on without me." I listen. "Do you understand?" she says. "What a good marriage can be like?" I tell her that I do. I am grateful for my training that teaches a lie is not just a lie, but something we've named unconditional support. He calls out to us. We go in.

"Give Annie one of the glasses," he whispers. "Tell her to hold it to the moon."

MY HANDS are limp, my gut clenched tight. I breathe down to the knot. I listen for the plastic card sliding in the door. I breathe. I listen. Mozart has faded away. Vivaldi takes its place. The water begins to cool. The candles burn straight and true, the hotel wine glass a perfect bell of golden light. I set my hand on my belly. I breathe into my touch. None of this does any good. I sit up, slam down the last of the wine, and stand.

I wrap myself in one of the huge towels and lean toward my reflection. The mirror is fogged with steam. I open the bathroom door. Cool air pours in and the mirror begins to clear. I see my face flicker in the candlelight. Plain. Tired. Bewildered. I lean forward and rake the tips of my fingers through what's left of the fog. I write. *I want to go home.*

I carry the candles to the low dresser, then turn toward the bed. The maid has laid out my night-gown, the waist pinched in, the skirt spread wide, a woman formed of silk. Naked, I climb into bed.

The candles gutter. A chunk of moon burns zircon through the window. I pull the blanket up to my chin as though to shield against that icy light. I wonder what time it is. The moon has moved clear across the pale sky. I have, again and again, walked to the window and looked down on the river. I have compared it to a silver ribbon, an icy mountain highway, a huge shining serpent. I have imagined telling all of that to Richard, maybe even writing a poem, as I once might have. All of that seems pathetic. At least I have not, as the marriage counselor I once visited alone cheerfully suggested, "made love" with myself.

Nor have I held the wine-glass to the moon. It lies, shattered, in the bottom of the wastebasket. The moon disappears to the west. The room goes not-quite-dark. I turn my face to the window. Far below, a scarlet light flashes off and on. I close my eyes. A Wild Rose flickers behind my eyelids. I know what is happening. I know, without question, why we are here. At last, I sleep.

RICHARD BENDS over me. I do not open my eyes. Behind my lids, I see a pale glow. I imagine morning pouring up beyond the river.

"Hello," he whispers, "hello, my friend."

I hold myself still, keep my breathing slow. I hear him retreat. The far side of the bed shakes. "Oh my god," he whispers and falls back on his side of the bed. More than a desert, more than a continent, lies between us. I do not move.

WE WAKE and dress in silence, not unusual, nor unfriendly. I face the window and button my blouse. The only light I see is sun pouring down on the river. The jade water is lower. I remember something about dams, something about electricity and power. "Richard, did you tell me something about this river? About dams?"

He moves to my side. "The Colorado once ran wild to the Pacific. There are twenty dams, maybe more. It's all about electricity and power." He touches my shoulder.

I turn to him.

"I love you," he says, "because of all the questions you could have asked this morning, that is the one you asked."

I look back at the water.

"Then," I say, "how much did you lose?"

"Eight thousand dollars."

"A nice neat figure."

We are quiet. This silence is not unusual. Nor unfriendly.

I put my arm around his waist. He bends and kisses the top of my head.

"Remember Atlantic City?" he asks.

"Our common-law honeymoon?"

"Yes, and more."

"Big," I say, "trouble."

Richard leans into my embrace. I hold him. He kisses my hair. "Yes."

MY HUSBAND and I are in the endless $2.99 all-U-can-eat breakfast buffet line. I read the menu. Eggs and meat and fried potatoes, scratch-baked pastries and fresh fruit. I watch old couples and single old women exit carrying as many apples and bananas and day-glo kiwis as they can. I hold Richard's wrist. His pulse beats wild against my palm. A bank of fully occupied nickel keno machines buzzes behind us.

"Coffee," I say. "Now."

He nods. He turns and studies the keno players.

"Christ," he says and turns back to me, "I can't not watch. They are my people."

I look ahead. A couple walks slowly out of the buffet. The man is jowly, his whitehair combed perfectly, his Haband slacks pulled up around his big belly. You can see his maroon socks, and the white sneakers in which he shuffles up the carpeted incline. He smiles at his wife. She's leaning on a quad cane and she clutches her plastic bucket of coins against her hip. They move toward us.

"Look," Richard says. "Her blouse."

She wears a dark blue tunic. Full moon, comets, and stars blaze across her bosom. Tiny sequins glitter in the comet's tail. She catches us looking and pats her heart. "My lucky shirt," she says. Her husband winks.

"There you go, Annie," Richard says gently, "absolute proof of the cosmos in life."

He sets his hand in the center of my back. I want to turn into the long curve of his arm, press my face against his throat. Instead, I look straight ahead.

"Richard," I say, "I'll tell you my wish if you tell me yours."

"But then—"

"It's just superstition. It's not probability."

He begins to speak. Somebody behind us hits big. Richard looks over my shoulder, forces his gaze back to my face. I listen hard. Under the murmur of a hundred hungry people, through the din of the pay-off, his words drop into place, welcome, dangerous, the impossible odds of a miracle. I touch his face, and we are kin.

Binky

THEY'RE GUTTING THE Bluebird. Every morning when I walk to work, I see my cousin Raymond on the motel roof, hacking at the old red tiles. He wears a doctor mask, wrap-around purple shades, and a muscle top, usually black. I like to watch his shoulders move. He's pretty, like a lot of the Rez boys 'til marriage gets them, or T-Bird, or college.

"There's poison in the insulation," he tells us, "that asbestos. We gotta wear a mask and take a shower as soon as we get home." My aunts nod. My uncle died from mining uranium. We're glad Raymond is being careful.

This morning, Raymond sees me. He waves. "Hey, girl, 'sup?"

I wave back carefully. I'm chunky and I don't want him to see the under part of my arm jiggle. I think where I got my sweet tooth was from the little bitty Indian part of me. What I got from my white part is the lonesomeness.

I head up the highway into town. I'm not on my way to work today, though I wouldn't mind. The cafe's fun. We bake our own pies and the customers are all kinds, tourists, Indians, hippies, geezers, and a lot of those rich people who dress like they're going to work on a ranch. The other waitress, Shanti, is my one almost-best-friend. She is a college girl and is what she calls "totally passionate about the earth." Shanti is also part of an Indian religion, not out-here Indian, but curry Indian. She says they believe, like us, that the earth is our mother and we are here to love and serve her. Which is why I'm walking downtown on my day off to meet her at Cody Park.

Yesterday, Shanti came to work crying. She handed me a flyer. It said that the Forest Service was going to cut down most of the trees where there was a forest fire near the Grand Canyon. That made sense to me, but Shanti explained that it was just an excuse to let the timber companies make money off the forest and that we, the taxpayers, were actually paying for them to kill our home. I don't pay taxes because I don't make that much plus I've got the two kids, but I saw what she was saying. Our favorite customer, Deacon, got so mad he wrote a letter then and there on one of the cafe's napkins. Shanti told us that there was going to be a demonstration at the Forest Service office right down the block from Cody Park and would we be there?

"Groovy," Deacon said. He is about nine thousand years old and wears beads and side-burns, and we don't have the heart to tell him people don't say groovy anymore.

"Sure," I said.

Shanti said she'd made animal masks so we could be creatures of the forest and would I be willing to wear one?

"How about rabbit?" I said, because that's my grandma's favorite stew, and Shanti said, "You bet."

I AM THINKING about being a rabbit when I come up the hill to the park. I *am* shy and I *love* fooling around. It's the most beautiful day, where the sky is really turquoise and your shadow moves ahead of you like it was glad. I see Shanti sitting under a big old cottonwood. The situation looks skimpy. Only Deacon is there and two other guys. Shanti wears her religious head wrap and she's practicing finger cymbals. The sound is silvery, like the cottonwood leaves catching light over their heads.

"Hey," she yells, "it's a perfect day for a demo."

"Groovy," Deacon says. We all shake hands like the AIM bros still do, grab wrists, elbows, then power sign.

"Tina," Shanti says, "this is George and Larry." The two guys duck their heads. I can't tell if that means "hi" or "get me outta here." George looks like Brad Pitt if he'd done a lot of speed and lost his teeth. Larry's weasel skinny. He's sprayed on his jeans and he keeps throwing his long greasy brown hair back like he was cute.

"Hi," I say. "Are we it?"

"Well," Shanti says, "Rosie told me she and a few others would meet us at the Forest Service office."

"Actually," George says, "me and Larry'll meet you over there, too. We haven't had our coffee yet. We'll head over to the Jesus Mission and catch you guys up later."

Shanti smiles at them. Nothing fazes her. I look down at the table and see that somebody has written *Binky* in that sparkly pink nail polish my cousin Leela wears. I run my finger over it. I don't want to look up. I'm feeling stressed about this whole thing. It doesn't seem to me that three people will make a very good demonstration, even if one of us is a rabbit.

"Shanti," I say, "do you think we ought to call some other people, like all those Earth First! kids? I'm kind of nervous to do this just the three of us."

"Solidarity," Deacon says. "That's all it takes."

"Three is better than nothing," Shanti says. "In the beginning, the only person who really cared about the trees was this old guy, John Muir. But he kept saying what he believed and the next thing you knew, there was Earth Day."

"There it is," Deacon says.

I look at Shanti's round face. She has freckles and when she gets fired up, they turn brick-red. Her eyes are blue, and, even now, with one of us not-quite ready to march for Mother Earth, they are fierce and determined. She pulls the rabbit mask out of her backpack. One ear is bent. She's painted a pink nose and crinkles so you can imagine that the rabbit is actually sniffing the air.

"Try it on," she says. I hold it and she ties the strings behind my head. I see Deacon in front of my left eye, Shanti in front of my right, both of them looking flat as cartoons. I remember Raymond telling me about a peyote meeting and how, for a long, long time, he thought he was seeing like an animal. Shanti picks up a bear mask and hands a raven to Deacon. I tie her mask while she ties Deacon's. She hands us a stack of flyers and a poster. Mine says: *Don't kill my home.*

I take a deep breath and say, "Okay."

Then bear leads rabbit and raven up the street.

 The Most Amazing Thing

Back when they were Mom and Dad, my mom and dad named me Linc. That's for Lincoln. As in Abraham, as in freed the slaves. They did that because my Mom was carrying me in her belly the first time she got busted in a demonstration. That used to happen a lot more back then, back ten, fifteen years ago, demonstrations, naming kids weird names, thinking you could change things if you cared enough.

In fact, I'm lucky I got named Linc, which is almost normal. My best friend when I was five in San Jose was named, this is the complete truth, Star Fire Lee. And, we knew a kid whose mom named herself Hawk and the cat, Sillysibin. So, the fact that my older brother is named Dave, my sister, Sarah, and me, Linc, is something for which we are all eternally grateful. Those are my mom's favorite words. She says them a lot.

"Well, Linc, guess what? My best Pigma One Ought pen was right where I left it last night. I was able to actually walk right in to my desk and pick it up in my hand. (pause, pause) For that I am eternally grateful." Or, "I notice, Sarah, that someone, some kind (pause, pause) stranger came in and made a fresh pitcher of orange juice before the slime on the bottom had begun to crawl up the sides. For that, we should all be eternally grateful."

Sometimes, we all think she thinks she is just too hip to be true. It's very weird when your mother is really sarcastic and funny and likes rock and roll and only wears blue jeans and flannel shirts and won't do anything formal with her hair. She raises us by herself and she works with people in a nursing home. She used to cook great food, linguine with clam sauce, chicken with little pieces of garlic stuffed under the skin, peppers and sausage she got at this real Italian butcher. But lately that's been fading out. More like Chinese take-out and bad Mexican, that's what's been happening lately. She's also a poet, not as good as Baudelaire, who I think is beyond most humans, but, good for a mother.

She's the only parent we've got. My dad, Eddie, is in an urban zendo. That's a Buddhist monastery, except instead of being on the side of some beautiful mountain or by the ocean, it's right in the middle of Dayton, Ohio. I visited my dad there a few times. It was actually pretty cool. Shaved heads, outer space eyes, staring at a wall for hours. People think stuff like that went out at midnight, December thirty first, nineteen sixty nine, but it didn't. In fact, if my mom would let me shave my head, my life wouldn't be that different from the zendo. But, she won't. Whenever I ask her, she says, "I draw the line."

My dad even gave me one of the robes. It's got samurai shield designs on it and rabbits and a moon with clouds. I go up to my room, which is where I am right this moment, put the robe on, and do nothing. Usually. Except it's different today. What I am doing today is sitting here in my regular clothes, feeling the last of being high and trying to know for real that Doc is dead.

My mom left my dad when we were little. Professor Lennie, the human entrail, left her about six months ago. In between my dad and Lennie was Doc. My mom left Doc for Lennie. If I ever get around to hating her, it'll be for that. Doc lives…Doc lived in Maine. When he and Mom lived together, he was a printer. They lived in an urban guerilla commune. Once, when I was about eight, he and I drove all the way across country and back. He played jazz trumpet and blues guitar and he was no-way-fake cool.

Now, he's dead, which I found out two hours ago, which caused me to come up here and smoke a doob and look out over the tree tops and be glad I have my own room in the attic. Up here, I can't hear anything, except maybe Dave and his buddies when they pound up the stairs. I can't see much but house tops and trees and light. My room's on the east side, so I can watch the sun come up, which, though I am fifteen and you would assume I'd sleep late every chance I get, I frequently do. It's just the best time.

I got pretty messed up from the doob. I keep wishing I would look out of the window and see dawn breaking up from the horizon and it would turn out that what I heard two hours ago in the downstairs hall was all a bad dream.

When I came in, the first thing I saw was my mom. She had the phone pressed against her ear. She was smoking a cigarette which she never does. Her hair was a mess, which is almost always the case. She was listening

The Most Amazing Thing

very hard and kicking the door jamb. The ugly old goldfish sconce over the phone trembled every time she kicked. She was covered with little diamonds of light from the beveled glass in the door. She taught me all that: sconce, beveled, how to find the words to describe something clearly. She thinks words are better than money. I agree. She turned to look at me and covered the phone with her hand.

"It's Maia," she said.

She stubbed the cigarette out on the heel of her boot. That was the kind of thing that had driven Dr. Lennie, the Sucking Wound, crazy.

"Stay here," she said. She doesn't usually give us orders. Bribes and sarcasm are more her style. I dropped my pack on the stairs and leaned on the railing.

"Okay," she said, "we'll be there quick as we can." She nodded.

"Okay," she said, "I gotta get off. Get tickets. Decide who's going. All that stuff."

She nodded again and frowned. "Yes," she said, "I know. You, too."

She kicked the wall extra hard. "Maia," she said. I'd heard that patient tone before. Maia was Doc's lover. She was very spiritual. "Yes," my Mom said in a tired voice. "Okay. Blessed be." She hung up the phone.

"Now, she's a witch," she said. "Wiccan, *excuse me.*"

I laughed. "What happened to *you can be anything you want through visualization?*" I asked.

My mom laughed. Then, she scared me. Her face went gray. She came towards me and sat down on the step at my feet.

"Oh, Linc," she said. "Doc's dead."

I still had the laugh from my remark on my face and that felt really weird. I couldn't seem to get the muscles of my face to do what they should. My mom took my hand.

"Well, piss," she said. "I pissing well just don't know."

I didn't even think to ask her if it was a joke or a mistake or some kind of awful psychological game. I knew. It was real. I looked down at our hands. We've both got long, skinny fingers and they were intertwined and very cold. One of her rings, the silver badger, was sort of cutting into my skin, but I let it be.

"What happened?" I asked.

"Heart attack," she said. "Bim bam boom. He was out running. They found him on the road. Face down. Maia tried to give him breaths. The doc…" She shook her head.

"The doctor said his heart exploded. He probably raised his foot for the next step and was dead before he hit the ground."

"That's fucked," I said.

"Yeah," my Mom said. "Truly. Deeply."

She hugged my shoulders, got up, went into the living room and put on The Who, which is this pissed-off, great, geezer music, and punched the air for a while with her fist. I came up here but not before I went through Dave's stash and found this neatly rolled doob. That's how he is. Everything done perfect. Later tonight, when he notices the joint missing and slaughters me, he'll do a perfect job. He'll say quietly and carefully that limp-wristed jerk-off that I am, I had better learn the difference between borrowing, and taking something that goes up in smoke.

When I first got up here I could hear the faint echo of my mom's music, that's how loud she had it cranked, but it's totally quiet now. I've got my guitar out, not playing it really, just holding it and I've got myself to the point where the high is almost gone and I can think about real life. Real death, no joke.

Doc was the best. He talked real slow. He liked the blues, even the ancient ones where you can't tell for the life of you what those old guys are saying. "Gwidowderibgogemmeamojohan." He was a skinny, freckled, red-haired guy who looked like he was about seventeen even though he was more middle aged, thirty when my mom first met him. As I said, she left him for Ph.D. Lennie, the tortoise-necked old fart who walked out on her, who she still misses so much that we, as a family, have to eat lukewarm Chinese take-out every other night because she doesn't care to cook. We all hate his guts. He'd do stupid shit like confiscate our stuff if we left it around for more than ten minutes. He'd even charge us part of our allowance to get it back. He was a walking hemorrhoid. I can't believe my Mom still cries about him. I'm drifting. That's the trouble. Here I am trying to remember all the great stuff about Doc, and Lennie's still oozing in.

First thing in the morning, we have a family meeting. We all hate those, me and Dave and Sarah, but it isn't so bad this time. My mom went out early and got some fresh bagels and some stranger has made fresh orange juice without being asked and Dave hasn't noticed that superior doob is gone, so I don't feel bad on top of feeling bad. I squirt some honey into my coffee and wait to hear the plan. The funeral. Who will go. How. My mom says it all fast and choppy. Of course, only one of us can go because, surprise, there's nothing in a Zen student's budget for child support and my Mom feels guilty that she left him, so she doesn't push and there's never much extra money.

We discuss it, though everyone knows who will go. Ever since Doc

The Most Amazing Thing

and I took this big cross-country trip, it's been known, not decided, just known that I am like his real kid. Dave doesn't mind. Neither does Sarah. You can't really mind something like that, because it's so natural. It's not something you can make rules about or learn how to do in some workshop on step-parenting. So, we agree that Mom and I go and Dave and Sarah watch the ranch, which is this big old three-story house between a park and a bad neighborhood. My mom believes in loyalty to the urban life. We finish our breakfast and hop to it. Mom's wandering around asking us if what she's put on looks decent. We keep saying, "Don't worry, you'll look awful no matter what." And she does. She's gray and bag-eyed and her hair's gone dull and limp.

"You're supposed to look awful," Sarah says. "Your best friend just died." She and Mom hug each other and cry for a while. I go up and take a shower and poke around in my room to find the important things to take. I get my tapes and my headset and my journal and my pen. It takes a long time for some reason, which is good, because this way I won't have to sit around waiting. The worst.

I'm having trouble keeping my mind on things. I keep straying back to that cross-country trip, to these beautiful horror-show lightning storms out on the plains and you're on a flat road and always the tallest thing around for miles and you don't believe that stuff about a car being safe. I think about a tornado we watched and how the air was yellow green. I keep seeing the little gray ghost ponies we saw on the coast road between L.A. and San Francisco and I wish I could see that long-haired, scrawny, grinning demon behind the wheel of that rusted out Saab.

But, more than anything, I look at my guitar and remember sitting on the front porch of this house last spring, a year ago, and me and Doc playing guitar and watching this moth dive bomb into a candle my mom had set in a cup. It died right away. Then it started to burn and next thing you knew it turned into a perfect little torch. It was still burning when my mom called me in to go to sleep. I felt sad for the poor moth, but it was the most beautiful light, clear and white and very steady.

Those are about one ten-thousandth of the memories. The earliest one I don't even remember. I've just heard the story so often, it's as though I remember it. I guess I was about three and Doc was in the tub and I walked in. We've always been pretty casual about gonads, etc., until the dread teenage years arrived. Anyhow, I walked in and looked into the tub and said, "Hey, Doc, how come you got a mutash on your peepee?" He never told that story in front of me but, when I was older, Mom told me he used to laugh 'til he got tears in his eyes every time he thought about it. He tell people in his slow, soft voice. He'd say "mutash" like I had. Then, he'd always say, "That kid's the kid I wished I'd sprouted."

That guy is dead. He is dead. And I am alive. That's what is slamming into me right in the middle of the memories. That's what's jamming the tears like rocks in my chest. I hate it.

DAVE DRIVES us to the airport. We all hug goodbye. Dave makes some joke about driving carefully, which is what my mom always says when he goes out, though he mostly walks or takes the bus, though she always worries about being over-protective, which she says is the absolute double bind curse and resulted in Lennie, Ph.D. So, it's this inside out, turned around backwards joke, Dave's favorite kind. He looks down at her when he says it. She's not that big though she is sturdy. "Welsh pony," Doc used to call her. And, "eight-track stereo baby," because she gets a little speedy and random now and then.

So, we are on the plane and she is helping them fly it. I point out to her that gripping the arm rests so hard that your knuckles go blue-white doesn't really hold the plane up.

"Yes," she says in an absent-minded voice. "I feel so helpless, Doc." I must have jumped a little, because she looks at me funny and says, "Oh, dear, Linc. Oh god, I'm sorry. I've got two brains cells left and they're not speaking to each other."

"No problem," I say.

Actually, I feel kind of proud. Besides, I'm watching the green fields around the airport fall away and thinking about the last time she and I visited Doc and Maia, how all of us had eaten in this restaurant that had Greek vegetable things and home-made bread and how Maia had corrected Mom's pronunciation in front of the waitress, so that every time we were alone after that, my mom would say to me, "Moo sa KA, you got that, Linc?" Then, Doc and I had gone off alone to a huge aquarium and he'd taken me straight to his favorite fish, the Clown Fish, who were fat and day-glo and would come right up to the glass and stare you in the face, so that Doc and I would make fish faces right back and laugh ourselves sick. Between keeping those fish in mind and the view out of the window in sight, the rocks in my chest are staying put.

We land in Boston and everything goes like it's supposed to.

"The miracle of plastic money," my mom says. We grab a couple of frozen yogurt hot fudge sundaes and pick up the rental car. It smells so weird. I guess most people know how they smell, but it's the first time I've ever ridden in one. Last time, Doc and Maia picked us up in the Saab. The

Rent-A-Car people have sprayed this car with something doubtless toxic, something doubtless to result in my never being able to father children, should I ever be so lucky as to have the opportunity.

It is pretty embarrassing altogether to be in this car. It is a sparkling dark blue 1977 Monte Carlo. It looks like the kind of car Tony Manero would give his left nut for. He's the guy in *Saturday Night Fever*, a swill of a movie my mom, for reasons beyond my imagination, loved enough to see three times. She played the sound track over and over 'til Dave started to retaliate with Blue Oyster Cult, which he actually hates and had to borrow off a friend.

So, this car is without smear or fingerprint. You can see buildings reflected off it when we stop at lights. Then, you can see highway overpass signs, while my mom clenches her teeth and goes white around the jaw. These Boston under-over-up-the-ass overpasses are brutal. Finally, you can mostly see sky and I can smell the salt from the ocean and that brings back so many memories that I forget about being disgusted by Tony Manero, who actually looks good in Sansabelt pants and still doesn't get laid.

I smell the air and I think about hiking with Doc on the brand new trails at Wolf Point Beach and digging clams and cooking them in sea weed in the sand. He taught me the names of the sea birds; not scientific names, like you might think, smart as he was, but names like Looie Long Leg and Bert Big Beak and Lola, who was sort of a hookerish looking bird who seemed to attract more than her fair share of male gulls. We didn't tell my mom or Maia about that, since both of them were getting in touch with themselves as women and didn't have great senses of humor about words like "hooker" or "hussy."

"Holy shit," my mom, Protector of Language says, "this sucker jumps!" I look over at the speedometer. The needle tips past ninety-five. My mom grins. It's the first time I've really seen her look normal in months. "Oh, well," she says and taps the brake.

"Doc would've loved this machine," she says. "Watch the speedometer for me, would you? I keep forgetting I'm not in The Roach."

Our normal car is a white Ford Aspen with half a bucket of brown semi-gloss spilled all over the back floor, which is not the reason it is a piece of shit. It is a piece of shit, as Doc would have said, because all cars made after 1950 are pieces of shit, some are just more expensive pieces of shit. Sometimes I think that between him and my mom and, in an opposite way, Tumor Lennie, I am ruined for life. What will I get to like? No boojie cars, no sexist remarks. Sometimes I think it's possible that a person could get so enlightened that they'd have to go out, buy a Camaro, load it up with beer, and go out and make rude, unbelievably seductive remarks to cute girls with big breasts.

I happen to know that Doc once owned a red Alfa Romeo when he was in the Army. There's a picture of him sitting in it, with this big shit-eating drunk grin on his face and a bottle of beer in each hand. He's got an awful Army hair cut, which looks worse on redheads than any other race. He looks completely normal and completely happy. That's what was so excellent about him, you could be like him, no big deal, you could grow up to be just like him if you just let it happen.

I have a rubber band keeping my journal shut. Every now and then I plunk it. I miss my guitar, which I was encouraged to leave home for some mysterious reason. Space, maybe. Memories. Mom clicks on the radio. I glance at the speedometer. It would be more appropriate to say that she clicks on the radio as we approach launch speed.

"Warp seven," I say.

She slows down. I tune in the radio. It's some hard-core station out of Boston. It thuds and whines along with us right up to the turn off to Pownal. My mom keeps slamming her fist on the steering wheel, speeding up and slowing down. I just plunk along. Once she turns to me and says, "How much should a person lose?" I shake my head. I like that she treats us like buddies, and I don't. I mean, old as I am, there are questions like that and sometimes, I would like to just put my head on her shoulder for a while. Sarah feels that way, too. We have discussed it.

"Minerva the Moose," Mom says, "and Lennie and Litter Bit and Doc. Spare me!" Minerva was a Siberian Husky with one brown eye and blue, Litter Bit a stray kitten, and now, her best friend. Shit, my best friend. Yeah. How much? I promise myself never to use her pens again and if I do, to put them back right away.

Next thing I know we're at the turn-off. I haven't been up in a couple of years. In fact, the last time the Phlegm's Kid, Stephen, and I had gone up there for the summer. It was a great and a disgusting time. Great, because among the wonderful things we did with Doc was the night he got fed up with all the stray dogs coming on the property and scaring Maia's ten cats, so he had us drink beer and walk around the boundaries pissing every few feet. When we ran out, we just had some more beer, 'til Maia got concerned and motherly and cut us off. Disgusting, because Maia was just about to start hating men, so she was always accusing us of being MCPs and because she had just discovered tofu and served it at every meal. It is unbelievably tasteless and disgusting, like slime. It is, as it comes to mind,

The Most Amazing Thing

the perfect honorary title for the Phlegm. Lennie, the Tofu. It sounds like an evil Chinese emperor.

That's the only bright spot in turning the corner and bumping down this two-rut dirt road. I don't like to think it, but it's the one Doc died on. There's a really beautiful late-morning light coming down through all the million kinds of trees.

"Wish we could go back," I say.

I didn't really expect to say anything like that. My mom looks at me.

"It gives me the creeps," I say. "I might have to sit in the car a while before I go in. I mean, he's not here, you know?"

"Yeah," Mom says. "I keep expecting that old Saab to rattle up the road." She shakes her head. "Ah, shit! I'm numb, Linc. I don't feel a thing."

"Yeah," I say. "Me, too," and realize it's true. My mind's going a mile a minute and I'm made out of rock from the throat down. We swing round a corner, through a clearing, over the old bridge and there it is, the beginning of their land, the gaping wood fence, the boulders that are all that's left of the original stone wall, and Doc's sign that says, Posted: No Hunting, No Fishing, No Rules.

One more bump and there's the run-down chicken coop held up by morning glory vines. Me and Stephen ate a bunch of seeds and got nothing but sick. Stephen was in his highly experimental phase that summer. He looked like Eric Clapton and knew about those Heavenly Blues and he was only fifteen years old. Amazing. Maia used to look at him and laugh and say that. *Amazing.* It's her favorite word.

The cabin looks great. Doc just finished covering it with fresh split shakes. He wrote us about it in one of his great letters. He always put pictures and curlicues around the first letter on the page just like a medieval book. In the cool light, you would think the cabin is made of gold. I hope he heard me think that. Maia is standing at the gate.

She's got her big, wide, bare feet planted in the dirt. She looks like a sturdy tree. She's got a big goofy smile on her face and, as always, her big tits are half hanging out of her shirt. She used to drive Stephen crazy. She'd hug him and he'd have to jerk off immediately. There's embroidery all over her shirt, which is a faded blue work shirt, what else? She has feathers from some poor dead bird hanging in her ears and a little tattooed woman's sign on her cheek. My mom sighs.

I can't believe the clearing. It's packed with trucks and V-Dub vans and old cars. It looks more like a co-op pot luck or some Women against Whatever than a funeral. There are crystals and feathers hanging from the rear view mirrors and bumper stickers on any spare space. There's about five dogs flirting and menacing and sniffing in disgusting places. There's no sign of cats.

My mom shuts off the engine. It's nice for a second, quiet, the sun warm and gentle, a hint of pine drifting in. Maia waves and walks toward us. I slump down in my seat. I mean, I love her, I really do. She's smart and she's the world's greatest cook and pun maker and she is careful to treat everybody as though they were a person. Which, I think, is the problem. That "as if." I mean, I am one. I'm young and I'm a guy, but I am a person.

She tugs the door open and pulls my mom out, no small feat since my mom is, as Doc says, sturdy peasant stock. I heave myself out the door and there we are, hugging. Between Maia's tits and Mom's big bones, I could get killed. When I come up for air, I see Mom look over Maia's shoulder and I know what she is doing. I am, too. What door did he leave from? Did he look back? How was his face? Did it hurt when it happened? I shiver. Maia steps back and smiles at both of us. Her eyes are shiny. I think she might be a little stoned.

"Oh, Linc," she says in her tiny voice, "don't be scared. Don't shiver like that."

"I'm okay," I say.

"For sure," she says. "You're more than okay." She holds me at arm's length. Her glittery eyes make me feel funny. She turns to my mom.

"Martha," she says. "Linc, this has been the most amazing thing. All of it. He's gone home. I just know it."

She grabs both our hands and pulls us over to a bunch of those old wall stones.

"What do you mean?" Mom asks. She perches on the boulders. Her back is very straight. Maia laughs.

"Relax," she says. "Let's sit here a minute. You look wiped."

"I'm alright," my mom says. "I just don't know what you mean. That's all." Maia pats her hand.

"Do you remember?" Maia asks. She sounds very excited. "That card you sent? A few weeks ago? The one with the Red-tail?"

My mom nods. There's this family story about Doc, about him and Mom being in this ancient, weird, horror-show museum, looking at a case of stuffed birds and my mom suddenly realizing that Doc looked just like a red-tail hawk. Once you heard the story, you could see it. His nose, his orange red hair, his forehead, which was definitely hawk-like and noble. I guess she'd sent them a card. She is the world's champion card sender. She even sent cards to The Tofu when he was on the coast with his secret girl friend.

"Well, something must have happened in the mail," she gives us this oh-yeah-it's-actually-karma look. "It came this morning. Two weeks late. And, as I was walking back to the house with it, the most amazing thing happened. A little sparrow hawk flew right past me, smacked into the garden fence, and dropped down dead at my feet." She looks at both of us.

I must admit, I am impressed. My mom ducks her head. She's not crazy about death and she thinks these ideas about rebirth and past lives are nothing more than people being disturbed by the mess of it all. As in "Hey, we got painless dentistry and painless religion and painless divorce, why not painless death?" We used to talk a lot about it when I was eleven and used to wake up in the middle of the night and wonder about life and what it meant and why bother?

I turn away as though I'm just looking at familiar surroundings, just sort of scoping things out. Rupert, the massive orange tiger cat, comes around the corner and saves all of us by being terrifically cute and affectionate. He's not really like that most of the time. Surly is weak word for his personality. He's got these huge ears that many important battles have turned into ragged banners. They flutter when he walks. So, his being adorable just adds to the miracles.

Maia leads us up the dirt path to the cabin. We go in through the mud room. The rocks in my chest turn into a blocked-up avalanche because there is Doc's old chamois jacket still hanging from its peg. I swear you can see the shape of his shoulders and his arms in how it hangs. Maia touches it gently and smiles back at us.

"He would have loved this," she says. "You guys here. All these friends. Really, it's more like a party."

We walk into the living room. I have my journal in my hand and if I wasn't able to keep plunking that rubber band, I would go crazy right there. My mom stops dead in her tracks. She looks weird out of her jeans and flannels. She'd finally dug up some awful shapeless gray-speckled skirt and a black blouse and jacket. She can't really wear black. It makes her look old and hungover. She looks around the big room kind of like a cat does when you put it in the car to take it to the vets.

There are a million people in the room. I know maybe two of them, Jeanne, the poet, and Duane, who works in the rope factory where Doc had done the night shift for the last two years. Everybody else appears to be ten years late for a TV special called, "The Sixties: Decade of Outrage." I don't mean pissed off. I mean outrageous. I don't know why women who hate men start to wear overalls. As a fashion statement, they are the worst. Half the guys are wearing purple. The other half are wearing camouflage.

Everybody's got their crystals. They're even wearing them, which Doc told me was a sacrilege to the people who really use them. With the light coming in through the big windows that Doc had put in himself, it's like we're in the middle of the beginning of a migraine headache, all these rainbow colors and flashing little flowers of light. Believe me, I know. One pinch of MSG and I'm in for a free total bummer trip.

There's this one girl with five earrings in one ear and a pierced nose. She's wearing a little ball of jade in the hole, which if you think of the color of jade and the color of snot, is pretty gross. It's 1978 and you can smell patchouli, which my mom gave up years ago, for which we all are eternally grateful. I can smell Buddhist temple incense. An unbelievably tall man is wandering around, carrying a stick of it and inviting people to wash the smoke down over their bodies. I do everything to keep his eyes from meeting mine. I think I remember him. His name is Gabriel and he knows The Way. He spots me and stares at me. His eyes are really creepy. They're gray and they seem frosted, like grapes look if you put them in the freezer, which Dave and I do because they become perfect little deadly missiles for food fights.

I pretend I am interested in the book case, which I actually am. Doc and Maia have the very best taste in books. There are great big art books that Maia buys marked down and Doctor Strange comic books and old classic comics and shelf after shelf of poetry. Maia is a poet, too. She actually wrote a very cool poem about periods. I settle down with good old Baudelaire and watch Maia work the crowd.

She's hugging everybody, those therapy type, "Have you hugged your kid today?" kind. She kisses a few people. Men. Women. Always on the mouth. She's directing things in her little voice. For a bossy woman, she's got an angelic kitten voice. I disappear into Baudelaire, which can happen, and the next thing I know, Maia is standing in the middle of the room with a cardboard box the size of a square bowling ball.

"It's Doc," my mom says and grabs my hand.

I drop everything on the floor but nobody notices. The box is wrapped in brown paper, like maybe somebody's cut up a shopping bag and used it for wrapping. It's stuck shut with masking tape and tied with brown string. I don't know what I expected. I knew he was ashes. I guess I just thought it would be wrapped different. He had a second-hand, offset press and he used to make this great wrapping paper printed with dragons and antique toasters and old letters and all sorts of weird stuff jumbled up together. I guess it seemed he should have been covered up with that kind of paper, by the kind of jokes he liked.

The Most Amazing Thing

Maia walks toward the door that leads to the garden. A young guy, my age maybe, steps in behind her. He's wearing a cape made from a quilt. He holds out his hands. The little hawk, looking like a feathered Cornish game hen on a plate, lies on top of a piece of folded cloth. I recognize the cloth. It was Doc's best-beloved scarf. It was from an obi. There were cranes on it and poppies. My mom had given it to him back when they were together.

"Oh, that poor little bird," My mom says in a vague voice. "If that fence hadn't been there, it wouldn't have died. "

"If that fence hadn't been there," I say, "the deer would have eaten the spinach." I hear Doc's words. It comes back to me, the argument Maia and Doc had and Doc's logic and how Maia had gone off to meditate on it and decided the fence was okay.

We all file out the back door and onto the path that snakes through the garden and up into the pines. One of the overalls ladies is waving incense and a guy with dreads is clanging little finger cymbals. My mom stops and a couple in back of us crashes into my back. My mom and I step off the path into the first shoots of the herb garden and wait until everybody has gone by.

"Okay," she says. I realize she isn't talking to me. "Okay," she says, "I can do this. I can do it for Doc."

We can hear the procession chanting something up ahead of us.

"Mom," I say. "He would have cracked up. He would be rolling on the ground, laughing. Let's go home."

"No!" she says firmly. "We'll do it for Maia. We'll do it for her. Or something. Got it?"

I don't, but she's looking very fierce and right on the edge of some kind of crying I really don't want to hear, so I nod and follow her up the path. It isn't that bad once we get into the trees. It smells good and there's pine pollen sifting down through the light. The shadows are the same color as the pine needles, sort of blue-black green. I make a mental note to myself to put that in my journal and snap the rubber band a couple of times, which always helps me stick some fact or observation in my memory.

Everybody is at the foot of a big pine tree that stretches up from a little rise. They are chanting and clanging and waving incense and doing all different kinds of dances. Maia calms us down and gets us started digging the hole, one person at a time, one shovelful at a time. It is a deep narrow hole. You can see a layer of brown pine needles, then a layer of rotting black leaves, then the gray stony dirt. I look down. Then I look up at the grandfather pine that would watch over him. The words in my mind surprise me. You wouldn't think I'd think of grandfather. Neither of mine were really visible, not like in some of the stories I'd read, where Grandfather takes the kid out to fish or hunt or shoot the shit. I'm glad Maia hands me the shovel. I dig deep and add the dirt to the pile at the side of the grave.

MAIA MAKES a little speech about how Doc talked sometimes about wanting to be buried at the foot of a pine, so he could go into the dirt and up into the tree.

"To feed it," she says softly. "To become the tree."

My mom nods. "She's got that right," she says gently.

I feel almost happy. Maia opens the box. She folds the paper into a neat square and wraps the string around her wrist. She's a careful person like that. She even washes out plastic bags and uses them again. She'll use that paper again. You can count on it. She tips the box in the hole. The ashes pour in a solid stream down into the needles and leaves and dirt. The young kid in the cape carefully sets the hawk on top of the ashes and lets the scarf cover it up. My mom presses something in my hand and moves forward. They are wilted violets. She must have picked them in the park the day he died. We scatter violets over the scarf and bird and ashes. I think maybe I see a white glint of bone, but I think it would be too weird to look in there for very long, so I back up.

Maia sifts a handful of dirt into the grave and everybody, one person at a time, does the same, some in silence, some whispering something, one little girl in checkered stockings humming to herself. We all get in a circle around the grave, which is almost filled up. I set my journal at my feet and hold hands with Maia and my mom. A song begins. That's just how it happens. I couldn't tell you who starts it. Mom's jaw is set. She probably would have brought a ghetto blaster and played the Ronettes or the Big Bopper or early Coltrane, but she isn't doing this. Maia is.

So, we sing this airy rainbow "we're all brothers and sisters" song about souls into souls and never forgetting, never forsaking, which despite its hippie musak melody, almost breaks up the log jam in my chest. Maia says, "Blessed be," and we start to march back to the cabin, some of the people pretending to play Dixieland jazz on air instruments. I am moping along, twanging the rubber band in my journal when I realize I'm in the middle of the jazz band and my mom is gone. I glance back. She's sitting by herself at the foot of the grandfather pine and, for a person of sturdy peasant stock, she seems very small.

I stop and watch her. She doesn't move. She just keeps looking down at the grave and up at the sky. I want to cry so much I stop thinking poetically of the sorrow in my chest as rocks. I wish I had some kind of magic dynamite to blow it up. I am plunking the rubber band the way Pete Townsend does at the end of *Not Gonna' Get Fooled Again*, when I feel a hand on my shoulder. My eyes are closed and I squinch them shut and see sparks. I can smell rosemary shampoo.

When I open my eyes I see Maia's smart, kind face. She is crying.

"Oh, Linc," she says. "Oh, sweetie," and puts in my hands Doc's perfectly tuned, hand-made twelve string guitar. "It's for you," she says.

I see Mom start back down the path toward us. Maia steps back. I stand there between them, Doc's guitar in my hands, the piney air moving into my lungs so fierce and clean I think it could bust me open.

 Luzianne

S EVEN YEARS AGO, my brother called me from clear across the country to tell me that at thirty-nine, he had finally figured out what he really wanted to do. I was happy for him. It had been a long confused haul and he deserved a little clarity. Which, as he told me in his thin, tight voice, was sitting in a rocking chair by the window of his second story bedroom, in the old Southern Tier farm-house he'd bought, and taking shots at a three-pound coffee can. It was a twenty-two rifle and the coffee had chicory in it. When I asked him what brand, so maybe I could picture it, he said he didn't know and, what's more, it didn't matter.

All that mattered were the soft, green-gold, long, long summer evenings you get down in the Southern Tier of New York State and the way the wind teased the can. Gently. Seeming to slip in from every direction, so the can danced around in ways he couldn't predict and he had to concentrate, to see, to aim, to shoot. He said that he sat there for hours, and in that time, now and then, tears would run down his face and he didn't have any words for the sorrow. Did I? Was it like mine? Could I tell him?

I told him the truth. That I couldn't quite get the picture and it's the pictures that matter to me. I told him that he'd probably have to sit there a while longer and see for himself. I'm the older sister here, by five years. He turns to me about once a decade and, sure as shit, I seem to always let him down.

I must have blown it big on that one because I didn't hear from him for ages. Except for times I called our folks and he was there, like Christmas '85 and '86 and '87. He'd be all warm and almost teary and he'd want to talk a long time. On my money. Finally, I was so pissed off by him never calling me on his own dime, that, in '89, when my mom said, "Do you want me to put Rick on the phone?" I said, "No, I don't think so. Not this time. No." I could hear her breathe. I could hear her swallow her words. I almost wished I'd swallowed mine.

But I thought about all the Christmases and birthdays he'd messed up and the time I'd sent him a Lackawanna & Erie Railroad key chain and he'd never even written to say *thank you* or *remember when we used to go down early morning to the station and watch the trains and we were always scared the trains would suck us under or remember how when Mom was nuts Dad would buy us breakfast in that little wood shack on the way home*, so the hell with him. Anyway, back then, back two years ago, with me it was *don't get mad, get even* that guided my path. Especially with men. Especially men who didn't call. Every now and then, I'd think about Rick up in that rocking chair, plunking away at some coffee can and I'd feel a little sad, but, it was his turn, it was his time to stick the dimes in the slot.

Besides, about then, my life got lively. Out of nowhere, there was this unexpected miracle of tele-communications. My ex-boyfriend Scotty called up and showed up and, somehow, he and I were different this time around. This time we went slow. This time we could stand the silences. This time we actually talked. He started telling me Nam stories and I had to think about them and see the pictures they made. And I had to face that I had no picture of my brother. Not a snapshot, not a home movie, not any way to see him at all.

So NOW, time's gone by the way it does when you're happy with it, when you don't have to figure how to fill up the empty places. Scotty is solid in my days and nights, and my brother's still out there somewhere. It's funny how that kind of absence of someone who wasn't ever really there feels. It's not like a hurt, it's more like a bruise you don't notice 'til you bump it, when you're floating in and out of sleep at night, or waiting in the grocery line, or road-tripping one of these Southwest highways, with your mind drifting from exit sign to exit sign. Then it aches. But, only for a second, only for as long as it takes me to put my mind on happier things, like how Scotty Desmont is lover and pal and story-teller and brother enough.

Scotty Desmont. *Day-mon*. Of the mountains. Actually, of Ohio. Actually, Rupert Desmont 'til he sprouted to six foot two and one hundred-ninety pounds his high school sophomore year and no way were the cheerleaders going to shriek "Rupert" every time he completed one of his shamanic passes. That's how he tells it, how his mom, Myra, tells it whenever we're snug on the couch in her Tempe condo, swamp-cooler purring, lizards blissing on the patio wall, the photo album in our laps and all those pictures of Rupert-Scotty. The three of us are flipping the pages and that kid, that place, and that weather seem more like a galaxy away, than the two thousand miles and twenty-plus years they really are.

I still do not quite trust Scotty, but being a mom, actually a grandma myself, I trust Myra. I trust most Moms. At some level, no matter how the surface looks, a lot of us are alike. We know about the bruises that lie under things. We tell magic stories about our kids and, sometimes, about the bruises. Most of us have been less than magic and, real shamans nonetheless. I think of my own mom, of her young face pale and slack from too many Seconal, and even with that I see her tan hands moving over the piano keyboard, playing *Satin Doll* on a drenched August evening. I think of her laughter, hear her and Aunt Marge telling the stories of their flapper girlhoods. I wish I'd been there and when Myra tells me Scotty was something special, I wish I was back two thousand miles and twenty-plus years, except I'd be twenty-three and he'd be illegal and we'd both be back East, a fate we've agreed that's worse than death.

Myra doesn't use the word shamanic. Neither does Scotty. That's more mine. What she says, causing him to look at his shoes and go red in the ears, is that he was flat-out magic there on the field. She'd watch him running and dodging and blocking and she could hardly believe it was the same skinny kid she'd pulled through pneumonia for three winters in a row. Scotty hates that part. How she says that and how she pats his balding head and gets this wet look in her old blue eyes.

It took Scotty and me six years and four false starts to get together, six months for him to decide to haul me south to meet his folks, six months for me to agree to go. All of that was longer than this most recent silence that stretches between me and Rick, my brother. I notice I talk about Rick so infrequently that I am careful to say Rick, my brother. I do think about him, about Rick, my brother. My brother, Rick, who is frozen in my mind somewhere around 1968, when he slid into a marriage long-since trashed and sent me the pictures, him with a white-boy afro and a paisley cummerbund, her in a pink cotton mini-dress, her belly pushing out, raising the hem even higher above her sturdy legs; my brother, Rick, who didn't raise the kid I hardly know, who sits, instead, alone in green-gold dusk and raises some kind of gun to his shoulder and listens to the ping of the bullet hitting some kind of coffee can. I think of him at the strangest moments, like when I smell pine and it has that gold-green perfume, or when Scotty and I are tramping around the Mogollon Rim in hunting season and hear gunshots and we both speed up a little and, most of all, when I hear Scotty tell me a story and I realize I know more about twenty-four-year-old Scotty and his Special Forces Medic year than I do about my brother and whatever he did or didn't do in those same, strange days.

In truth, on the other three go-rounds that Scotty and I stumbled through, I didn't have a picture of *Scotty*. He was a stranger to me. *A stranger in a stranger land,* like this great country-western song says. I was a stranger to his thoughts, his secrets, his stories, to everything but his body. That solid home land, that flesh and smell and hunger, known as though never not known, was enough to snag in my memory and draw me back. The way some little canyon can tug at you, the way a sandstone arch can call back your heart. And, finally, you go.

Now, having gone, everything with Scotty and me seems to be easy and, amazingly, after a year, still hotter than a FNG on his first night in Saigon. Fucking New Guy. Saigon. Saigon, 1969. Ancient history to most people, that time and that weird war, practically last week to Scotty, who was in that war, who was more *there* in that war then he's ever been since. My brother wasn't there, in that war. Though he's two years older than Scotty and he could have been. He was somewhere else. He was somewhere, year after year, that wasn't quite *there*. That much I have guessed at.

Wherever my brother was, Nam would have been better. Scotty doesn't know he's convinced me of this, but he has. In the albums his mother spreads out in front of me, there is one picture of that time. Scotty's ears stick out, which they still do, and he is a big fellow, which he still is and you can see the man he will become. I can't see his eyes behind his glasses, but I can guess that he's looking straight into the camera, no flinching, no turning away. I think Nam gave him that. I think he brought it away. A hard gift. A difficult treasure.

There is only this one picture of that time in his mom's album and she knows zero of the stories that might go with it. I think it's her loss, but I understand. I don't want to know how my youngest got on and off cocaine and I don't want to know what happened in the hours right before my middle daughter took her gorgeous kid and left her mystery marriage. But with Scotty, late at night, when we're worn out from our fine loving and we can't listen to another song by people who now have gray in their beards, or silver in their long, straight hair, he tells me the stories, one after another, sometimes repeating them two or three times, the way old people will tell stories, the way that gets you to see the pictures behind the stories. I listen, and, as I listen I see these are the pictures that are not in the album. It was, it is too dark under the triple canopy, there is too much flesh, too much blood and bone for them to have ever been developed.

I'm willing to see those pictures, to let them come up out of the dark, to watch the boys and men and mess take shape. I'm willing to secure the hot light and shadows in my mind. I'm willing to remember the stories that go with them, picture for picture, word for word.

I think we human beings have a gene for both those things, for telling stories and remembering. It may not kick in 'til we're old or scared or we've been through something that must not be forgotten. Then that story gene floats up out of the old animal soup and we tell and repeat, and those who listen start to remember, so when it's time for them to pass the stories on, they mostly get it right. Maybe they add some things in, you could do that, out of love, out of respect, out of hatred or pain. But, when that gene is working you have to listen, and you sure as shit have to talk.

"It wasn't patriotism," Scotty tells me. "It was other things." He pulls on his beer. Beer lubricates the story gene, especially late at night, especially when talker and listener have exchanged longing and satisfaction—and breath and whispers still drifting over their tired bodies.

"Mmm," I breathe against his chest.

"Can you hear me?" he says. "Put that thing in."

I reach up and take my hearing aid from next to the mirror and the candle and the baby oil, and put it in my ear. I turn the little dial, hear the air crackle and rest my other cheek on his skin.

"It wasn't patriotism," I say, "It was other things."

"Right," he says. "It was friendship. It was the buzz. It was clarity."

I wait. I love his breathing and his smell, our smell, and I love his room that has no pictures and a 9MM automatic in a holster on the headboard shelves and a shotgun down alongside the waterbed. It's like being on an ocean, in a boat with a strong, well-armed friend. I feel warm. I feel safe.

"You were with these guys," he says, "and all of you were with death, twenty-fucking-four hours a day…"

He stops. I wait.

"You were so tired," he says, "every one of you. See, because what you'd been doing was this: maybe you'd been up three nights straight, with that lousy Army amphetamine, did I tell you about that, we called 'em Green Hornets?"

I nod. He ruffles my hair, pulls me in a little closer.

"So, you spent the day digging holes and stringing wire and, then, you go out on ambush," he says quietly.

I can't imagine that fatigue. I think maybe a little, when I remember walking point as a single mom, hitting the floor moving at 6 A.M., getting the kids out to school, myself to work, then back, buying groceries, maybe doing a wash, cooking dinner, then night school and study 'til one, and still, nobody was trying to kill me.

"And you're all the time, scared to death." He stops.

"You…are…scared…all…the…time," he says again. Scotty is a calm, understated guy. In six years I've seen him mad maybe twice, heard him be scary once when he told me that if anybody had spit on him when he came back, he would've shoved his or her nose into the back of his or her head. I've seen him be outrageous plenty, but even that is gentle and silly. All three times when I told him that due to his hopeless insufficiencies I couldn't see him anymore, he had the grace to walk away. And stay away. His favorite mental health advice is "Lighten up."

I know *scared…all…the…time.* I can see, can smell, can feel *scared… all…the…time.* I did that. For fifteen years. Panic disorder. Agoraphobia. Scared shitless syndrome. SSS we called it in the funny farm, those three times I went, those times I was happy to be locked in. Now and then, if I haven't been taking care of business, if I let myself get too hungry or tired or pissed-off I go right back into it. Can't think. Can't move. Can't breathe. Can't do anything but stay still and do what passes for prayer 'til my heart lays off and I can swallow past whatever it is, I still don't know, from being little, a little girl, a spooked and furious little girl, that blocks my airline, that cold-cocks my heart.

"I know some about that," I say. Scotty is staring up at the ceiling.

I can hardly see him. We talk about getting a Lava Lamp so we can watch the shadows play off our bodies, but we haven't done it. He told me it was a great relief to tell me things from those late sixties, early seventies and not have to explain. So, we miss Lava Lamps, and tie-dyed bell-bottoms and pony-tails. When we're out in the high canyon sun he still wears a bandana. He wonders if they came from Nam, from how the guys kept the sweat out of their eyes, so they could see, see to stay alive.

Once, a little before Christmas, which we both hate, we had our own celebration out at his house on the Rim. I remember the clear morning light pouring in through the picture window and the pines outside. He put on my gift, the patchwork skirt my friend, Crazy Sue, had made for me in 1968, and a purple bandana, and we took my holy beads from around my neck and hung them around his. We were listening to Steppenwolf and Scotty sashayed around, into the sun and out, across the living-room shag onto the gritty kitchen tiles, up and down the long hallway, 'til he stopped at the wall cupboard and took out his green beret and a couple medals and the death's-head plaque the guys had given him in '70. *Rupert "Dark Cloud" Desmont,* and the death's-head had fangs, and the grunts and officers thanked him for his work.

Now, lying pressed against his warm body, the memory sings in my blood. *Brother,* I think in that old dreamy stoned way. *Brother.*

"One time," he says, "I was with some Vietnamese regulars and a bunch of 'Yards and we were going through this elephant grass."

It's the trip-wire story. I wait.

"Did I tell you how that grass could cut your hands to shreds? You had to wear gloves. When you got it bent down, it was so fucking slippery to walk on that you had to grab what was left standing around you to stay off your ass. You wore canvas gloves. In that heat. That's how bad it was." He doesn't wait for me to tell him that he's told me. I wouldn't anyhow. The gene is jumping and I need to listen to the stories, to how they change, to how they stay the same.

I don't have any big need to tell him mine, the ones about the Draft Board bust and the bail fund benefits and the teach-ins and sit-ins and die-ins and the marches. The only one he knows is the time I stepped out to walk ten city blocks, knowing that somebody had called the cops and threatened to blow away one of those peace cunts. Just that time, that's the only one that really seems important these days. I can still hear the slow, steady thump of the single Buddhist drum. I can still see how everything was blurred because I was so scared. I made my feet step in time to that dark Buddhist beat. That's the only way I kept moving. That's the only story he's heard.

"I couldn't see anything," Scotty says. "I heard a pop. I heard somebody yelling, '*Bac se. Didi mau. Bac se.*' That's 'Doc'…'run fast.' I told you that once, right? And, I know that one of those fuckers has snagged a trip wire and is out there in a world of hurt. And, I know that because he is scream-ing, and these people don't scream. And, I know that this whole stretch of grass is rigged with trip wires and I gotta get to that little fucker. And, I know it's impossible and it don't mean nothin'."

He made himself lift up one foot, then the next, then the next, one step at a time, forcing himself to walk, forcing himself to breathe. Going forward, breathing in, breathing out, going, breathing. His skin is soft and warm against my cheek. He's put on weight since that don't mean nothin' stroll. I love his bulk. He is a bear or a tree in my arms. I imagine him in that cruel grass, young and thin and hard, his skin clammy, his muscles frozen, his heart racing inside his ribs. I can see how he might have moved, not a machine, no, he would have been fully human, but slow and stiff as any robot. I can see how his eyes would have been behind his fogged glasses, how his breath would have moved choppy and short and stubborn around his heart.

I cannot hear what he heard. I have never heard that sound. I have not even come close. And the smells that he tells me were there, never.

"Did you get to him?" I ask. He doesn't answer. I hear him begin to snore. Later, he will deny it. He will tell me that he doesn't snore. It's me who snores. And, we will have to wrestle about that. It will be dawn and we will be laughing and wrestling and not kissing because we haven't gotten out of bed to brush our teeth, and, you see, we will have already made love at least once.

MAYBE THOSE nights and mornings have given me the courage. Maybe it's the stories, the way Scotty's stories fill me with pictures, the way they light up the dark empty spaces in my heart where my brother ought to be. Maybe it's this new war that's just begun and the television pictures of rockets over Baghdad like hot jewels against the midnight sky. Maybe it's how I watched and remembered a comic book I'd loved when I was eight.

Each of its hundreds of pictures was framed in flowers and jewels. There were only six stories, not the full thousand and one that Scheherezade had told to save her life, but I read and re-read 'til the six were a thousand and the last story was never told. I read over breakfast. I read in the car. I read crouched under my bedroom window after lights out, squinting in the last of the summer dusk, so sleepy the pictures blurred and shimmered before my eyes.

I read in the waiting room of the psych hospital while my dad visited my mom. I knew the endings by heart and, on that old maroon leather couch, under the thin fluorescent light, only grown-ups around me, I made myself forget. I surprised myself, again and again. I traced the jewels and flowers with my fingertips. I studied the flying horse and turned the pages fast past the terrible djinns. Two of the stories began in Baghdad. With all my young heart, I wanted to fly there someday. I wanted to fly to Baghdad, to a place where a girl could tell stories to save her life.

Now, watching the rockets, knowing how far we are from their scream and dazzle, and how close, I begin to see something. I know it's not a huge deal, not life or death, not *didi mau, bac se*, but I see how I have to do something about my brother. One of the Sundays when I'm at my place and Scotty is denned up out in the pines, I find my photo album and I make myself look at the pictures. There's formerly crazy Mom. There's Dad who, right this minute, as I tell this story, is not going gentle into that good night. There's Rick. He's blonde and round-cheeked and you can see that the dark little girl on the sled next to him, the frazzle-haired kid who's squinting at the camera, is less than thrilled about something. You can tell that she might be the kind of sneaky little shit who would tell her kid brother ghost stories and then holler to her parents that he was crying and keeping her awake. You can tell that she would be pissed at getting caught, and she would not have one, not one-half a baby regret that she'd done such an awful thing. You can tell that she's already made up her mind that life is not a square deal. You could guess that she already tells herself stories, none of them ghostly, all of them full of jewels and magic carpets, and captive princesses and brave peasant boys who set them free and love them forever.

Scotty has an older sister. She's far away. He doesn't write. One night, I start to tell him about Rick, and I stop. There are stories that happen across an ocean and there are stories that happen in your very own back home back yard. I can see that yard as a bunch of vines, all tangled together, thicker than any jungle and ten times as scary. There are wonderful blossoms and unbelievable birds and there are trip wires, folks. If you go back into that jungle, if you keep breathing, if you listen to your racing heart and lift your foot up and go forward, sometimes what you step over still blows up in your face. Sometimes, the screaming never stops.

I'm having those deep thoughts as I look at the picture of my family, and the ones after it, and, finally, the one taken last Christmas: my folks, my kids, and Rick flashing a peace sign at the camera. There is no triple canopy. There are no flares. There is only the flashbulb reflecting off Rick's glasses. So I can't see his eyes. I can only see his scared grin and how he's facing square into the camera.

I pick up the phone and he's there. I tell him about being mad and he says he doesn't blame me. I tell him I miss him and he says he knows that he's the one that's got to break the silence. I start to cry. He says that sometimes he goes to this island where our family used to camp and he sits on the big rock and he cries and cries. He says he's found the little boy that lives inside him and he doesn't know whether to kill him or give him a hug. I, for once, wisely keep my mouth shut. We're quiet for a minute.

"I've just got a couple questions before I hang up," I say.

"Go for it," he says. I see him there, in that rocking chair, with the rifle, sighting out along the barrel, watching the can twist and sway in the soft air.

"What brand is that coffee?" I ask. "I need to know."

"Luzianne," he says. I see the shiny white-and-red can. I see how it might catch the sunlight, how the earth would keep circling toward dusk, and the light and colors fade. I see how, at the last, there would be just that black shape dancing against the pale sky.

 Monsters

It's not that Jen wanted pity. That would have been too embarrassing. She'd gotten herself in this mess, plus pity was for victims, she'd been totally a volunteer. She didn't even want understanding. To get that she'd have to explain things to someone. She'd have to say it out loud. *All* of it. No, forget that. What Jen wanted, plain and simple, was an easy, safe, painless, and absolutely secret abortion. What she wanted was to be a kid again.

Easy was easy enough. She was nineteen. The state had yet to do whatever they kept threatening about parental permission, so it was just a matter of signing on the dotted line. *Safe* was what Family Planning Center was all about. *Secret*, no problem. She was three months into her first semester at college, so hardly anybody knew her. The town was little enough that she could walk to the FPC clinic from her dorm, through pine trees that smelled like vacations. If anybody saw her, she was just getting birth control. Lots of kids carried something. It was the days of AIDS, whether you liked it or not. *Painless?* That was another story. A girl in her high school had cruised into the clinic one afternoon and been back in school the next day. Another was like it was totally the worst experience in her life.

What was totally weird was that she was crying a lot. Not that she was sad about the situation. It was one of those things you had to deal with. She'd stayed awake through the X-rated parts of high school health class so she knew we were not dealing with quite a real person here. We were, basically, dealing with a little It. And still, she'd be studying or waiting in line at the bank or picking up something at Circle K and, all of a sudden she's crying, tears running down her face and she has to find the ladies' room and wait out the storm. She figured it was hormones. Her body, her self, all complicated and not-her.

One time, she was crouched over herself in the Circle K ladies' room and, out of nowhere, in the middle of the tears, she started thinking about what was inside her and she remembered being a little kid and going to the museum in D.C. with her dad. He took her and her sister, Trish, and her brother, Jason, in this room that had all these pickled babies in it. Why she'd never know. Her dad *was* a doc, but still, it was way gross. Even if the babies had been normal, it would have been weird because the room smelled like chemicals and the babies were all gray and wrinkled up. But, those pickle babies were *really* strange. Little stub arms, and one with no legs, but a tail, and the worst, a tiny monster with a huge head and one eye in the middle of its face.

Later, out in the more modern, more cheerful rooms about Colonial America, with the videos you could work yourself and the voice-overs that told you about beeswax and handmade cradles, she'd felt better. Dad had taken them out for lunch at a fancy French restaurant and he'd let them order whatever they wanted. When she tasted the chocolate ganache, which was easily the best thing she'd ever eaten in her life, somehow the tears started and her dad had walked outside with her and listened and he'd told her that people didn't have those kinds of babies much anymore. Modern medicine saw to that. There were ways to monitor the fetus, ways to know if something was going wrong and, mercifully, ways to stop the mistake. He'd hugged her and, when they'd gone back in, her dessert had still been there and she'd eaten every spoonful.

She could almost see the whole thing, almost as though it was projected on the backs of her eyelids, on the white, white walls of the Circle K john. When she finally felt the tears stop, she flushed the toilet twice, so maybe the people outside would think she was ralphing, not in there doing something weird, and then she had washed her face and come out into that always bizarre Circle K light and all the people had looked strange to her. Their normal two-eyed faces, their regular-shaped arms and legs, the way they were putting cheese goo on their nachos or a lid on their coffee, they looked like perfect Disney robots. She'd gone outside and stood in the noon sun, watching the traffic move along the street, feeling grateful that the cars and trucks didn't do anything out of the ordinary. She watched the light change a few times and that was normal, green to yellow to red, and she felt calmer and she realized, for half a second, that she was way scared—and she didn't know what of.

The weirdest part about the weird feelings was that they would come up out of nowhere. When she was talking to the in-take counselor at the clinic, she'd been totally calm. She'd been totally honest. The whole business had been her own fault.

She could not blame the guy. And not like some of the other kids in the dorm, she couldn't blame a broken family or an alcoholic father or no mom in the home or anything like that.

In fact, though she didn't tell the sweet-faced counselor this, she had only gone through one major tragedy in her life, when Tracey had died. And, bad as that had been, you couldn't say it caused Jen to do what she'd done. Besides, right after the news about Tracey got out, the counselors at school had helped everybody. They'd had these grief groups and she'd cried a bunch, so she couldn't blame her weirdness on "unresolved sadness," or "stuffing feelings" like the counselors had kept talking about. Though, she had to admit, sometimes when those stupid tears started dribbling, it was Tracey who came to mind. It was the way it had happened that still seemed really bizarre, like something you would see on television or read about in the *Enquirer.* Teen-ager dies in graduation-gift sports car while family watches TV one room away.

No, she couldn't really say that her childhood had anything to do with it, or a bad school, or living in the kind of neighborhood where girls got pregnant as a usual thing. It had been all her. The boy, whose name she hadn't got, had been the one who suggested condoms, who said he'd go to the all-night drugstore to buy them. It had been *her* who hadn't wanted to stop. It had been her who couldn't stand to feel him move away. She hadn't even taken a breath to figure out when her period was due. They'd been kissing and touching and, why she would never know, she had wanted just for that minute to do what *she* wanted to do, right when she wanted to do it. So they had.

And now she was ralphing in the dorm john and lying about how much she'd drunk the night before, pretending it was *piña coladas.* Her roommates were like they didn't notice, but when you were three girls in a two-girl room there weren't any secrets from anybody. Luckily, Susan was Mormon and Vivian was Hopi. They might as well have been born on planet Xenon. They saw nothing, they heard nothing, they knew nothing but good grades and happy families. So, hopefully, for all she knew, she'd gotten by.

But them being so innocent about life, which could seem like a good thing, was really the bad thing. With Tracey gone, she had absolutely no one to talk to. She had hoped she might meet somebody at school, somebody she could *begin* to get to know. She'd figured maybe your roommates could be like sisters, but even better.

Jennifer'd known it wouldn't be the same as her and Trace. Probably, there would never be anything like her and Trace ever again in her life. K–12, every single year, same home room, same sorority, same clothes, same color phones and rooms, same everything 'til the last six months of Senior year, when Tracey's mom had kicked out her dad and he had almost immediately moved in with this college intern from work, who was FOUR!! years older than Tracey. Tracey had talked like that, with capitol letters and exclamation points and her long, tan fingers flying around, pointing like, *"Is that fair, you guys? Come on, is that fair?"*

At first, Tracey had stayed at Jen's. Night after night, they'd talked 'til dawn. Trace had said that helped her, to be sitting there together, so sleepy you could pretend you were calm, watching for the first desert light. She'd loved dawn and sunset and monsoons and anything that was a change from ordinary. She said that no matter how weird things were, that dawn light was always hopeful to her.

They'd finally hear Jen's mom moving around in the kitchen. They'd go out to the breakfast counter and Jen's mom would have special almond coffee and real cream, and croissants. She'd be "no big deal" about whether they'd slept or not. Jen's mom and dad were cool about that sort of thing. They didn't treat her like a baby. No curfews. No family counselling-type questions. Jen's mom was big on boundaries. So, in a way, it was her and Trace alone with it.

Over and over, Tracey was like, "I should do something," and Jen was, "Right!" but they couldn't come up with what that something was. So, finally, she went, "What, Trace...what are you going to do? Why do you think it's your business anyhow? It's not like he was *your* husband."

"No," Tracey had gone, "you're right. He wasn't. He's just my dad and it's not my business, not anymore, not at all." And, that night, for the first time, she'd turned out the light before midnight and she'd gone to sleep.

In the weeks that had followed, she'd just sort of faded out of Jen's life. Jen had tried to talk with her. Tracey was like, "No, really, I'm fine, just busy, just got tons to do, you know?" Jen had tried a few more times, sent some notes, put one of those "You're my friend no matter what" cards in her locker. It was a really nice one with calligraphy and a butterfly, but Tracey hadn't even mentioned it. Gradually, without really noticing, Jen drifted off herself. Those last months of school, that summer in between high school and college, you could go non-stop if you wanted. You could just cram in all the stuff you'd wanted to do for four years. She wished now she'd seen what was happening, because if she had, Tracey would still be alive and Jen would be calling her down in Tempe and telling her what was going on. She'd be able to say everything, how it was her fault, how those stupid tears kept coming, how, though she didn't want to admit it, when she thought of the "It", she saw that poor little gray monster baby in the museum. Tracey was absolutely the *only* person Jen could have told that to.

THE DAY for the abortion came closer, except they didn't call it an abortion. When you caught it right at the beginning they called it a menstrual extraction. She hadn't waited at all to set an appointment. She'd waked up the morning after the big event and she'd cruised right in to the clinic. She'd known the second she'd felt the guy cum in her that she was in trouble. She wondered how you knew that sort of thing. When she thought back, it had been an incredibly weird feeling, as though she'd opened out, as though he'd sunk something deep in her and she'd felt it take root. They'd told her at the clinic that she had to wait ten days for the test, so she'd gone to the drug store that minute and got one of those kits, so what? The stupid kit hadn't worked. Then, her period was late and she began to wake up with her stomach feeling awful.

The rabbit died. They couldn't take her right away. They had some rule about six weeks at least, so here she was, with five weeks of Circle K boohoos and morning prayers at the porcelain throne, and all those weird flash-backs of bottled babies and Tracey dead in her beautiful, little red Honda CRX, and the words, *I should have done something,* chasing themselves around in her brain, as though they'd cloned themselves, as though they were little animated guilt-trips, like some dumb video game characters that you couldn't beat.

"I should have done something," she wrote in her diary. And, sometimes, when she'd run out of tears and still the sobs were wrenching out of her, worse than dry heaves, worse than anything she could remember, she'd say the words out loud and there'd be nobody there to say, "What? What could you have done?" And, she couldn't even go to her room and put out the light and sleep the pain away, because Vivian and Susan were in there, studying all the time. You didn't want to lie there in that cold fluorescent light, with your eyes closed and the things you couldn't help projecting themselves on your eyelids, while you listened to the beeps on Susan's PC and Vivian's whispery voice going on and on, talking to her Mom or her sisters or her cousins or any of the ten million people she seemed to have for family. It was too weird, hearing normal life and not-quite-seeing things that could have been out of a nightmare.

And what she seemed to see got worse and worse. First, it had just been the look on her mom's face when Mrs. Richards called about Tracey, then it had been watching her own fingers dig into the desk, seeing how her nails broke, one after another, and still she was gouging scratches in the wood. Then, it was the stupid funeral. And, voice-over came in, the flabby priest saying all this boring stuff that had nothing to do with Tracey, not one fucking thing at all and you could hear kids crying and Tracey's boy-friend kicking the back of the pew, his mom trying to hush him up, her whisper hissing so everybody could hear it. "Stop it, Corey, act like an adult."

All that was bad enough. But, what was really causing Jen to doubt her sanity was that she'd begun to wonder about what Tracey had been thinking, how she'd come up with it, how she'd felt when she finally got the vacuum cleaner hose hooked up to the exhaust and running in through the back car window, how she'd felt when she could smell the fumes starting to fill the car. Why had she worn the prom gown? Why had she washed her hair and set it and sprayed it with that glitter stuff? Why did she have her little velvet purse in her lap, with gloss and blusher and liner and five dollars, folded into a tiny wad? Why'd she have that really stupid rock station on her Walkman? Why wasn't she listening to *Offspring?* They had meant so much to her, they could have brought her some comfort, made her change her mind.

And, even if you could never answer *those* questions, there were all the others ones. Did it hurt? Did you just get goofy and groggy and go to sleep? As you were drifting away, could you actually *hear* the radio? Were the last more-or-less human voices Tracey heard the ones of those totally white late-night d.j.'s, thinking they were so cool because they played hip-hop and every other word out of their mouths was def or homey or dissin'? God. Tracey would have hated that. Did she? At the last second, did she hear those whiney, bogus voices and wish she could have changed her mind?

Compared to picturing that, thinking about the abortion was nothing. Crying and seeing monsters in the Circle K and terminal ralphing and somehow getting to class and getting papers written, even in English where you had to write personal stuff right when you didn't want to think about anything in your life at all—that was Baja Spring Break compared to the hours she lay in her bed, half-seeing, half-hearing, whole-hearted imagining what might have been.

The only decent part was it made her absolutely sure about not having this baby. It made her even wonder if she would ever have one, if she would ever trust a guy enough to let him be a dad. Because, though she didn't have any proof, she had some guesses about why Tracey had done what she'd done. And, if she was right, no way was she ever going to risk putting a little girl out on this planet. Imagine if you were your daddy's special most darling absolute little princess. Imagine if he left and never said a word to you until after he was gone. Not one.

Then, as though seeing stuff wasn't enough, Vivian and Susan started acting strange. Jen would come in and there'd be one of those murky silences, where you knew you'd been the topic of conversation. They still acted the same. Real polite. Not pushy or anything. It was creepy. You started to wonder if you'd left your diary out or maybe talked in your sleep. Jen forced herself to stay awake pretend studying 'til they put out the light. In a way, it helped. Reading, even if you read the same page over and over again for an hour, kept your eyes busy, and it shut off the voice-over going in your head.

A WEEK TO the Big Day and the roomies asked her to go for pizza with them. At first, she passed, then she thought about being in the room not quite alone, just her and the *Friday the 13th: Part Ten Million* her brain had become, and pizza sounded like a good idea. They walked over to Paulo's, which, of course, was in the same shopping center as the Family Planning Center. Jen really needed that. It wasn't that she was scared, that wasn't quite the word for it, but when she saw the gray-curtained windows and the plain sign, her stomach jumped.

"Did you hear about those pro-lifers?" Vivian said. "You can hear them from my History class."

Susan glanced at the place. "I've *seen* them," she said. "Big old signs and handing out stuff. I saw them screaming at a lady who was trying to get out of her car."

"My cousin went through that," Vivian said. She turned her face away. "I shouldn't have said anything. My aunt'd kill me if she knew I told."

"Is it a sin in Hopi to get one of those?" Susan said.

"All my cousin was doing was getting checked out to see if she was pregnant," Vivian said. "They scared her real bad."

"*Is* it a sin?" Jen asked. The question just seemed to jump out of her mouth. She tossed back her hair and hoped she looked casual.

"Not the way you might see it," Vivian said, "besides, me and my whole family, we're Christians and our preacher says it is a sin, so I go along with that, but not big time."

"Mormons, too," Susan said.

You can feel like a one-girl plague at moments like that. Jen shoved her hands in her pockets and made sure she was walking right in step with them. After they got into the pizza place and settled in at the table, it went better. Susan said that she hadn't actually made her own mind up about stuff like that and Vivian said what other people did was their business. So, they got a Large, with half sausage and mushrooms, and half pineapple and ham.

"My Comp class," Jen said, "that abortion stuff and legalizing marijuana were the only two topics our teacher could get the class to talk about. Some of the girls were real mean about it." She wondered if she'd said too much. She couldn't seem to shut up.

"My Comp teacher is a radical," Susan said, "keeps talking about that kind of stuff, too, that and women's lib and gays even."

"If they don't hurt anybody..." Jen started to say. Vivian and Susan looked at her. The pizza guy called their number. You could be grateful for small miracles like that. She went and picked up their stuff. By the time she got back, they had changed the topic. You could be grateful for that, too, even if they *were* talking about religion, even if you couldn't think of anything to say, miracles or not.

OF COURSE it was this perfect day when she went for the abortion. FPC told her to have somebody drive her back, but she didn't know anybody, so she told them that and they said they could call a cab for her and to be sure to have cash for the cab, because she might be too groggy to write a check. She wasn't that scared, but she tucked what was left of the woven friendship bracelet Tracey had given her not even a year ago into her backpack, along with five dollars for the cab and her identification and she headed out on the dirt path.

You wouldn't believe the sun, especially in November, or the way the mountains were just as clear and big as if they were in the middle of town. Ravens were screaming in the pines on the edge of campus. She wished she'd saved some corn chips for them. She'd been feeding them. There was something about sitting under a big old pine, letting the sun beat down on your head, watching two of those rude dudes fight over your left-over lunch. Besides, she'd given herself too much time to get to the clinic and the thought of sitting in that cozy waiting room was weird.

She got a diet pop from the laundromat and sat in the sun. She wondered if she should do something like say good-bye to the It, but she wasn't feeling like doing that, or much of anything but swallowing her pop and letting the sun touch her face. She wondered if she was stuffing feelings or if she was just a heartless monster. She knew that in the months to come what was really going to bother her was not the fact that she'd voided the It, not even the fact that she'd been stupid enough to start the whole thing in the first place. It was how even in the middle of those stupid tears, she would feel nothing for the It.

She crushed the pop can under her foot, tied Tracey's bracelet around her left wrist, and headed for the corner. The pro-lifers were out there. They were silent. They were dressed boring and they were carrying neatly lettered signs. The signs asked you to think about the little babies. They asked you to look into your heart. Jennifer stopped. She wondered if she should just act casual or if she should hug the buildings, go past the lifers to the drug store and around the back. They were lining the drive into the shopping center. She saw a hippie girl in a pick-up throw them the finger. She saw somebody else stop and take a flyer. She saw a cab pull in and a woman get out and the lifers huddle up and move toward her. All of it, the pro-lifers, woman, the cars, the sunlight pouring down on them, reminded her of that weird Disney time in the Circle K. She wished she could push a button, like in an exhibit, and watch them all fade out.

She moved her pack square onto her shoulders. An earring caught in the strap and it took her a minute to fix it. She was glad for the minute. For the time to breathe, to watch the pro-lifers. They never stood still. They were going up to people and huddling together in little groups and, even if one of them stood alone, she'd be all jittery, moving from foot to foot, poking around in her purse, waving her sign, looking up and down the shopping center, as though she were an old-time scout. Jen thought of ants, like there was one big ant brain running the whole show. She took another deep breath. She wished that her high school Health class had prepared her for this, but it no way had.

She started walking along the front of the deserted supermarket. Through the dusty windows, you could see shopping carts still lined up. Somebody had swept the floor. Big sacks of pet food were stacked by the registers, as though any second people would be coming in. For a minute she felt safe. Her Comp teacher had said something about that, about how the ordinary works, how it can bring you back, be a comfort almost.

She saw that the people she was walking towards were real people. There wasn't going to be any button to push, to start the exhibit, to make it stop. No voice-over was going to explain how in the late 1990s some people had to have abortions and some people didn't want them to, some people bombed clinics and killed doctors, some people, dressed nicely and carrying signs that talked about babies and listening and heart, started walking toward an eighteen-year-old girl, who put on her shades, who tossed back her hair, who managed, somehow, through the tears that were blurring her eyes, through the gentle voices that said "Baby-killer" and "Murderer," to walk *through* those people, past them and their huge poster of a little gray fetus, and into the warm safe waiting room that was not the end of the thing.

THE ABORTION did hurt. It was over quicker than she might have guessed and she was back on the turquoise couch in the waiting room, sipping a mug of herb tea, too groggy to care that the people outside had started to chant. The sweet-faced counselor sat next to her. She held Jen's hand. She touched the woven bracelet.

"It's from an old friend," Jen said. The words were thick in her mouth. She felt tears slipping down her cheeks. The tea smelled like cinnamon and oranges. "Her name was Tracey. We used to drink tea like this."

"Someone called," the counselor said. "But it wasn't Tracey."

"No," Jen said. "Who was it?" She couldn't think how to tell this woman why it couldn't have been Tracey and how much she wished it was.

"Susan. She said to tell you she and Vivian were on their way over. She said they didn't think you should go home alone. She said to tell you so you wouldn't be surprised."

Jen swallowed her tea. It was too confusing to do anything but that. She could taste tears in with the spices. Her insides felt salty and raw, as though there, too, she was crying.

"I'm feeling something," she said. The counselor nodded. "I was afraid I wouldn't." The counselor was quiet.

"Sadness," Jen said. "Not so much for this. Not yet."

The door opened. Susan and Vivian stood there. You could tell they were bummed. Vivian had on her dark glasses. Susan's hands were shaking. But, they were definitely there. The counselor stood up.

"Is it okay if we sit down?" Susan said. She started to cry.

Vivian took off her shades and half-smiled. Jen set the mug on the low table. She patted the couch on either side of her. They both sat down… carefully, as though they were the ones whose knees were wobbly, whose insides were waiting to hurt. The counselor started straightening up the reception desk. You could see the light through the blinds begin to cool. They heard a car horn beep. The chanting got louder. Somebody leaned on the car horn.

"It's the cab," Susan said.

Jen looked down. She saw their feet, her beat-up Doc Marten's, Susan's low-heeled boots, Vivian's spotless Avivas. You would have thought they were at a Junior High dance, waiting to be chosen.

"You guys," she said. "You guys are the best."

"Whatever," Susan said.

Vivian looked away. She grabbed Jen's hand.

"You guys," Jen said, "I want to go home."

 Armageddon Coffee

I've HAD THREE DATES in the last two years. More accurately, three endless dinners from which I drove myself home—one in a veggie cafe, the second at the VFW fish fry, the third, a theoretically charming picnic on the floor of a divorcé's condo. Here, verbatim, are samples of what the gentlemen said: *I'd love to hang out with you...not romantically, just as good friends, I haven't given up on finding a maiden to braid my hair...*

...can't cut the mustard like I used to, but hell, honey, we're getting kinda old for that ...

And, my personal favorite: *I like women. All my best friends are women. I can't really talk with other men. Especially about how I feel about Jennifer.*

Three guys in twenty-four months. I'm 57, the guys were 56, 58, and 54. The so-called Sexual Revolution was 35 years ago, as were the first days of Women's Lib. About fifteen years ago, guys started trundling off to the woods to beat drums, talk openly about their penii, hug each other with A-frame hugs and say things like, *When you said you were afraid to hug a guy because people would think you were gay, I related.* By my math, none of this adds up.

My hair-dresser told me I should look at the complete weirdness of all the numbers and he knew a great numerologist in case I wanted to check that out. I don't. Where I live 45% of the people still believe in all that New Age caca, 45% want to burn *them* at the stake; the other 10 percent are hard-core rock climbers, river-runners, and back-packers who basically don't give a shit. I wouldn't call myself hard-core, I climb easy stuff, 5.7, 5.8, mostly indoors, I've run a few Class IV rapids, and yet, due to my three mid-life dates, I *have* found myself pretty much not giving a shit.

My neighbor Dan, who is forty-one and my best friend, says his gender is probably doomed. He too, hasn't had many male buds, but because we're writing/road/Scrabble pals and not dates, it doesn't bother me. Besides, we recently met Baker.

"A gift," Dan says. "The older brother I never had."

Baker is a poet, and an old trad climber, which, if you are part of the ten percent that doesn't give a shit for anything but granite, pain, and terror that feels like prayer, means he started climbing before the advent of drilling bolts in mountains and wearing Eurotrash black and pink lycra. Baker resembles an otter who has been weathered by a particularly hard and rewarding life. His eyes are hawk-gold and he uses them like a raptor. He hangs out with a gang of middle-aged delinquent trads who call themselves The Boys.

Baker lives in a trailer as weathered as he is. The first time Dan and I visit him, we drive the long way out to his place, through shadowy Ponderosa forest, out into prairie just beginning to shimmer with wildflowers. There are mountains all around and dirt roads and like metastases on a CAT scan, real estate signs everywhere. Baker greets us at the gate. He's fenced in the trailer so that Harriet, his ancient Navajo Rez dog, and Wingnut, his brain-damaged Lab, don't take off toward whatever promise of bliss calls dogs toward highways.

"Check it out," he says and gestures east. Last light washes over the Peaks and flows down the long volcanic south slope. Fuji. Kilimanjaro. Mountains made of fire, sunset burning on bare rock. Baker loves the Peaks. Rafe, his dead best friend, put the profile of the mountains in the eye of an eagle he painted as a trailer-warming gift. You don't notice it at first. Baker tests people with the painting. You walk into the trailer. He waits. And then, if you're a potential one of The Boys, or what The Boys call a REAL WOMAN, you see, you're struck dumb, or you gasp and say something like,

"Holy shit, that's beautiful."

Dan spots the eye-mountains instantly. He doesn't say anything. Baker grins. I glance at the painting, look around the trailer, at the bears cast in the sides of the old iron wood-stove, the single head-high shelf of books that runs clear around the kitchen-living-dining room, the altar of photos above the tiny breakfast nook.

"That's Rafe," Baker says. He moves next to me and points. A red-haired kid soldier in Viet Nam. Then, the guy in bedraggled bell-bottom cords grinning at the camera. His arms are piled high with firewood. Behind him there is a house angled and beautiful as an old crazy quilt. Physically, Rafe could be Dan's older brother, his copper hair wild, his eyes intent, his

Armageddon Coffee

body the compact muscle of a natural athlete.

"He never finished the house," Baker says. "Twenty years and he never finished it."

Dan and I are quiet.

"You guys," Baker says, "the two of you are so much like Rafe."

Wrong, I think, *I finish things. I love to finish things. And start them. It's the middle parts I hate.*

I turn back to the eagle.

"Rafe was amazing," I say, and then I see the Peaks, moon-silver in the bird's pupil. "Holy shit," I say, "this is astonishing."

"Welcome, Lizzie," Baker says. "Let me make you guys coffee."

BAKER TELLS us to consider his home ours. He tells us we'll never have to worry about having a place to rest our heads. He says the meadow is ours, the lightning-struck juniper, and the tacked-on ramada, with its plastic-sheeting walls, its beat-up futon, meticulously piled firewood and porcelain bathtub catching rainwater from the roof. I want to believe him. Ever since I was a hippie mom with three kids, sleeping on gritty kitchen floors, in the backs of cars, in hotel rooms, courtesy of failed musicians and pot dealers, courtesy, just once, of the old Chinese night-clerk with whom I bartered a blow job, I am terrified at the idea of nowhere to sleep. Three years ago, after Grady, my last love left, I bought a pick-up, slapped on a camper shell, loaded it with sleeping bag, Coleman one-burner stove, and kitchen supplies and was able to finally relax a little. The only shelter I believe in is shelter in which I can drive away.

So, when Baker puts his arm around Dan and me and says, "*Mi* trailer, *su* trailer," I smile and tell him thank you and look out at my truck parked in the wildflowers. We take Baker's fierce coffee out to the juniper and watch last light go amber, go moonstone, and gone.

"Rafe didn't like twilight," Baker says. "He liked noon. In the Mojave or on top of a mountain. He hated shadows."

We are quiet. I look for Orion, realize it's June and He's south, visiting His other fans. I'm crazy about that big diamond guy. I love that what He hunts he never catches. I love that He's a zillion miles away.

"I hate people killing themselves," I say. "My mom was a wannabe suicide—and she lived to be eighty-five."

"Not Rafe," Baker says quietly. "The first time he tried was the last time he tried."

Dan looks at me. He's told me there are times he wants to die. It's a sign of our friendship that I am sitting here, with him, listening to our new friend talk about his dead friend.

"Yeah," Baker says, "he was all alone in his trailer. They think he sat in full lotus, put the gun to his heart and pulled the trigger."

"How old was he?" Dan asks.

"Forty-eight, two years younger than me." Baker stuns us by taking our hands. "I feel like Rafe gave you to me, so I wouldn't have to be so alone."

Hang on, Baker, I think. *Being around me, half the time, is like being alone. That's what Dan knows. That's what he signed on for.*

"Baker," Dan says, "you add up Lizzie plus me, and you got somebody who's maybe, some of the time, some places, in the right light, if you're willing to look past a few things, a whole human being."

"Suits me," Baker says and he starts to cry.

LATER, DAN and I drive home under New Moon and mountain stars. I'm half out the window, comet-hunting.

"Jesus," Dan says, "I hope I can live up to this."

"You better," I say. "I'm about out of crying shoulders for mid-life males."

Baker's lover, Sparrow, is younger—by twenty-seven years—but he's told me he is different from all those other middle-aged men chasing young pussy.

"She's special," he says. "Smart, funny, you should see her paintings. Plus, she followed the Dead for six years when she was a kid. She's paid some dues."

"Yeah," I say. "I understand." What I'm actually thinking is: *Dues, I bet she paid 'em with Daddy's Visa.* I've met Sparrow. She's willowy and peachy-pink and cute.

This is nothing new for me to be a double agent. I've always been the kind of Feminist to whom guys say, "You're not like other Feminists. I can talk to you." Only since the break-up with Grady have I begun to question that distinction. Only since he walked out into the arms of my Total Woman best friend, Sharon, who was, incidentally, Grady's best friend's wife, have I made myself stand in front of the mirror and say, "You, Elizabeth, are a hypocrite. You, while you were with Grady, sold out everything you know about being a woman. And, it didn't pan out." *Pan out* being defined as Grady staying with me, who looked, at the time, exactly like a stocky, plain fifty-four-year-old woman. *Pan out* being defined as Grady not leaving me for Sharon, who has a Siamese kitten face, digital calculator eyes, and twenty fewer years than me on her long-legged body.

Dan is the only person who knows I am a double agent.

"I always lie to men," I tell him.

"Always?" he says.

"Absolutely," I say.

A WEEK LATER, I'm belaying Dan up the rock gym wall. We're connected by a sturdy rope, me solidly planted on the floor, him moving off tiny holds. As long I never take my right hand from the rope, he is safe. An old Junior Wells tape is on. Dan is bopping up the 5.11 route, nodding his head like an ancient Delta bluesgod. Baker walks up.

"Bam," Dan yells. "Got it." I ease him down.

"Beautiful," Baker says and starts singing. "*Allons enfants de la patrie…* *Mes amis, c'est Le* Grand Weekend *de le* Granite Gang Joy and Annihilation Bastille Day Reunion. You are invited. No, you are commanded. You will be there. You will meet *Les Garcons!*"

I DRIVE TO Baker's alone. Dan's gone on ahead so he and The Boys can climb a sweet little wall just off I-40. It's Bastille Day. I am, as usual, grumbling in my head about the filthy rich and patriarchy and pig real estate developers, and did anybody notice there *was* Earth Day, whatever? As usual, I stare down the highway and think about running away to another planet.

"Dan," I say, as though he were in the passenger seat, "sometimes I just want to take off on a terminal road-trip."

"Hey," imaginary Dan says.

"No," I say, "not suicide. I mean just hit the road while I get older and older 'til I can't do it anymore. I'll be a little gray floating speck not attached to anybody or anything."

"Except petroleum," my friend would say, as usual. "Nowhere to run, baby."

BUDDY GUY and Junior Wells blast out over the twilight meadow and the lightning-blasted juniper. I pull my truck in behind a '74 Chevy van painted with daisies. Baker walks toward me, his arms held wide.

"Check out the van," he says, "it's Sally's. It's cherry. I want it to have my child."

"You know, Baker," I say, "if you could just get into your sexuality a little more, you'd be a real hot daddio."

He hugs me. Full-body warm, no sneaky shit, no A-frame. "Come on, meet The Boys and The Other Real Woman."

"Woman? Singular?"

"Sally."

"What about Sparrow?" I ask.

"She hates me this week," Baker says. "She'll get over it."

"Sally and I are the only women?"

"Come on, Lizzie, you like it that way, even if we're all old geezers." He gestures gallantly toward the ramada.

"Wow," I say.

The ramada shimmers like a nomad's tent, if a nomad's tent held a shower of blue-white meteors.

"What *is* it?" I ask.

"It's The Boys," Baker says. "Let's go."

I go in. Somebody grabs my thigh. I look down. A boy is sprawled on Baker's beat-up futon. His left arm waves helplessly. He can't be more than fourteen. I think he's drunk.

"He.......lo...lady," the kid says and I realize he's retarded. His long face twists into a smile. I detach his grip from my leg.

"Hey," I say, "I'm Liz. What's your name?"

"Ed...die," he says and stares down at his right hand.

"Is this a good party?"

"Good party," he says, "doin' shots."

The ramada lights up as though a monsoon has rolled in.

"My dad," the kid says, "doin' shots." He flops his hand toward what's behind me. I turn. A stocky guy crouches near a smoking hibachi in the center of a small circle of people. He toasts them. Blue flames flicker across the surface of the glass. He tilts back his head and swallows.

"Yeahhhhh, Dad!" the kid warbles.

Dan touches my shoulder.

"Welcome," he says.

Baker crouches next. Flash, whoosh, his head is back and Eddie whacks my leg.

"Ba...ker," he says, "doin' shots."

"You bet," I say. Eddie pokes me.

"You gonna do shots?" he says.

"No," I say. "I can't drink." I look down into his wild eyes. I suspect, as I always do with those who we call the developmentally challenged, that he can see clear into my heart, where, just now, I am a clueless kid at a party where everyone else is cool.

"Can't do shots," Eddie says and nods. "Bam bam bam."

"You got it," Dan says. "Bam bam bam." Dan hasn't had a drink in fifteen years. He quit when he was twenty-six, due to the loss of the previous decade. I quit when I was forty-seven and doesn't a day go by that I don't think about booze, how it takes the edge off—or hones it.

"What's in the glass?" I ask.

Dan grins. "*Cuervo.*"

"Oh, goddamn," I say. "I want some."

Baker steps back from the hibachi. He nods to the next fire-swallower. The guy is short, wiry, balding, and pony-tailed. He picks the glass up with two aluminum hooks where he's supposed to have hands.

"He climbed a 5.8," Dan whispers. "Left blood on the rock."

Baker lights the tequila. Captain Hook throws it down. Eddie cheers.

"That's Ray," Baker says. Hook glances over and bows. "Ed, Eddie, Dempster, Sally, Jake, this is Lizzie. She has seen the mountains in the eagle's eye." Everybody grins and raises glasses. Ed is Eddie's Dad. He's got a big, square face and he's grinning lop-sided.

"Join the party," he says. "There's charred chicken and home-made ice-cream and, and, and…fire."

"Alright!" I say. Dan looks at me.

"Home-made ice cream," I say. "Give me a shot."

"Bam bam bam," Eddie says, "give her a shot."

Dan and I take our ice cream into the trailer. Baker's kid, Shane, and Jake's kid, Gidger, are leafing through Baker's old Dr. Strange comics. Shane looks like Nijinsky, elfin face, mop of dark curls, the grace of one of the antelope that have gathered in the twilight meadow. Jake's kid, Gidger, is older, maybe fifteen. He's got a peace sign earring and the look of a kid definitely ready to get laid. He nods to me.

"I'm gonna do it," he says.

"Do what?"

"Shots," he says and steps down into the ramada.

"Jesus," Dan says.

I look at Dan. Five years of Alanon and all I want to do is jump out into the middle of the ramada, dump the tequila in the hibachi, and scream.

"Do we just stand here?" I ask.

"Jake's his dad," Dan says. "I think we just watch."

HOURS LATER, I've found out Gidger's name comes from Jake having to say "Gidger sneakers on, you're late for the school bus," every morning of the kid's life. I've watched Dan watching, and huddled twenty times with him while one of us said, "I gotta do something," and the other said, "No."

Baker and Shane have built a huge bonfire. We're all gathered around it, except the kids. Shane's holding a flashlight for Gidger, who's heaving ninja throwing-stars at a home-made target. The silvery discs glitter into the white beam of light and are gone, glitter and gone, again and again. If I look to my left, I see the perfect line of the Peaks against a brilliant midnight sky. I am using that pure beauty like I used to use Tanqueray.

"I'm tired," Dan whispers, "but weirdly I don't want to miss anything."

"There's no point in whispering," I say. "Everybody else is bellowing."

Ed stumbles past us from his camper. He's just tucked Eddie in. He lurches down next to Ray.

"He's a great kid," Ray says.

"You're beautiful, man," Ed says and punches Ray on the arm.

"No," Ray says, "*you're* beautiful, man."

"No," Ed says, "*you're* beautiful, man."

Dan punches me on the arm.

"Lizzie, he says, "*you're* beautiful, man."

Ed and Ray laugh so hard they nearly fall off the bench. When I look away from the mountains back toward Dan, I see he is grinning. Pretty soon, all four of us are howling at the Milky Way.

"Oh god," Dan says, "I miss getting loaded."

Baker walks toward the fire. He holds something black in his hands. Ray sees him, puts his arms over his eyes.

"No," he wails. "Not tonight."

"It is time for The Ceremony of the Holy Leathers," Baker says. He crouches next to Dan.

Ray uncovers his eyes and shrugs. "Hey, Baker," he says, "ain't it about time we retired this? It's been a fuckin' long time."

Baker doesn't move.

"Come on, man," Ray says, "I know. We'll run The Leathers up the flagpole and see if anybody salutes it." He giggles. "If anybody can. My flagpole's pretty wilted." He turns to Sally, who's snuggled next to him. "But—morning will come—and the cock will crow—" She pats his knee.

"There you go," Dan whispers. "You're not the only real chick left." I look at her. She is a round, sweet-faced woman, her gray hair frizzed like Janis Joplin's used to be.

"God," she says, "remember? *Let your freak flag fly?*"

"*Let your freak flag fly,*" Dempster says. It's the first thing he's said all night. "Dempster, the dumpster," Baker told us, "he'd put anything in his body."

"*Freak flag,*" Dempster says. "That was twenty million years ago." He stares into the fire. "What the fuck happened?"

Baker stands up. He holds the jacket out toward the shuddering flames. What's painted on the beat-up black leather leaps in and out of focus. I'd swear I see the tiny soldiers moving, the jungle shining day-glo green, the red-brown river flowing south.

"Ray," Baker says. He's swallowed eight shots and he's dead sober. His gray eyes catch fire-flicker and go scary. "Either you put this sumbitch on, or you're right, a long time has passed, and I sacrifice The Leathers to the flames. Total annihilation."

Ray leans forward. Without a sound, he lip-reads what's written along the river's shoreline: *To free the oppressed, human or river—that is our vow. Mekong, 1967-68.*

Ray pushes himself to his feet and snags the collar of the jacket with his right hook. Baker lets go. Dempster lights a shot and hands it to Dan. He sets it on the ground and watches it burn.

Ray smoothes the jacket across his lap. He shakes his head. Sally looks up at him. Her dark eyes are tired.

"Honey," she says.

"It seems to me," Ray says, "that a man oughtta know when it's time to move forward." He tilts left, catches himself on his hook and sits up with that rigid dignity you get one beer before passing out.

"Wait," he says, "hang on—Sally, Lizzie—I mean a woman, too. A human person oughtta know when to leave the past behind."

"Right on," Sally says.

I raise my hand in a power salute.

"Groovy," Dempster says.

Ray tosses the jacket behind him. Baker nods.

"Acsh'lly," Ray says, "those days are long ago. We are in new times."

"Oh god," Baker mutters, "here he goes."

"I remember that Billy Joel song about Viet Nam," Ray says, "*...and we'd all go down together...*, but, you know, here we are. Buddies. We're alive and we don't need no war."

Ed lights a shot. "I'll drink to that."

Baker picks up the jacket and slings it from a juniper limb. He comes back and crouches next to me.

"That's the Ceremony?" I say.

"That is the ritual," Jake says. "We do it every year." His bony face is peaceful.

"Oh god," I say. "Every year?"

"For twenty years."

"I told you," Baker says. "The Boys are not your average middle-aged men."

I'm so tired my hands are numb. I start to get up.

"Lizzie," Ray says, "how ya doin?"

"I'm pretty whipped," I say. "I think I'm gonna head home."

"No!" Baker says. "You can't do that. You haven't tasted Jake's coffee."

Jake lurches to his feet and bows.

"I'm a speed freak," I say. "I gotta wake up and have my coffee before my feet hit the floor."

"Me too," Dan says.

"You will," Baker says. "Jake brews. I personally bring your coffee to your camper."

"I don't know," I say.

"You cannot deny the Brotherhood of Coffee," Jake says. "Uh, sisterhood, too."

"Wait. Wait," Ray wobbles up and walks over to Jake.

"Lizzie," he says, "Jake here. He is the King of Coffee."

Jake punches him. "You're beautiful, man." Ray pulls Jake into a bearhug.

"Jake *always* makes our coffee," Ray says. "He's got 'spresso coffee and decaf coffee and he's even got that kind tastes like almonds, what you call…"

"Bailey's?" I say.

"Naw, naw," Ray shakes his head. "Amar. Amarillo. Armadillo. Naw, naw, Ar…maged…don coffee," Ray says proudly. "He's even got that kind."

"Armageddon coffee?" I look at Dan. He sighs and nods.

"I'll stay," I say. "No way I'll pass up Armageddon coffee."

Ray lets Jake loose. He and Jake and Baker high-five each other, power salute, grab elbows and wrestle each other to the ground. I hear Ray's muffled voice, "Lizzie. Lizzie. You're beautiful, man."

DAN ROLLS his pad and sleeping bag out near the juniper. I lay out my gear in the camper, leave the back window open so I can watch the sky. Shooting stars ninja above the black mountains. I hear fire crackling, and the bellows of The Boys.

"Hey, Rafe. Here's to Rafe. Hey, Rafe, we miss you. You're beautiful, man."

I think of Grady, telling me war stories, and fucking his best friend's wife; of Baker, across from me in a cafe, his head swivelling every time a girl walks by and later he'll write a poem about geodes and how true beauty lies inside. I think of Ed, totally shit-faced, gently leading Eddie to their camper. I imagine Ray's blood drying on the mossy limestone. I think of Shane, poised in the summer dark, a silver star in his hand, his eyes intent on the target, and I see Gidger, pouring fire down his young throat. The night grows still. Cold air moves across the meadow. I hear Dan settling into his sleeping bag, rustling like something wild in the wild grasses.

"Hey Dan," I whisper.

He sits up.

"Don't say it," he says. "I gotta pee. I can't laugh. I'll have to get up and freeze."

"I have to," I say. He snickers.

"You're beautiful, man," I say.

"Noooooo…" I see his black shape rise and move toward the juniper. He stands, pissing into the wildflowers. I look up at the sky. And then, his head is between me and the stars.

"Good night," he says and kisses my forehead. "I'm glad you're my friend."

"Me, too," I say. "And that's the absolute truth, man."

 What They Write in Other Countries

"**I** WAS BORN IN Sausalito," the Kid says, "in '66, on a houseboat. My dad was an artist, called himself Peter Saturn. Even us kids didn't know his real name. He used to go to Volunteers of America and G.I.N.A. and the Sally Army and get great stuff and stick it together and display it on beaches. My mom left him when I was three. She took me, my older sister, the orange cat, and a vase of peacock feathers, which somebody later told her was bad luck."

He pauses. He's got a paisley bandana tied round his wrist and a silver feather hanging from his ear. He's stopped me in the hall even though classes didn't start until next week and I am clearly impatient. He fiddles with the bandana and studies my face with his gray-green eyes. You can't help but notice him. The eyes and something prematurely ironic in his face, they draw you.

"Write it down," I say. He bows and leaves.

HE'S THERE the next week. On time. Holding his printout as though it were a ticket to something magical, something more filled with possibility than I know this seminar to be. Creative Writing One. All over the country someone like me is sitting down with someone like him, one of us filled with resignation, the other filled with what must seem like beginning. His classmates straggle in. Most of them are on time. They must have heard about me. And they are looking sharp; Hilfiger and Gap and Fresh Jive and denim baggies that somebody has washed in a vat of stones.

They are about to be surprised. They are about to discover that I don't have an opinion on our racist governor or hip-hop, that I don't give a damn if they saw *The Color Purple* and that though my son is named

Bobby and my daughter Angela, I am resigned to living in a decade when the aforementioned Bobby has been featured in an article in the *New York Times* Business Section on barbecue magnates. Indeed, I let my hair do its do and, yes, my butt is big and I refuse to give up dashikis because they make little of what's big. They are going to discover that they are going to call me Ms. and that I am not particularly eager for them to know my first name, much less use it. It's all going to be less predictable than they might have guessed coming through that door for the first time; if, in fact, they bothered to guess at all.

The Kid gives me a funny look. "Are you alright?" he asks and I start the first category of the semester: Pure California. Mom's post-modern Martha S. There are hundreds of books lying around the house, which has huge windows, the windows hung with little stained glass symbols of things hopeful, things vaguely mystical. The books have titles that indicate that men do not much like women but that women can do many things about that.

"I am fine," I say to all of them and smile my smile that involves only the lower half of the face, the smile that is cliché and judgement in itself. "And I am Ms. Green and this is Creative Writing One and it is my hope that we will surprise each other before the end of the semester."

A skinny redhead to the left raises her hand. She has managed to mismanage her frizzy hair into dreadlocks. She has even wrapped four little braids with colored yarn. It must have required the stoned concentration that only a dedicated follower of Jah could sustain. She is wearing a tie-dyed tee shirt with a skull silk screened across her bosom. I can't bring myself to check her feet, to see if she's wearing those thick German sandals that make everybody's feet ugly. I nod.

"Will we read some Third World writers?" she asks.

The silvery blonde young man who's just come in the door glances at her, glances at me, smiles carefully, and settles into the desk in the farthest corner of the room. He's already bored. I can tell because he pulls out one of those things you hold in your palm so you know what your life is. The Kid is watching me intently.

"I don't care what you read," I say. "I care what you write." She blushes, the pink washing up behind her freckles. I pull the first class assignment out of my old briefcase. Angela, my daughter, wishes I would get rid of it, the briefcase. She says it's ostentatiously po' folks. She wishes I would get my hair cut and buy some new clothes and realize that the old days are nothing but old. She's living in D.C. with her husband. He's going to Howard. She sends me pictures of the two of them, of their townhouse, of the Akita they have named Patrice. They do look good. All of them. She reminds me it's different now. When I visit, she takes me to some wonderful restaurants where they serve black-eye peas garnished with cilantro and spoonbread hot with chiles. She laughs when she tells me that Eldridge has designed a new line of men's pants.

"You will write," I say, "on the theme of your summer vacation." The redhead looks worried. Bored writes my words down, maybe, in his Life Plan. The Kid laughs.

"Alright," he says. "Alllllright!"

I realize that in the excitement I have forgotten to take attendance, so I do. The redhead's name is Rain. Bored is Toby. The Kid won't tell me his first name. Must run in the family, that hip coyness. All the printout say is "Saturn, N." In addition to these three, there are two Jennifers, one of whom is dressed from barrette to ankle boots in sherbet yellow. There are Corey and Chris, Lupe, and a Farrah Fawcett look-alike named Debbie Yazzie. Steve and Rick and Jon and Randy all have perfect haircuts and wear baggy pants in terrible colors. There are two no-shows. I encourage those present to leave early. The Kid hesitates at the door, checks out the set of my shoulders, and leaves.

NEXT CLASS, the two no-shows show. They've even done the assignment. One of the no-shows, a tiny woman in a very large shirt, develops an immediate and obvious case of something for Toby and spends the entire class carefully ignoring him. He is busy studying his palm. I read them an early story by Doris Lessing and when I call on him, he gives me a gorgeous warm smile and says he's sorry but he drifted off for a minute.

The other no-show is, for some reason, dressed all in beige, in cotton shirt and sweater and pants and shoes that have an unusual, in my view, number of flaps and snaps and loops. He, himself, is also in beige: hair, skin, eyes, eyelashes, even the fine fuzz on his arms. The Kid stares at him. Those orbs of his, they seem to eat up everything, hungry shining, long-lashed, gray-green holes in space. He's got a funny, almost sweet, smile, like he can't quite believe what he seems to see.

My Angela comes to mind. I remember shopping with her in Tucson. We'd stuffed ourselves on tamales and were walking in that big airy mall. She plunked down on a bench near the fountains and started people-watching. That's her favorite pastime next to talking trash about what she watches. She shakes her head as they parade by, the young ladies in aerobic gear, the poor old souls in Bermuda shorts, the college kids who appear to have been computer drawn and die cut.

"Why do they try, Mama?" my child says. "Why do white people even try?" She hauls herself up from the bench, eyelids drooping, every muscle in her body declaring great weariness. "I swear, Mama," she says, "I've got to get me one of those big old gourmet chocolate chip cookies just to stand this mess." That's how we are, my child and her mother. Cookies. Social commentary. Declarations. Of difference, of kinship, of love.

The Kid taps the beige one on the arm and smiles. "David Byrne, I presume?" he asks.

"No," the beige one says nicely. "My name is Mark. I think you've mistaken me for someone else."

The room has gotten awfully quiet so I run on for awhile about Lessing and how she can make you feel a place and how they might want to think about how she does that and then do it. Next assignment, I want them to make me want to visit someplace they treasure in their memory.

"Does it have to be real?" Rain asks.

The Kid is studying me again. I start to move down the aisle to pick up their work. Rain has woven some feathers in her braids. She touches them nervously as I approach her seat.

"I'm sorry," she says in her high little voice. "That was a dumb question. I didn't think. Really. I bummed." She starts to hand me her paper and ducks her head.

"If you can make me want to be there, honey," I say, "I don't care how you got there." I tuck her assignment into the pile in my hand. It's on notebook paper. The child has hand-written it. She has dotted her i's with little circles.

THAT NIGHT, I spread their work out on the cleared surface of the old roll top desk that takes up most of the living-dining room. It had been my grandpa's desk. Some of the cubbyholes still smell like his old sweater, snuff, pencil lead, the salve my grandma used to brew up to spread on his bony old chest when he had catarrh. I've got a big mug of milk and molasses. She knew that, too. Long before the scientists and the ladies' magazines starting telling us, she knew that milk and sugar would make you sleep good. A splash of rum doesn't hurt. That's my discovery.

"Make you sleep good," Angela says I'm trying to talk down home when I say stuff like that. She's never forgiven me for growing up in Evanston, for her grandpa being a dentist, for me having no trouble getting into a good school, earning a good degree, getting a mediocre job. She keeps wanting to know about her *real* roots. Milk and molasses. Gospel. Greens and ham hocks with lots of black pepper.

I remember my mama's church clothes, the print dresses, the fine sharp hats, the white gloves, the brooch, not gaudy, but with real gold shining against her shoulder, the strong, sweet, clean smell of her, I tell my daughter about that. And me, that too, my baby's mama, standing politely outside the dime store on Fifty-third Street on an August day, the Chicago soot hanging in the wet air, me dressed in a tasteful skirt and blouse and low-heeled shoes, staying calm, keeping my eyes carefully focused over the customers' shoulders while they read my sign, while they walk away or shake my hand or spit at my feet. It worked. A year later, anybody could buy a bad hamburger anytime in an Atlanta lunch counter.

Rain's hand-written sheets are on top of the pile. She has gone to every Grateful Dead concert in the Southwest summer of '92 and she wants me to know the totally unbogus energy of those shows. She wants me to know that at those shows there are people actually old, there are men with gray braids, there are African American people and Chicanos. Twice there were rainbows. Once, at Red Rocks, it rained right in the song where it talks about rain. The Dead want One World….really, a Dead show is one world…that's what they want, like Bob Marley, Peter Tosh, like all those dudes. Jah!

I add a little more rum to the milk. I truly don't want to grade these things. I correct all the spelling errors. She's got the hard ones right, like Rastafarian and Ethiopia and synchronicity. It's the small words, the ordinary ones she can't handle. I start to play with the punctuation and lose heart. My children's father, Leon, my ex-husband, he had teased me, then nagged me, and finally gotten so he'd just slip out of the room when he found me muttering over their poor papers. It was only one of the ways we had not been able to keep it what?….keep it kind? I still think of him nights like this, because at least when I was done, he had been in there, asleep, his fine-boned body warming the bed. Uh-uh! I will not give in to that shit. Done is done.

Toby has written a cool, tight, tense, polished chrome and enamel, nasty little jewel on Europe on two hundred dollars a day. He hadn't missed a trick, in his travels, in his style. I give him an A-. It'll drive him crazy. Debbie Yazzie starts off slow, then gets me right there, on her grandma's ranch. She's got a problem with paragraphs, somebody taught her to put exactly four sentences in each one, but she gets me to smell the juniper, the dust, the rank fat perfume of the mutton broiling on the wood fire. I clean up the paragraphs and give her a B+.

I pull Rain's paper back out and give her a double grade: C for writing, B for politics. That'll bring her running. If I've got to hold office hours I may as well teach these kids to debate. Not dialogue. Debate.

The others do the predictables: Puerto Peñasco, kiddies' camps, Volunteers in the Parks, back packing, river running, "Salad or curly fries with that burger, ma'am?" The Kid's paper is last. The Kid's papers. I open the stained envelope and a wad of paper cut-outs fall out. He's read Burroughs. He knows Dada. He's cut up old Patti Smith lyric sheets and thrown in some early Leroi Jones for good measure. There's more. If I read the mess right he's spent the summer as a male hustler or a French sailor or a Manhattan litter box. The word "spike" appears frequently and I can't tell if it's slang for syringe or an inadequate male organ. He's poured ink on some of the sections and labelled the blotch "random censor."

I find myself saying "Have mercy" out loud and with the last sip of warm milk, invoking the puzzled ghost of my grandma. I fail the Kid. "See me soon," I write, and go to bed.

THEY ARE puzzled, surprised, disappointed. I know how they feel. Writing what have been described as "elegant, somewhat detached" essays, I more often than not open an envelope and let a rejection slip fall out onto my grandpa's desk. And, now and then, I sit with my sleeping potion and let it rest on my tongue and, even sweeter, let the printed page I hold in my hands, rest in my mind. "June Jordan: Plain Talking," by Antoinette Green. I sleep the good sleep of the worker on those nights. So, when they glance at the last page of their papers and let their eyes rest briefly on my face, with pleasure, with petulance, I know how it is.

Later, they come to my office, that small room with no window, that neat room without posters, without clues. I sit in the straight backed chair and I listen. Toby is charming. He mentions Zoetrope and his hope of being a successful screenwriter at twenty-one. He waits for me to appreciate the joke. I smile. He leaves with his A- intact. I've brought an apple and yogurt for lunch. In the silence, in the solitude, they taste clean.

I smell patchouli. Rain follows her scent. She pulls her paper from her peasant bag and sets it on the desk.

"I wonder," she says, "like I was kind of bummed, no big deal, really, but, hopefully, we could talk about my grade?"

Her nails are bitten to the quick and very clean. She tucks her feet up under her and perches on the chair. I know that any minute she will hunker forward and hug her knees. I wrap the apple core in my napkin and toss them in the waste basket. She unwinds and leans toward the basket.

"I can use that for my compost," she says. "I mean, like if you don't mind."

"No," I say, "hopefully, it will be good for your garden." I feel a mean little charge in my gut and surprise her and myself by apologizing.

"I'm sorry," I say. She looks eager and puzzled. "Rain," I say, "you don't use 'hopefully' that way. You can say 'I hope' or 'one hopes', but if you are serious about this course, you will not use 'hopefully' in that way. 'Hopefully' is an adverb…'She said hopefully'…something like that."

She mentions another instructor and points out that he uses it all the time.

"He's wrong," I say and, again, tell her why. She gets confused. She's not real sure what an adverb is. I realize she has no foundation and I start to think of language in just that way, as a structure, as a home. I imagine a new essay and forget her for a minute. She pokes around in her big bag and pulls out a bandana. She wipes her eyes. I realize that she is crying.

"I'm bummed," she says. "I've got so much inside and I can't get it out so other people can hear. Like my mom. I go home and I play the Red Rock tapes and I try to show her some things I wrote about them, about the Dead. I mean, she's your age, right, so she was my age when they were starting. And all she can talk about is how I should shave my legs and that if I took off all my earrings but one pair I'd look so nice. So, I go…"

I hold up my hand.

"Stop," I say. "In the first place, you don't 'go', you 'say.' In the second, you and your mom are not my business."

"Oh," she says. "I'm sorry." She starts to get up.

"Wait," I say. "If you want people to hear, write so they can hear. Rewrite that piece. Write only about what you heard, about how you heard…not so much the people on the stage, but the people around you… Okay?"

"Far out," she says. She flops the bag on my desk and begins rummaging in it. "Here," she says, "this is for you. I got it at Telluride. Purple's a high healing power." She sets a little amethyst crystal on my desk. I pick it up and hold it in the fluorescent light

"Sunlight," she says. "Natural light, that's what works."

"It's pretty," I say. "Thank you."

"Blessed be," she says, blushes, and leaves. I rub the crystal along my temples. It's not much more than a small cool sweetness.

The Kid is next and he's carefully carelessly beautiful. He's wearing sleek shades, the mirrored kind. He's got a long tweed coat on over beat-up Levis and a clean, clean white, button-down shirt. I have to look away. How he does what he does, put that surface together without a flaw, it scares me. He's braided his hair and when he pulls off his shades I can see that he's lined his eyes with indigo pencil. He's got those rich bitch fine ass features that our poor Michael J. had to carve from his living skin and bones. There's a silver moon in the Kid's left ear. It's curved up. My friend Ramona once told me that kind of moon was a sign of withholding.

"I didn't expect you to deal in success or failure," he says.

"You're too damn young to be so damn hip."

"Who judges?" he says quickly. "I like to shatter things."

"Honey," I say, "you've got make 'em before you break 'em."

"I didn't sign on for political theory," he says and smiles. "But, Ms. Green, while we're at it, what are yours?"

"A," I say. "And I am Ms. Green and this is office hours for Creative Writing One."

"A for anarchy," he persists.

"A for apolitical," I say. "You're too damn smart for this."

I watch him shape himself back into what he thinks I want to see. He takes off his coat. A scent rises from him. It's bitter and piney and somehow comforting.

"It's juniper smoke," he says. "I got smudged before I came here."

"Are you Indian?" I ask.

"No," he laughs. "But, I might wannabe."

It's a joke here, a slur. Rootless white kids, some of them left over burnouts from the old days, middle-aged left-wing politicos who wannabe, you can find them at Big Mountain rallies, up on the mesas at the dances. Navajo, Hopi, Yaqui, that's what they wannabe. Usetabe me they'd wannabe. Back in '61, back in SNCC, in Chicago, in Detroit, in little southern towns, the white girls in cotton shifts, the boys in overalls, the ones who said "Right on" and "yo mama" and learned to signify. I wonder where they are.

"Well, you ain't," I say. "You are what we refer to these days as a son of the dominant culture. How'd you find out about Burroughs?"

"He was a friend of a friend of my dad's," he says.

I know he's lying. "Whatever," I say. "Cut up ain't nothin' but t.p. to me. What are we going to do about this?"

"I'll write something different," he says. He looks down. There's a copy of an international literary magazine on my desk, one of those with photographs so technically perfect that they seem to float up off the page and with monstrous stories of those who disappear and those who disappear them. I'm reviewing something for the magazine, a book on South Africa, on women; on a country far removed from me, on a sex I've come to believe I barely know.

"Is this the kind of stuff you read?" the Kid asks.

"Sometimes," I say. I check my watch. "Time to close up shop," I say and nod at the door.

He's staring at a page in the magazine. "Can I borrow this?" he asks. His voice is thick. When he looks up, his eyes are trancey.

"Be careful," I say.

RAIN MISSES the next class. The Kid hands in his rewrite and the new assignment in that same stained envelope. I feel a little lump in the package. That night, as I take out his work, a sprig of juniper falls out. I crunch it between my fingers and rub the oils into my wrists, along my temple. I can smell a place I'd like to know.

I'm a little surprised when I see most of the accompanying pages are blank. I take up the rewrite with the juniper scent plain and strong in the air.

"In the pines out behind my mom's house," the Kid has written, "there is a trick of light in early evening so that suddenly I am walking through flowers. A moment before, a moment after, there's only a different light and dry grasses."

I write "more please" and give him an A for the juniper.

Three days later, the Kid stops me after a graduate seminar and asks if we can talk.

"I'll listen," I say. We go to my office and he waits politely 'til I'm settled in. Then, he slaps the magazine down on the desk and just looks at me. He's drawn a tiny silver star on his left cheekbone. It's terrific against his olive skin. It works like a TV screen in a gloomy bar; my eyes are pulled back to it, again and again.

This stuff is true?" he says.

"Yes," I say.

"They could really take a person and shove, you know—a boiling hot rock up their ass? They would do that?" he asks.

"And more," I say.

"Okay," he says. "How did I miss all this? I read. I watch TV. My mom's real aware of things."

"Who would want to know about it?" I ask.

"Right," he says. "You got any more stuff?"

I hand him a pamphlet on Chiapas. One of their finest journalists, now dead, wrote it. Someone here, a woman who has left that country, translated it. The Kid thanks me and leaves the second rewrite on my desk. When I finish, I truly want to be on that north California coastline. I want to see the great blue heron. I want to smell the salt and pine of the air.

A FEW CLASSSES later, we are starting to get to know each other. None of them have withdrawn. They have turned in their poorest, their okay, their on-the-way-to-good, and their surprising work on how it might be to be a visitor in a foreign country where one could not speak the language and where one was immediately identified as a stranger. Jon, one of the white hip-hop boys, wrote about visiting the girl's locker room. They have begun to critique each other, to be very harsh or silent, to say what they would like to hear and, sometimes, to say what I could not.

Debbie Yazzie has tapped on my office door, that door being wide open, her being unwilling to raise her eyes to meet mine, which I understand. A century ago, I might have been seen by her people as some kind of witch, possibly one of those who is so dreadful that its name is not spoken. She wants to know if I ever read Ntozake Shange's *For colored girls who have considered suicide/when the rainbow ain't enuf*, and she wonders if I know that it isn't so different sometimes for girls of her background. She tells me her favorite sister has gone east to school and that her professor is a Japanese woman, born in California, and had suggested the book. I have to smile. So does she.

"You know about not looking in the eyes?" she asks cautiously.

"We were slaves," I say. "Different danger, same doorway."

"ANGELA," I e-mail halfway through the semester. "Help me, child, I am pre-ju-dissed. I look at most of the white kids' papers and all I can see is weak sentences, bad spelling, arrogance, can't think and don't give a damn. One writes this thin stuff about perfect people in perfect marriages with perfect children who suddenly have a DISASTER! and prevail. Another one writes fairy tales. This young man, the clone with the perfect bone structure, keeps writing this obscene elegant mess about dope and cars and pussy. I can't tell most of the rest of them apart. I am a failure of compassion."

"You need a man," she writes back. "Swear to god, Mama, you truly need a man. It's been eight years."

I'm so mad I send a telegram "Like hell I do." She knows my ups and downs so she calls and we talk for two hours. Later I wonder if I'm having one of those mid-life crises people are getting rich writing about.

NOBODY COMES in during office hours. The mail is a joy. U. of New Mexico Press wants to publish a small collection of my essays on barely known women writers of color. *Harper's* buys a short piece. There is an invitation from my chairman to come in and discuss a few things. I lock up and head down the hall.

He is free. He smiles, offers me sherry and tells me he's delighted to hear the news because, frankly, he has become concerned about my failure to make certain linkages between teaching and publication. It appears that my priorities are skewed. I dare not drink the sherry or I will have to ask him in a plainly nasty way what the fuck a linkage is. They all talk like that these days, not just the Education faculty.

I MEET MARGOT for lunch to celebrate New Mexico and *Harper's*. I bitch clear through her Chardonnay and soda, my rum and Coke, both our salads, and the chocolate suicide we split. I tell her about Angela's diagnosis. She laughs.

"Caroline tells me the same thing," she says. Caroline is her twenty-year-old going-on-ancient daughter who lives in Seattle and knows about securities and pork bellies and dot-coms. She's on two phones eight hours a day and in the company library six more. She tells Margot that she's too busy for a man but that Margot, being advanced in years, has the luxury of kicking back and "drawing in" the right one. She, like Angela, believes we draw in the events and people in our lives; draw in negative and uh-uh!, draw in positive, well, my my my! I think living with the threat of nuclear annihilation has softened their brains.

"I got to start drawing on those positive men," I say to Margot, "all those smart, healthy, horny, available, middle-aged Black men."

"Are there any?" Margot asks.

"I believe they are out there on the astral plain somewhere, just waiting for us positive women, along with all the smart, etc., etc., white guys."

That's when we order chocolate suicide and two spoons. Draw in positive and you get chocolate suicide and two not-so-bad-lookin' women laughing and a lunch check for thirty dollars.

THAT NIGHT when the phone rings I almost don't answer it. It is the Kid. His voice sounds funny. At first I think he's high and start to tell him that Ms. Green and Creative Writing One do not exist for students messing with drugs.

"Something happened to the beige one," he says, "to Mark." I realize he's absolutely sober.

"What?" I ask.

"He jumped out of the ninth floor of the Math tower," he says.

It happens twice a year at this school. I stare up at the ceiling. "Do Lord," I say before I can stop myself. I suddenly wish I had white gloves and a good hat and someplace to wear them, someplace where people sang, where people knew each other. I can hear the Kid make some muffled noise.

"I'm here," I say.

"We went for coffee a couple of times," the Kid says. "No big deal, I think we were curious about each other. I used to tease him and he got so he'd tease back. He'd been so tight, so safe. I played one of the early Talking Heads tapes for him once. He liked it. I told him he looked like David Byrne. He finally got the joke."

"Listen," I say, "I don't mean to be cold, but there's nothing left to do....if there ever was."

"I know," he says. "I just wanted you to know." I feel my belly tighten. There is a chill up my back. Some feeling starts to crawl towards the surface. I notice the phone is slippery in my hand.

"Write about it," I say. "I've got to go."

"Wait," he says. "I knew you'd say that. That's all there is to do really, isn't it? I've been reading those plays you gave me about South Africa. I thought it was all some nice safe liberal hands locked in solidarity in front of the embassy deal. It's not, right? It's about people being trapped, right? People being killed by something that sucks the air out of them?"

"Write about it," I say. "Like that. That's all I've got to give you."

After I hang up the phone I start to think about chocolate suicide. I don't mean to, but the phrase keeps coming back and back and then I start to laugh and then, to cry. I've been working on an article on linear plotting vs. flashback. I shut off the typewriter and slip an old tape into the deck. The mechanism lurches and Aretha Franklin's voice, the young Aretha Franklin's voice, finishes me off. I flop on the couch and let those damn tears run down the sides of my face.

"Bridge over troubled waters..."

I asked for this. I'm crying so hard my chest hurts. My nose is running and I can hardly breathe. If I had the Kid's number I'd call him back and I don't, so I just lie on the damp couch cushion and imagine my grandma sitting in the room, wiping my face with something wet and good smelling, telling me to hush, calling me "child."

THERE'S A hole in the seminar. You can't miss it, and you can't say a thing about it, especially me. We're rolling on toward the last few classes. The Kid is writing about the early days, about the smell of the Bay and about the new people who began to move in and the divorce and split custody and always being the new kid in class. Rain is dotting her i's with dots.

Toby has almost ceased to remind me of an oil slick under a Lexus SUV. Every image I arrive at for him is a sleek cliché and I give up, wondering if that failure isn't the definition. I think of *The Shining*. I imagine him peeking round the classroom door, his perfect hair a mess, his gorgeous face grotesque, him whispering, "Heeeeeeere's Toby!"

Debbie Yazzie comes to my office and walks right in. She looks me in the eye and hands me a paper.

"It's called the *Lady in Turquoise*," she says. "I was thinking about sending it to her, to that Shange woman. I wanted you to read it first."

"I'll read it," I say. "But go ahead and send it. I bet she gets lonely out there."

"Alright!!" she says and pauses. She's looking at me like she's measuring me.

"Listen," she says. "If you want to try some of our food there's a restaurant up near that old grade school. You could go there." She says the next part quickly. "A lot of the neighborhood people do. Doesn't matter, you know."

"I'll do that," I say. "When I used to live up north, I used to go to Gray Mountain."

She smiles. I see clearly how beautiful she is, in her torn Blackfire tee shirt, with the lean flawless line of her perfect belly visible, three woven Guatemalan bracelets on her wrist, her hair bleached and permed into that Farrah Fawcett flip the girls on the Rez seem to love. She unties one of the bracelets and hands it to me. We tie it around my wrist.

"'Til it falls off, right?" I ask.

"Uh-huh. I may have to miss the last class. My grandma might need me up there. She's getting really old." She giggles. "She's so little. Her head comes to my shoulder."

"Same as mine was," I say and I think of that proper fierce woman.

Debbie reaches out her hand. "I want you to know I learned a lot." We shake, her grip gentle as a child's.

She is gone by the second-to-last class. I give them their final assignment. It will count for half their grade. Pastel Jennifer raises her hand.

"Is that fair, do you think?" she asks.

"Yes."

"Like, why?" she asks.

"Because I am Ms. Green and this is Creative Writing One."

"Well," she says, " I can see why you would say that, but you know, you work real hard on a class or something and you really try to get something out of it. I mean, you do your best, you know, like you really care a lot about the assignments and your grade and everything and it seems you ought to get something out of all that that's really fair."

"I do," I say.

"No." She is blushing behind her blusher. "I mean me."

Rain is nodding her dreads vigorously. The Kid looks at me and shakes his head. "That's cold, Ms. Green."

"True," I say. "However, when one uses 'you' for 'me', I stop listening. I get bored. I don't like to be bored, okay?"

I hate myself for that "Okay?" and the Kid knows it. He grins.

"Jennifer," I say. "Come and see me. I won't change my grading system, but I'll tell you I'm sorry for what I just did."

"Okay?" she says.

They leave the room with the assignment, which is the standard one. I want them to write a short story, no more than twenty pages, no less than ten. That's all, except that I want it to be of content and quality. If they don't know what I mean, it's too late.

JENNIFER NEVER makes it to my office, but Rain does. She's tucked her dreads up into a knit tam-o'-shanter. It's red and black and green and I can hardly stand to look at it and her pale face, woebegone and hopeful beneath it.

"I don't know if you can help me with this?" she asks and perches on the chair. She pulls off her tam and her hair tumbles stiffly down around her shoulders. She's strung some tiny bells in her braids. I wait for the sound to fade.

"That carries our prayers," she says firmly.

"I've never heard of that one," I say.

"It's Tibetan," she says. "We're all *metis*. Mixed, you know. Like we suffer the same; we pray the same."

"What if I reject that?" I ask and wish I hadn't. I know what comes next.

"No problem," she says. "It just is."

I am spared more because she folds her thin hands in front of her and says, "I have a problem and I wonder if maybe you could help me?" She smiles a genuinely wistful smile.

"Hopefully," I say and, for the first time in the semester, I hear her laugh. It's a good laugh, straight from her chest. The bells chime along. She takes a deep breath and closes her ginger eyes. "My old man left me." She suddenly begins to sob. "Don't worry," she says, "it's good to cry like this, to let your feelings out. It clears the fourth chakra."

I hand her a tissue. I wonder how they get out of bed in the morning and find their way here, the kids who live in a maze of other peoples' teachings.

"Really," she says, "it's okay. Besides, I drew him in, you know, and everything that happens works out." I see that it isn't even teaching, it's a cheerful chaos of beginnings of teachings. And the others, the ones who look burnished, who believe they know where they'll be in ten years, I cannot bear to think of them.

"Your father left?" I ask, though I know better.

"No, "she whispers, "Miguel, my old man. He went back to his old old lady. It's not him, it's me. I don't know how to let go." She starts to sob again. She is so tiny, the noise so big. I'm glad it's early evening and we're alone in the building.

"Rain," I say. I think I'm going to firmly suggest that she take a deep breath, sip some water, go home, take a hot bath, medicate and listen to the Dead, and I don't. I say, "I know how it is."

"You do?" she says, and I realize that she cannot imagine how anyone as hefty and middle-aged as me could know about any of this.

"Yes," I say. "It's happened more than once. I hate it every time except that I usually lose a few pounds. It'll probably happen again."

"What did you do?" she asks. "Like, how did you let him go?"

"I drank," I say. "I lived on yogurt 'til I could eat too much again. Chocolate. Work. I moved two thousand miles once. I don't recommend any of those options."

"But," her voice rises to a wail, "how did you stand it?"

"I waited for time to pass," I say. "And I wrote about it."

She takes a green crystal from her pocket and rubs it on the place where I can see her heart pulse in her throat. "Sometimes this helps," she says. She hands it to me and I rub it over my throat. It feels good and clean and smooth, a little warm from her skin.

"Yes," I say, "my Grandma had this herb tea she made for heart troubles—not for the physical kind—for the man-woman kind. She died before she taught it to me."

Rain tucks the crystal back in her purse. When she closes the bag, a puff of air carries the scent of old leather and patchouli and herbs.

"My mom takes Pro-whatever," she says and giggles.

"Different strokes."

"Well, hopefully," she grins.

"Write about it," I say. "Content and quality."

"Did you really drink?"

"I still do. Rum and warm milk. Almost like medicine."

"Well, like, I don't want to butt in," she says, "but you should try ganja. We believe that alcohol harms the physical envelope." She unwinds from the chair and stretches. Under the layers of scarves and sashes, her body is lovely. She tucks her dreads up into her cap.

"Ms. Green," she says, "can I ask you something personal?"

"You can ask," I say.

"What's your first name? I mean like if it isn't secret or ritual you know, or something like that. I'd just like to know. I mean, what you told me today, it was more like we were friends."

"Antoinette," I say. "Tony, sometimes." She leans down, kisses me on the cheek and is gone.

THE LAST class is a long one. I ask them to read five minutes of their story. I time them. I cannot believe how slow the minute hand moves. I don't want to feel this way. By the time the Kid stands in front of the class, the setting sun gilds the room. The Kid is wearing a silver dragon on a chain. In its claw, an opal burns. It is an old one, fiery and deep, not like the new pale stones built from layers of inferior mineral. The Kid touches the dragon once and begins to read.

"My name is Mark and sometimes people mistake me for David Byrne."

The Kid's voice shakes. I have watched him grow ashen through the other's readings, as though their words were shrapnel, as though he bled. I wonder if the others see that. Their themes frighten me, not because they are horrifying, but because they are complacent. Each year it has gotten worse. At the end of his five minutes, the Kid has let us begin to be curious about Mark. The sunset is fading. The opal has gone flat, like one of the faked-up ones.

"Thank you," I say and the Kid nods. The others look up at me. I thank them. All of us realize we are not going to discuss the work. They begin to pack their things. Rain wipes her eyes with her sleeve. I start down the aisle to collect their papers and see the Kid rise up to meet me. His fine-boned face is swollen and red. He slams his paper down on his desk and brushes past me. I hear him stop. Even Toby looks up.

The Kid starts to cry. He's gasping a little. He can't get his breath to speak. "Do you know?" he asks. "Do you know what they write about in other countries?" He points to Jennifer. She giggles, then starts to cry. He points to Corey and Steve and Jon.

Jon says, "Oh, maaaaan, lighten up!"

The Kid points to Toby and repeats the question.

"Do you have even one idea of what they write about in other countries?"

Toby looks at him, then me. It is as though he is calculating something. The Kid's hand shakes but he holds his stance.

"Tell me," he says.

Toby gets up and saunters to the door. Just before he exits, he looks straight in the Kid's eyes and says calmly,

"Yo mama, suckah."

The Kid's arm drops. In silence, the students file out. Jennifer touches the Kid gently on the shoulder. He nods. He and Rain and I are left in the silent room. We each gather up our papers and pens and various packs and bags and briefcase. The Kid is a little wild-eyed, but he moves with grace through these small ways to put things right. Rain moves between the Kid and me.

"Nick, Tony," she says, "Miguel left some chocolate behind, some beautiful Mexican chocolate with cinnamon in it. He showed me how to cook it. I could make us some?"

I nod.

"Okay," she says. "You'll love it. It's not like Quik at all."

"Nick," I say, "so that's your name." I turn back to Rain. "And yours," I ask. "Is it Rain?"

"My name is Linda," she says. She touches the back of my hand, takes Nick's hand in hers.

"Really," she says. "Please. I'm glad to have you visit." It's become dark. We stand in the dim room a minute. Nick shakes his head the way an animal shakes off pain. And together, we three go out.

Riv

B Y THE TIME my wife Jenny and I got to Gene and Terree's Second
Annual Labor Day party, the backyard spigot was on full blast and
the mighty stream was already running. It snaked through the backyard, through mud and old volcanic cinders, made an ox-bow, a rapid,
and flowed much-diminished into the bathtub Gene had buried and covered with redwood slats.

Jenny dropped a juniper twig in and watched it sail along. Gene stood
next to her, sipping a beer and grinning. Jenny grinned back. "What do
you call it, captain?"

"The Riv," Gene said happily. His wife, Terree, walked up with a tray of
munchies.

"Just like the mighty Colorado," she said. "Just like the real thing!"

Jenny turned to their kid Squeak. "You gonna run it?" The kid nodded.
He was looking real confident. He was even keeping his pants up over his
skinny butt.

"Looks to be about a 2.5 degree of difficulty," Jenny said. "Colorado
scale."

Squeak nodded again, serious, slit-eyed, scouting the water like he was
twenty years older and a hardened river rat.

"Go for it, Squeak," Jenny said, in a tone I knew well, "you can do it.
Run that sucker!"

The kid trundled over to his Big Wheel and peddled it through the
gravel shoreline right into the channel. He was a somber, snot-nosed kid,
pale blue eyes glittering out of his mud-caked face. He was three and he
said only two words: Out! and Mine! He did great 'til he hit the ox-bow,
mired in the muck, and went over. Terree stood there, her arms folded

over her chest, holding herself back. She'd been the Great Rescue Mom and she was forcing herself to let go. Squeak tugged the Big Wheel upright and rode off to sit under a gnarled juniper. We could see his little shoulders shake. I could feel him gather back his dignity.

By the time Rusty and Lila got there with their baby Dante, Gene and I were at least a six-pack to the wind. Squeak had dumped more than once. Terree had finally gone into the cabin so she wouldn't have to see him and struggle with the part of her that wished he'd never left the womb, the part of her that wanted him cradled in close to Mom, the way Gene wanted to be, the way, tell the truth, I think everybody wants to be.

Gene started dragging pine deadfall to the fire. He was clearly in one of his arson moods. It looked like the Great Labor Day Conflagration might become an annual event. The year before, the Pines Park Volunteer Fire Department had arrived and ended up getting loaded with the rest of us, while the fire roared up into the obsidian sky and in all that red light, the moon flat disappeared.

My wife had begun her business of studying everybody. She does it whenever she's nervous or put-out or disapproving and at one of Gene and Terree's get-togethers, she's usually all three She doesn't drink anymore or smoke, so social events are hard for her. I cracked my fourth Moosehead. She gave me a fierce look and went out to help Lila bring the baby's stuff onto the back porch. Gene had built it and it was one of the prettiest places you could imagine, all redwood, Terree's plants growing magically in this dry air into a jungle of greens and reds and purples.

I don't know how Gene does it, I can't even begin to guess how Terree does, how they've made this little paradise out in the middle of the cinder cones north of town. There's a sky-light observatory on the roof, a school-bus turned into a greenhouse, and this new tribute to stubbornness named the Riv. You've even got to wonder how they had time to make Squeak. Gene and I work five ten-hour days a week roofing the developments that are infecting the east end of town. And Terree, she works too. She's a School Aide, so Squeak ends up in day care five days a week.

Jenny and I are past the kid part, thank god. Ours are grown. We're in our forties and more or less free. I really don't know how Gene and Terree do it. I wouldn't want to try.

Rusty dropped himself down into the busted deck chair next to me. He's tall and skinny and you can't tell he's half bald because he almost never takes off his truck hat. He keeps what's left of his red hair long and one of those drake's tails sticks out the back. He's only twenty-eight and it chaps his ass to have to do that, to wear that hat. Lots of things chap his ass. He worked a month or two with Gene and me, 'til our boss, Dave, let him go. "I think you're suffering from terminal dissatisfaction," Dave had said to him. "I don't have Workman's Comp for that."

"Shit," Rusty said. "Look at that sucker go." He waved at Gene's fire. Sparks were shooting out tree-top high. I forgot about the danger. The sparks were too pretty, and there was that excitement that rises up in humans around fire. We were just starting to lose the light, the sun setting behind us. The top of the nearest cinder cone must have had busted glass on it, because it was winking red-orange against the pale sky. Kids go up there to drink beer. They think nobody can see them. I think we're a little like ostriches at that age, maybe even now. Hide in the sand, think nobody can see us.

"Why's he always build these hormongo sons-a-bitches?" Rusty said. "Dumb son-of-a-bitch'll set his little paradise on fire."

"Have a beer," I said.

Rusty grabbed a Moosehead. "I'm in AA," he said, "but that shit's Canadian, so it don't really count."

I felt Jenny move up behind me. We've been together about six months, married three, and I'm getting so I can sense her, I can sense her being there, I can sense her moods. I'm not sure whether that's good or bad. As long as I don't go numb, that's the part I worry about. That's the part that's killed all of it before. She bent and kissed the top of my head. I felt warm there. That was a good sign.

"Hey, amigo," she said, "Terree wonders if you'd come in and check the turkey. Gene's disappeared."

"Hey," Rusty said, "which turkey?" He half knocked himself out with that.

"Huh?" Jenny said. Rusty handed up his empty Moosehead.

"No thanks," she said. I felt her stiffen. She's got ideas about Rusty and Lila, how Rusty gives these orders, how Lila snaps to and obeys.

"I'm not drinking these days," she said.

"Me neither," Rusty said. "Least not without getting up and getting my own." He poked my arm. "You gotta work on this woman."

I heard Jenny catch her breath. I wondered if I was about to watch Rusty die. I stood up. Jenny grinned.

"Yeah," she said, "you gotta work on this woman."

I realized I was the one not breathing. I couldn't take another weird evening. I didn't want another one of her silences. They weren't the "yes, hon" kind. They froze you out. They were the coldest, longest quiet I'd ever known.

"I do my best," I said and kissed her cheek.

"You do indeed," she said and surprised me by sitting down next to Rusty.

"Hey, bro," Rusty said, "would you get me a refill? Make it Canadian."

TERREE WAS wrestling the turkey out of the oven. She smiled up at me. She smiles more than any woman I've ever met, and I've met some smilers in my day. I've seen her smile while Gene drove the van into the brand new wading pool. I've seen her smile while he passed out in her lap, right in the middle of a room full of company. I saw her smile the day of their wedding when he fell towards the wedding cake and made, through no grace of his own, a bull's-eye face plant. The only time she doesn't smile is when she can't find Squeak or when she's got her arms folded over her chest and you know she's making herself let the kid run out his limit.

"Where's Pa?" I asked. She nodded toward the bedroom.

"He kinda got a head start on the party," she said.

I pulled the drumstick away from the great brown bird. She stuck it with a fork and the juice ran clear.

"Supper time," she said. "You'll have to carve."

They'd put the redwood picnic table up near the firepit. While I got the table set, Lila and Jenny carried out dishes and platters and bowls. Terree always cooks up a storm. We'd brought french bread and cheese and a more than reasonable amount of beer. Lila had packed a green jello salad with little curds floating in it. It looked pretty nasty. I was studying it, trying to figure out if I'd be able to eat it. She caught me.

"There's dessert topping in there too," she said. "And those red cherries. You can't see 'em, but they're in there. They sink to the bottom, but I'll make sure you get some."

She smiled at me. She's a plain woman, thin but flabby, and yet, the kind that must have been an amazing little teen queen. She still tries to dress that way and I can't look at her too often, because there's a sad sexiness in her tight jeans or the way you can see every feature of her mini-tits under the tube top. When she smiles, you forget everything else. Even Jenny's seen it, and she's a woman who will not admit to competition. "She looks like a Christmas tree angel," she's told me. "When she smiles I cannot take my eyes off her face."

Terree brought out Squeak's booster chair and Squeak. He was howling. He'd had a plan to haul his Big Wheel up on the redwood bench and sit right there for the meal. He kept glancing over at it and The Riv. I knew how he felt. Things that wonderful could disappear while he cleaned up his plate. Terree finally had to put the Big Wheel at the end of the table right where he could see it, right where he could know for sure no neighbor kid was going to sneak off with it while he was trapped with a full plate and a table of grown-ups. He set his plate down as close as he could get to it.

"Mine," he said.

I raised the carving knife and we got started. At least, me and Squeak and the girls did. Rusty never made it to the table. He'd pulled his chair over to the fire and appointed himself fire-keeper. He'd pull on his beer and throw on a branch, pull on the beer, throw on a branch. He'd about wiped out the moon.

"In good old Gene's memory," he said. "I gotta keep it burnin'."

"He's not dead," Terree said, "he just looks that way."

She laughed and filled up her plate. She'd made a great meal, something she called tabooli, with lots of chopped vegetables in it, and garlic bread that brought tears to your eyes and a fruit salad not from the cheap stuff like bananas, but full of pears and strawberries and melon and pine nuts. And, of course, there was the turkey. It weighed twenty-two pounds. It almost outsized the Big Wheel. I started to slow down on the beer. Jenny was working real hard not to give me the fish-eye and, besides, I wanted to taste the food.

I wish Jenny'd cook more, but she works and she raised three kids completely on her own, so I understand. And I've been rolling in most nights half-dead. It's one thing doing roofing in your twenties, it's hell on earth when you're my age. I haven't told her that yet. I haven't told her about slowing down, but I think she already knows it. It's not just before dinner, it's after. It's that part that's got me worried. She was with a younger guy before. She hasn't said anything, but sometimes I wonder. I don't like to admit it but I do.

It was weird being at the table with the three women. I think they forgot I was there. Usually, when we're out here, Gene's around, or Chick, our other work-buddy, or even Rusty, the more or less that he can be. So, we end up talking what Jenny calls constructo. And, the women chime in or buzz buzz about their own stuff. Once the food's gone, we'll play cards or just hang out.

Lately, Jenny's been bearing down on staying sober, so she's not really comfortable with partying. She and Terree usually end up out in the kitchen doing dishes. No big deal to that. She doesn't mind it and neither does Terree. "We talk girl talk," she told me. "You know, diets, about hair, the meaning of life, in other words, you boys."

But, this time, there I was all by my lonesome, and they launched into it. I'm not kidding, I could have been invisible...or deaf, for all they cared. They started with diets and that is some boring stuff. I kicked in a few observations about how some men like women who look like women. Jenny patted my knee. Then they got into the women in ads and how most of 'em were maybe fourteen years old, at most.

Lila said she'd thought about modelling once, but she'd got side-tracked by Rusty and then Dante had come along and that had put the stops to that. And now there was maybe a new one on the way.

"I'm jealous," Terree said. She and Gene had been trying for a while to get a second kid cooking and it wasn't happening.

"I'm not," Jenny said. She glanced over at me. That's one of her major dreads. Pregnancy. She wouldn't, she couldn't get an abortion. She's a strange one. She drove one of her best friends out of town to get one and she cried with her and she ran over there in the middle of the night when some problem kicked up, but she couldn't get one herself. I think I know why. There's something about a kid she gave up. She doesn't tell many people that. She's like a puzzle, pieces falling into place, sometimes slow, sometimes fast. And me, shit, I can't even find my pieces, but I hope there's something there.

"Now, Lila," Jenny said, "what I *am* jealous of is your hair. I am hair dyslexic. I truly am."

I've watched her stand in front of the mirror, trying to get combs in or putting that goo on it that makes it stay in place. And she is hopeless. Even I can see that.

"Well, hair *is* my best compliment," Lila said. "When my sister got married the first time, she would not go to a salon. My mom offered to pay for the whole works and Deb, that's my sister, she said no way, there was nobody but me was going to do the job. She looked like an angel, if I do say so. She completely did."

I had stopped eating. I don't know why I was doing it, but it was like I was half-memorizing what they were saying. Jenny and I are best friends and there's been other female best friends before her and we've all talked, talked a lot, but how often does a guy get to listen to ordinary girl talk. Never.

"Boy," Jenny said, "that's a real compliment."

She surprised me, because for all she gets crazy about her hair and her weight and her age, she thinks women are nuts for doing just that. "What you see is what you get," she'll say to me and she doesn't usually encourage that kind of sorry self-improvement talk in other women. I saw she might be doing something she sometimes does with me. It has to do with not quite telling the truth, but the other person walks away feeling like a million dollars.

I wondered when they would get to the part where they talked about the boys. I remembered being a little kid, being curled up in the corner of the sofa, hardly able to keep my eyes open, all the other kids in bed, me hoping my dad wouldn't notice me, hoping I'd get to stay up and see what magical things they did when we were asleep. He'd catch me at it and he'd carry me upstairs in his arms. "No you don't, Bub," he'd say. "It's the grown-ups' hour!"

They never got around to the boys. Almost as quick as I realized they'd let me be there, it was over. Gene staggered out from the house. Terree fixed him a plate of food. Rusty hauled himself up onto the bench, nudged Lila with his elbow, and she followed Terree's lead. Jenny had one of the most peaceful looks on her face I'd seen in a long time. Squeak had curled up on the bench and was sound asleep.

I wanted somebody to ask me what my best compliment was. I didn't know what I'd answer, maybe still having a full head of hair, maybe keeping on keeping on those damn roofs, maybe not whining most nights about just how beat I was, maybe taking my eyes off Lila's smile and turning 'em to Jenny's plain strong face. But, nobody asked, so I kept my best compliments to myself.

The fire was down to red coals. The sky was its pure black self, the moon almost full. I wondered about the Riv, if it was still snaking there, silvery now, across the black sand. And, when I turned away from the table, away from all the tired, gentle faces, and looked to see, it was.

M Y MOTHER SITS at the dinette table. She smokes her Camel, drinks her cold coffee. She has eaten half a powdered sugar donut. Her upper lip is frosted, her head shaking and her dark glasses are on her plate next to the donut. She glares at me.

"Your Dad's name is in the paper," she says. "Why is he in the paper?"

She presses *The Mountain Sun* on the table, running her ragged fingernail under my dad's name again and again.

"Edward Garnett, 226 E. Greenway, Mesa, Arizona, 86023. That's our old address. It's an article about mineral rights. Gold. Uranium. Thorium. What the hell is thorium? What's your dad doing with that stuff?"

"Dad's dead," I sit beside her.

She shakes her head. "I know that. I'm not feeble. Look, it says something about True Point of Beginning, '804.69 feet to the True Point of Beginning.' It sounds like religious babble. Your dad would hate that."

I try to slide the paper from her fingers. She holds tight.

"What is this, Barbara? I insist you tell me."

"I need coffee."

"Help yourself. It's de-caf."

"No high octane?"

"You know you need to get off that stuff," Mom says. "It makes you impossible."

I pour a cup of de-caf into a bone china cup painted with violets. She's drinking from a Lucky Bucks Winner mug. She dumps dry creamer out of a packet she's filched from one of her beloved casinos. She steals everything, toilet paper, sugar, even the lousy stationery. On the bluehair bus back from Nevada, she totes up what her loot would have cost at Safeway, and subtracts it from her losses.

"What the hell is wrong with me?" she says, "these are the flippin' tax sales."

She stands, totters and clutches me for support. "I get it," she says. "You don't fool me. It's Estrellas Ranchos." She pulls away from me and wobbles to the sink. "Not the ranch, you don't sell the ranch, my darling daughter." She fills a glass with water and throws it at me. "Dougie put you up to this, didn't he?" Her green eyes are shards, her upper lip drawn so tight you'd think she was a snake.

"No." I want a cigarette. I haven't smoked in thirty years and every time I'm with my mother I want a cigarette. "It was my idea. You've got no choice. Dad's insurance money is almost gone, the college just cut me to part-time, Bill's child support is fiction, and Dougie says he's tapped out."

"Ah," my mother sighs, "the golden years." She stubs her Camel out in the sink. "What ever happened to Honor Thy Father and Mother?"

She sits down, pulls a cigarette from the pack. "Okay, give it to me. I can take it. I knew this was going to happen." She puts on her dark glasses and leans her chin on her left hand. I know she knows I am looking over her shoulder at the sepia portrait of her as a young woman. In it, the woman not yet my mother sits at a piano, staring into the camera, smoke drifting from a cigarette held elegantly between her fingers, the sheet music for *Satin Doll* in front of her.

"I've lost everything," she says, "except you and Dougie, more or less. What's one more precious memory." She starts to hum *I'll Be Seeing You*.

"Won't work, Mom."

"My daughter the Feminist," Mom says. "Honoring women. Sisterhood. Hah!"

I consider taking the cigarette from her hand and letting the smoke burn harsh and soothing down my throat. "This isn't about theory," I say. "It's about economics."

"What isn't these days?" She shakes her shaking head. "I guess you and Dougie just see me as red numbers in your checkbooks."

"Mom," I say, "why can't you be some dumb old sweetie who lives for keno?"

"You got the keno right." She grins.

"And that's part of the problem. How much this year?"

"Five hundred bucks," she says, "Okay, a thousand. So what? I get on the Seniors Turn-Around bus. We ride through the beautiful desert. I look out the window. For three and a half hours, I forget everything. I pretend your dad is waiting for me. He's got the tent set up by a big old Joshua tree, and when I get off the bus it'll be just like it used to be."

She takes off her dark glasses. Her rattler eyes have gone soft and wet. "What am I supposed to do?" she asks. "I'll sign the papers."

"This is too easy, Mom."

She sets her glasses on her white curls. "For you, maybe," she locks eyes with me.

DOUGIE CALLS on the weekend. "Hey, Sis," he says brightly. This means he is scared to death and he knows I know it. When you live with a lady who is your mom three-fourths of the time, and a raving suicidal looney the other fourth, you learn to read everything, the flatness in the voice, the boneless droop of shoulders, the way a bathroom door can be closed and locked without a sound.

"It's okay, Dougie." I swear I hear his grip on the phone relax.

"Has she locked herself in the bathroom again?"

"Really, it's okay."

"Don't count on it." I hear the faint click of computer keys and I know he's working while he talks to me.

"Turn that off," I say. "Please just listen." The clicking stops. Dougie, aka Douglas Edward Garnett, works from the time his feet hit the floor 'til he collapses next to his sleeping wife. She is sleeping because she has worked since *her* feet hit the floor. She and Dougie run on empty so they can afford to live on Dougie's land in an upstate New York farm town in which the farms are gone. Everywhere are barns, rusting tractors, and a sign that says: Prime Real Estate. For Sale. Not Dougie's.

"Okay. I put it to sleep." I hear a muffled meow.

"You still using that kitty screen saver?" My brother, Dougie, fifty-one year-old barrel of a guy, rides a 750 Honda 'cause Harleys are ostentatious, and owns five real cats, four dogs, and a screen saver with cats you can feed, brush, and paint blue.

"Yeah," he laughs. "Jeez, what weird times."

"Maybe it's just us Garnetts."

"The Garnett family is a jewel. Flawed but beautiful." he recites. My mom's favorite joke. Happy families are boring, only in the cracked scarlet heart of a Garnett is there true beauty.

"So," Dougie taps his finger on the phone, "what now?"

"She wants to go to the ranch for one last night. I told her my only stipulation was we take real coffee."

"I wish I was there."

"No you don't."

My mom and I decide to drive to the ranch Friday dawn and come back next day. "There's more good light that way," she says, "you know, that long shadow light." I'm grateful it's early April. From May on, Estrellas Ranchos is a high desert inferno, bony piñon-juniper giving up more scent than shadow, juniper reeking like cat piss and wet Sixties dope, the kind of smell my mom would eradicate with bleach and elbow grease.

She cleans a lot. It holds sorrow at bay, and with two clandestine cats in the Seniors' Efficiency Unit, she has to. Murdoch, the greedy tabby, is on the table when I get there.

"Where are you?" I hear muffled noises from the thumb-sized john.

"In here. I'm fine, just getting ready."

I snoop. She's been unnaturally cheerful the last couple weeks. Clinic shrinks told us to look out for cheerfulness. "It is a deadly sign," the last doc said. He was Sikh, his dark eyes fierce as he sat my brother and me down. "These types often cheer up just before they…you know…krk-kkkkk." He drew his long finger across his throat.

"I'm not suspiciously cheerful," my mom yells from the bathroom.

"I'm snooping," I yell back. I've only got a few minutes. Her toilette consists of shower, running her fingers through her wet curls, brushing her teeth, somehow smoking a cigarette the whole time. I flip through the papers on her desk, a 1995 form X-miss letter from Dougie's ex-wife, a hummingbird feather and an unsealed envelope addressed to somebody in Oregon. I slip out the card.

Greetings, Sally, Another year has gone by so quickly it's hard to believe its almost 1998. I'll be 88 in March.

This year I've had three articles published in Better Days *maga-zine. I keep busy with garden work and volunteering—easy things like hostessing, changing the magazines in the hospital waiting rooms and lead a class for seniors called Sit and Be Fit. It's amazing what can be done sitting down. I've given up long trips do short ones with the seniors now. Boat or ships or buses I still can do and enjoy as once you are on board you can do as you want.*

Have you written any more stories? Have an enjoyable year. Mart.

P.S. Still smoking those damn cigarettes.

My mom sneaks out of the bathroom and catches me. I have my back to her which is good because that way she doesn't see my eyes are wet.

"Ha," she says. "Pay-back's a bitch." It was in my 1958 diary she found out I was pregnant, and later I found the check for five hundred dollars and the note, "This is enough to get you and Rick set up."

She fluffs out her hair. Her robe is half open. I look away. She laughs.

"Look," she says and opens the robe. "My breasts aren't much anymore," she says softly. "You know, your dad…"

"Whoa," I say, "More Than I Need to Know Alert."

She grins. "You'll *never* know, honey. You'll never know."

I've already loaded the truck: sleeping gear, classy caf and de-caf from the local espresso place, apricot scones, linguine, garlic, good olive oil, and real Parmesan. She won't let me cook. I know that, and this menu's easy. You drain the boiling linguine water into the frying pan, swipe out, and dry on the juniper fire you've lit to ease the evening chill. She never said, "This is how you do this." She just did it. I watched, learned. Camp cooking, naming cats, writing to save your life. Staying loyal to a mean man. I blew that last one. A blessed failure of domestic training.

Mom hobbles down the steps. She's wearing a plaid flannel shirt, her Wupatki National Monument Volunteer jacket, too-big Levis rolled up to the calf, and a pair of hiking boots I've never seen.

"Nice boots," I take her arm.

She shrugs me off. "I ask those kids over at Second Hand to hold size sixes for me." She grabs the truck door handle and winces. I bend to lock the camper, feel pain shoot down my leg and flinch.

"Thelma and Louise with arthritis," she hauls herself into the seat. "Let's hit the road."

Highway 180 north out of Flagstaff is gorgeous and deadly. You wind down off the mountain, through old gold Ponderosa, past cinder cones soft rose in the morning light. Shadows hold the chill. A late snow has powdered the highway and transmuted into black ice.

"Black ice," my mom says, "I always thought it was just like my friggin' depression. You can't see it, but…"

I nod and accelerate into the straight-away that runs by meadows pouring silvery-gold to the base of the mountains. There's a V-Dub camper parked by the Chapel of the Holy Dove.

"Honey," mom says, "will you ever forget that time?"

I won't. By the third mean man, I had begun to suspect something was funny. I knew I wasn't pretty, and plain women need to work just a little harder for love, but by the time my love told me he needed to explore his feelings with his new post-doc and would I mind if his son stayed with me and my kids over the weekend while he and Doctor Lisa examined neurological sub-strata and he didn't have time to talk about it, I wondered if a god in which I didn't believe had it in for me. I had hiked out to the

Chapel and pinned a note on the Messages for the Lord Celestial Bulletin Board.

Big Whatever, I doubt you're there, but if you are, please let me know what's wrong with me. Dubiously, Barbara

Mom had picked me up on the mournful hike back. My dad never let her drive. To this day, I don't know how she sneaked the old Buick out of the driveway. She beeped. I looked up. "You followed me," I said. She nodded. "I read your note. I want you to get some help. Even if it never worked for me."

To THE east, the tops of the mountains glitter, snow swirling up, rhinestone wraiths dancing into nothing. Mom sighs. "I love this."

We stop at Red Mountain. The parking dirt is deserted, Thunderbird bottles and Old Milwaukee cans sparkling, a pair of panties hanging from the sage. Two minutes out the trail is clean, the footing soft. New wildflowers spangle the sand, purple stars no bigger than your baby fingernail. The juniper are blue with berries, scent baking out. My mom lights a cigarette and breathes deep. "This is heaven."

We come to the opening of the crater. Red Mountain glows in front of us, basalt and iron oxide, pomegranate, cobalt, sunset, and thunderheads. We'll have to traverse the side of a cinder cone or climb up a dam an early rancher built across the arroyo. Mom leans on her cane and glares at the stone-work. "Flippin' busy-body men. They can't leave well enough alone."

"You want me to boost you up?" I ask. "We did it last year."

"Darling," she says, "eighty-eight is forty years stiffer than forty-eight. You go ahead. And get me some obsidian."

"Okay," I say. "I'll be right back."

Dawn or dusk, monsoon or clear sky, a wind swirls inside Red Mountain. If you try to camp there, a soft howling keeps you awake. You give up before midnight, pack your gear, stumble out, by full moon if you're lucky, by new moon if you're not. When you approach the opening and swing your gear down over the dam, you wonder what lies outside. You have forgotten.

I climb to the huge old pines standing like miracles in the crater's heart and say the only prayer I know. "Thank you."

I want to hurry. The crater is silent, the wind soft. This is heaven on earth. And still, I miss my mother. I scoop up a handful of obsidian and tiny red cinders. "For my mom," I say. "Okay?" The sky burns mountain blue. Only perfect silence answers my question.

BACK ON the road, mom holds the obsidian gravel in her palm. She has been picking out the red cinders for the last twenty miles, looking up to show me a jay's iridescence, wild-flowers bursting from a rusted truck chassis, how Grandmother Butte has just appeared on the horizon which means we are almost there and do I remember the Havasupai story about the rabbit old Supai Jimmy used to tell?

"The rabbit," she says, "was the scared one. The other animals made fun of him. There was a big forest fire. Rabbit ran and warned all the animals, led them to a big hollow in the ground near Grandmother Butte, and jumped in last. The forest fire roared over and burned his back. That's why jack-rabbit has a black streak down his back. That way you know the truth about his courage."

"There," she tucks the obsidian in her shirt pocket. She'll add it to the Laguna bowl in the middle of her dinette table. The bowl is unglazed micaceous clay, no design, only the earth's shimmer. It holds obsidian—arrowheads, needles, pebbles, black and scarlet, translucent slabs with what seem to be ferns in their hearts. The bowl holds Oregon noon, Sierra twilight, Mojave dawn, a thousand sudden stops on dirt roads. I hear my dad's voice, "Jesus Christ, Martha, you and your damn rocks. We're gonna have to get a new suspension."

"I just drove your old dad crazy with my rocks," mom says fondly. "Wouldn't he hate that I put him in the rock garden? Except for these." A plastic bag of ashes rests on her palm. "All that's left. He's going where he wanted to live forever. I'm putting him under the stars."

The sign hangs lop-sided, stars silvery against splintered wood. Estrellas Ranchos: Beautiful Vistas. $99 down, $99 monthly. Where the Real West Begins. Jim McHane.

"McHane," my mom snorts. "Damn fool idiot. Couldn't even get the sign right. Estrellas Ranchos! Sounds like a Nevada floozey-house. It's Rancho Estrellas. Ranch of Stars. Someday I'm gonna tear that flippin' thing down."

McHane thought of everything, advertising in eastern newspapers, roads in a grid across the rocky sand, street signs, Tonto Lane and Trigger Drive. The only thing he missed was the total lack of water. My mom and dad didn't mind. They bought #407 Tonto Lane, an Army surplus tent, two canteens, one big sleeping bag, and a Coleman lantern. Their third anniversary, they drank a bottle of fair champagne, poured the dregs at the base of the alligator juniper for luck, lay down on the warm sand and under a zillion diamond *estrellas*, made me.

I drive the crumbling asphalt around baby sage and sprouting datura to #407, and pull onto the cracked concrete my dad poured a thousand years ago.

"What the hell?" my mom says. "Look at that."

Somebody has taken a chain-saw to the alligator juniper. Most of the lower branches are stubs. My mom climbs out and stomps to the tree. A piñon jay scuttles off. Frost-blue berries rain down. "You're a dead man," she yells, "whoever you are, you're dead!" She hauls her backpack out of the camper and tears it open. "You misbegotten monster, take this." She pulls a tiny pistol out of her pack and, before I can stop her, shoots five times in the direction of town.

There is perfect silence. She clicks the safety and puts the gun back in her pack. "I will be glad to be out of this world," she says. "It can't come too soon." She grabs her cane and stomps off for firewood.

"Apparently," I yell, "rage is good for arthritis." She shakes her fist and disappears into a little wash.

"Nobody," I say, "cooks like you." I lick garlicky oil off my plate. Juniper flames flicker off the mutilated tree. Sunset burns cool, far mountains black against a horizon of drifting tourmaline light.

"I'll miss light," my mom says. "We've got so many kinds out here."

"Stop talking about death," I say.

"I'm not. I'm talking about light."

We hunker close to the fire. It's an Indian fire, tiny.

"Old Jimmy taught your dad," she says. "The white man makes a big fire, has to back up not to get burned, and freezes his butt off."

"You think those two are still hanging out?" We look up at the stars.

"I hope so."

She lights a cigarette. "Sixty-five years and the first puff always tastes like a miracle. Especially out here."

"I miss 'em every day."

"Good for you. I don't want you to go first."

"Mom."

"I'm not talking about dying," she grins. "I'm talking about love."

I roll out our sleeping gear. My mom adds sticks to the fire. We crawl into our bags. I watch the tip of her cigarette move in the dark and I remember what the Hopi say about *Masau'u*, God of Life and Death: "When you see little lights far-off in the desert and there's nobody there, it's Him."

"I miss your dad," she says. "The old fart."

I ask the question I've never asked. "Why?"

The cigarette glows bright as the North Star. For an instant, I see her face, eyes pure midnight.

"Because," she says. "He was my heart. And I was his. And you. And Dougie. And this place."

"But…"

"He couldn't show it. That's how men were. Honey, we never told you this, but he was scared to death all the time. My nervous breakdowns, flippin' psychiatrists, hospital bills—we didn't have health insurance. There wasn't any in those days. You know what that meant."

I turn on my back. "Maybe."

"Three jobs. No breaks. Me gone two months out of every year. Plus, when I was home, you know depression, no…"

She's sparing my delicate modern ears. *Sisterhood,* I think. *It's time for me to be her sister.*

"No sex," I say.

"That's right. No sex, no nothing. Baby, you sure you want to hear this?"

My childhood drops away and is gone. "I'm sure."

She tells me. Sparks and stars dance in the branches of the juniper. Her words pour over me, through me.

Finally, she says, "How could I not love him, faithful as he was? How could I not want to go be with him." Paper rustles. "Here, I never showed you this. He gave it to me a week before he died."

The hand-writing is a scrawl, the yellow paper unfolded and folded so many times, I see our camp-fire through the creases. *Martha. I love you. E.*

"Those were the last words he ever wrote." I hear her turn on her side. "Just like the old days," she says without a beat. "There's a cow-pie right in front of my nose."

I SLEEP AND wake. I think of the pistol, the one bullet, her calm, "I have the right." Our fire is out. I look into the desert. Nothing glimmers there. Above, the Milky Way slices open the black sky. I slip into it.

A SHARP CLICK wakes me. I sit up. I wait for the gunshot. I won't stop her. Hard hard sisterhood.

"Barbara. Baby."

She stands by the truck, the dome light on, and bends over something. "I know what I need to do."

I scramble out of my bag. "Mom. Stop." That much for sisterhood.

"Look," she says. Her Wupatki jacket is spread on the seat. On it lie four piles of obsidian. She sifts my dad's ashes into one of the piles and stirs gently.

"I thought you had the gun."

She straightens and holds out her arms. "Oh no, honey. Come here."

I stumble into her hug. "That's done for me," she says. "I woke up and knew I wanted to divide the obsidian. Some for you, for Dougie, for the bowl, and the rest for your dad." She gathers the ashy obsidian and gives me half. "Here," she points to the juniper, "we'll leave him here."

We scratch Dad and obsidian into the sand. Mom rebuilds the fire. I put a pot of water to boil. We watch dawn slither in over Grandmother Butte like a pewter snake, the fierce red eye of the sun burning low. My mom drinks her de-caf. I drink my high octane. We toast scones and pile on butter.

"I buried the bullet by the ashes," she says. "I thought you'd want to know."

"I'll see you through," I say.

"I know." She grabs the lowest juniper stub and pulls herself up. "I'm ready to go home."

We pull onto the highway.

"Stop," Mom says. "The sign."

She rummages in her purse, pulls out twine and a huge black marker. While I watch, she climbs out and goes to work. When she is finished, the sign hangs even and McHane's words are gone.

Rancho Estrellas, she has written, True Point of Beginning.

 Squirrel

J ULIA HEADS NORTH. She is in the middle of a decade hard as mineral, a time for surgery, a time to stay alive. In three years, she has lost five people to death, her desire to her aging, some of her hearing and sight to the same honest thief. She buys hearing-aids and new glasses. She does not take estrogen. Or a lover. She drives north, hunting obsidian.

Obsidian is black or red or gray, sometimes all three. You look into the heart of the stone and see a galaxy, distant, spidery, fiery as earth's core; you look at the surface and see yourself. Obsidian can be drab as a bad morning or brilliant as winter midnight. It can be sharpened to a finer edge than any other material and it can be used to shape itself, a blade for surgery, for hunting, for separating fur from flesh and meat from bone.

Julia stops to move a road-kill badger off I-95 out of Vegas. A broken obsidian point shines in the littered sand. A day later, Glass Flow thrusts up through High Sierra granite, moonlit boulders gleaming big, black, and sexy as Lincoln Continentals; then, two days of hard driving, a night of starry sleep and she is at Glass Butte, gathering lozenges of orange and black, gray chips containing ghost-ferns in the delicate Autumn light.

At Yellowstone she is told there is obsidian. "Go to Black Sands Basin," a bored ranger says. "Drive carefully. Have a nice day."

She puts the binoculars to her eyes and scans the basin. There is no black sand, no obsidian crystals shimmering like cheap eye make-up. There are only a cinder trail, charred pines, pools of oily iridescence, and people moving silent as shadows through pearly vapor. She can hear the true voices of this place, steam and boiling water and a raven shrieking from a skeleton tree.

She walks the trail to Emerald Pool. The pool is emerald only in its heart. Where the water is shallow, the pool is turquoise, then aqua, then the thin blue of Wyoming sky. There is a sign on the railing: *Danger. Do not go beyond boardwalk. Though the surface of thermal area appears solid, only a thin crust may lie above scalding water. Unpredictable shifts in the elements below can make sudden deadly changes in the area.*

Elk and deer shit are scattered between the springs, lie dark and ordinary at the chalky lip of a tiny geyser. She wonders how the animals know where to walk. Do deer test the surface with a delicate hoof? Can elk sniff out a change coming? Or, do aspen-white bones shudder in these brilliant waters? Are she, the two Dutch girls in Rainbow Tribe regalia, and the dark man with the camera bag gazing into a pot of elk broth?

Julia wants to move sure as a doe across the chalky yellow and white earth that does not look at all like earth. She thinks of old teeth, stained by sixty years of cigarettes. Her mother dead from an efficient lung cancer at eighty-five. "Not a bad bargain," she had said. "A lifetime of not one cigarette I didn't enjoy, for a quick and painless death."

The Dutch girl moves next to her. "It is scary? No?" Julia nods. The girl reaches out and touches the little leather bag Julia wears on a cord around her neck.

"It is for magic?" she says.

"Luck."

The girl touches the peace sign hanging from a black leather thread around her slim waist. She has pierced her navel. A zircon sparkles there. Her bicycle shorts are paisley and her striped tee shirt is cropped just below her young breasts. "I," she says, "wish for peace and, how do you say it?—fairness."

"Fairness," Julia says, "is, perhaps, a fairy tale."

The girl laughs.

"Sonja," her friend calls. "The bus is coming."

Sonja shakes Julia's hand firmly. "I think you would like Amsterdam."

Julia grins. "Perhaps."

"We *love* America," the girl says, "How you say? Totally?!" She hugs Julia, turns and runs for the bus.

The dark man moves next to Julia.

"Like something from another planet," she says.

He is off-beat good-looking. It's a long shot, but maybe he moved over because he had a similar thought about her.

"No," he says, "*this* is earth." He points to the pool.

He has a thick accent. She wonder if he is related to the girls and has just deliberately missed his bus. She wonders if she should feel flattered.

"I meant the girls," she says, "those kids are from some wonderful alien world."

He stares at her. She forgets about feeling flattered.

" Are you Dutch, too?" she asks. Her voice catches.

He doesn't answer. His bare arm is inches from hers. It is covered with the most wonderful tattoo she's ever seen. And, she lives in a town where rich middle-aged drop-outs sport Maori or Pocahantas logos and call them tats. The dark guy's tattoo refers blessedly to no Third World myth or Disney flick. It is done with craft. A perfect fir bough curves diagonally around his fore-arm. Gold and silver birch leaves drift between the twigs. Julia wonders if it is Norse. Her mythologies are not about tattoos. They are about what's standing in front of her, scowling, staring into the emerald water, Loki or Odin, as long as he isn't nice or available, he can be her hero, her wizard, her mischief-maker, her god.

"*That* is a beautiful tattoo," she says.

He turns and studies her face. He is not just off-beat good-looking; he is gargoyle gorgeous, his eyes furious and sad. *Not Loki*, she thinks, *Lancelot, Lancelot the scarred, Elf Arrow himself.*

"Squirrel," he says. Julia thinks she has misheard him. His words seem to jam behind his lips.

"Squirrel?"

He bends his arm. A gray tuft-ear squirrel is tattooed below the fir branch.

"That," Julia says, "is the best tattoo I ever saw."

He rolls his other sleeve up. His arms are powerful, not young, more the weathered sinew of an aging soldier.

"Old Faithful." He touches the tattoo on his left bicep. "And here," the words are more clear, "Prismatic Hot Spring."

She wants to touch the emerald pool set in his flesh, the pale steam drifting along his skin. She thinks of the delicately roiling water in front of them, of a tattoo of a woman standing transfixed near a green thermal pool, her name pierced into a man's skin. *Julia.*

"And here," the man says. An eagle soars along his other forearm. She half expects a winged shadow to drift across them.

"But this one," Julia says and points to the fir branch. She wants to touch it, but he is watching her face. She doesn't want this man to see the hunger. Her fingers burn. She imagines he would feel them searing the delicate fir needles, the soft curve of the squirrel's back, branding the tattoo doubly in his flesh. She looks up, studies his lined face, his raptor eyes.

"This one," Julia says. She touches the fir branch. "This one is art."

He nods, bends to gather his camera gear and walks away.

JULIA SLEEP-WALKS along the board trail. Sunset Lake. Rainbow Pool. The earth sighs into the cold air. Steam pearls on her skin. She moves through clouds of sulfur. People emerge. Vapor trails from their shoulders. They are angels in matching tee shirts.

Julia worries the sulfur will give her a headache. She imagines the shocking blues, the skeletal earth, the huge sky wobbling behind the acid-rainbow lens of a migraine aura. She comes round to where she started. The Squirrel Man is hunched over a camera in front of Cliff Geyser. It is a plain black box on a tripod, a Lindhof eight-by-ten. It is, for the photographer, a Stradivarius, a 1968 Stratocaster. The Squirrel Man does not notice her. He puts his eye to the view-piece, fusses with the lens, slides in a film-plate.

Julia remembers her first husband. He was a poet. It was 1958 and his best friend, Neil, was a photographer who, his bony fingers stained with nicotine and chemicals, prayed only to Edward Weston. Standing above this cobalt and gold and burnt orange earth, these lavish vapors, she remembers Weston's black-and-white, eight-by-ten photos. He cropped nothing. What he shot was what he printed; balanced, soaring, luminous, driftwood, bones, shells, a woman's naked back. Wood was wood, bone was bone, shell the pure calcium container for what had once lived and died. Woman was not metaphor, she was flesh.

Her poet wanted his friend to photograph her just that way. Ten shots. No fakery. No cropping. The woman he loved, essential as beach cedar, true as stone. While her husband taught Freshman Composition in a gloomy post-war Quonset hut, Neil and Julia had met on a long sweep of Great Lakes beach. Light flooded them. She leaned back against a huge drift-wood log. She wore jeans and a black sweater. Her dark hair was cropped close to her skull. She had outlined her eyes with kohl.

"Perfect," Neil said. "Look here."

He tapped the air near his left shoulder. Julia raised her eyes, not to the bright air, but to his intent face. He paused, then stepped forward.

She was twenty, already a mother. Her poet-husband was twenty-two, Neil twenty-six. On that shoreline, in that cool light, his shadowed eyes and the deep lines already marking his face seemed ancient. When his mouth touched hers, she was shocked at the softness of his lips.

"What will we do?" he said.

They left that afternoon. She mailed her husband her diamond ring.

He drove to Mexico, got a quick divorce and married a month later. His wife adopted their son. Neil left. In all the half-year they were together, he never photographed her. She moved to San Francisco, worked hard, made enough to allow her to buy one Weston print: black sand and a luminous shell that might have been a woman. She tested men with it. She hung it in the hall. If a man turned to it before he turned to her, she made him her lover.

THE GEYSER hisses softly, returns her to this fragile, violent place. She closes the gap between the Squirrel Man and herself. She wonders if he will look up, wonders if he will see what she saw as Neil moved toward her that first time.

The Squirrel Man stays hunched over the camera. Autumn sun glows silvery, the little geyser a plume of light. Julia walks to the left of the camera, sets her cold hands on the wood railing. She wants to kiss the back of the Squirrel Man's neck, press her dry mouth to the place where his dark hair feathers along his nape. She wonders, for an instant, if the sulfur has indeed poisoned her, if this desire is the sign of a migraine moving like cautery through her brain, cutting away caution fiber by fiber, cell by cell.

"Edward Weston," she says.

The Squirrel Man jerks his eye away from the viewpiece. She looks directly at the geyser. She knows he is watching her.

"You...know...Edward Weston...?" His words are broken gifts. She hears what they cost him.

"I didn't *know* him," she says. "I wish I had. I know that working with a view camera requires a great deal from the photographer..." She pauses. She has forgotten she is fifty-six. She is suddenly twenty and Arachne weaving with words, with what this man knows of light. She knows that if he turns and looks into her eyes, he will be caught. She imagines him walking into her apartment. He would go to the Weston. He would not hesitate.

"I know what you are doing," Julia says, "requires patience—and trust." She can almost see the web shining silken between his dark shape and her delicate craft, the geyser catching light, the web catching it.

He bends over the camera. The geyser sputters, feathers, hisses six feet of pure white steam. Again and again. The Squirrel Man doesn't take a picture.

Silence lies between them. She remembers she is fifty-six and the ten photographs that might have reminded him of her dark body, her gypsy eyes were never taken. And still, she weaves. The web catches on the wind.

"I can't speak well," the Squirrel Man says softly.

"Did you say you don't speak well?" Her hearing aids are in the car. She wants to laugh. *I can't hear you tell me you can't speak well.*

"Yes," he says. "An injury."

His jaw is set. Julia has had more than enough lovers to know when a woman speaks, and when she doesn't. But she is weaving and cannot stop. She looks past his shoulder. Steams boils in snaky caverns, twists up into the watery autumn light. The silence between this man and her is mineral.

"So what," Julia says. "I can't hear well."

He is quiet. She is ashamed. *So what. So what. So everything, you who have talked yourself into a hundred heavens, out of ninety-nine hells.*

"I envy photographers," Julia says. Her words rattle. "I'm a writer. This. Light. All of this. Steam, clouds, what we see through the vapor. It's nearly impossible to put into words."

He is quiet. She remembers that bright girl in the '50s Chicago coffee-house. Her husband and his best friend both wear black turtlenecks and baggy khaki pants. Her husband has a beard. His best friend's black hair curls along his collar. They smoke cheap cigarettes, lighting one from another, sometimes for each other, sometimes for her. They are discussing Celine and William Burroughs and how Minor White's pictures of ghetto walls remind them of Camus' sparse take on life.

The girl is nine months pregnant. This fact barely shows under her loose jeans. She wonders what it will feel like to be a mother. She knows only that she has no idea. The men seem to have forgotten her presence. She takes a deep breath.

"Do you think," she says, "that DeChirico's use of light reflects that same aesthetic, of austerity, perhaps?" Her voice is high and tight.

Her husband smiles. His best friend glances at his best friend's wife, a quick sharp look. "That's perceptive, Julia," he says. He runs his finger around the rim of the cheap wine glass and sets it ringing.

THE SQUIRREL MAN remains silent. Light burns on the mineral crust before them, glows copper in the dark stains. Julia remembers the absence of quiet at the coffee-house table and how, when silence came, she was afraid and studied the menu, the chipped Formica, the way the city light fell smudged across the striped awning. She thinks of squirrels, of how if you keep moving, keep chattering, you might think you can't be killed—and of her second-to-last lover and his cheery enthusiasm—twenty e-mails a day, a hundred plans for the future, a thousand reassurances that he was a good man and would not leave her and, how in the last endless month, she ached for silence. And he could not shut up.

Julia turns away from the geyser. She hears it sigh, then a sound like huge birds taking flight. The shutter clicks. She begins to walk away.

"Good luck," she says.

The Squirrel Man looks up. He steps from behind the camera. Julia stops. He moves toward her and rolls up his left sleeve.

"Old Faithful," he says and touches the tattoo.

"Yes," she says and points to Prismatic Hot Spring. "Prismatic."

He nods.

"Squirrel," she says.

Slowly he raises his other arm. They look full into each others' faces. Then, he flinches and turns away. Julia thinks that what is beautiful in an aging man's face can be terrifying in a woman's. She wants to set her hand on his arm and doesn't. He hunches over the camera.

Julia walks away. When she stops and closes her eyes, the light behind her lids burns scarlet. She hears the geyser behind her, the smaller unnamed springs bubbling on either side of the boardwalk. A bus roars up. The air is filled with voices. She bows her head and opens her eyes. Beneath her feet, the cinder trail shimmers.

 My Tree

W HEN YOU ARE A shepherd in the long green twilights high in the Toiyabe Range, you love the first week there. Especially if you are young and potent, and wise enough to love more than one woman. Three, perhaps. Two can comfort each other, and you can think of that while you are with the third.

Why, then, would that first week alone be perfect? Because although you are wise enough to love three women, and potent enough to turn Dona to flame, Loba to honey, and melt fierce Ria against your heart, the moon rules these women. When the moon rises full and their blood is an aching tide, the flame scorches, the sweet goes bitter, the soft becomes stone. Then, the moon rules you.

Up in the mountain meadows, one can be at peace. Joaquin Zillet is young and potent and wise, and he is far beyond serenity. A long month ago he rode into the aspen. On this Midsummer's Eve, he sits on the sheep-wagon steps and drinks cheap brandy. It warms his lonely belly. Just before the light goes silver, he wonders if he has drunk too much.

The air shimmers. Aspen trunks gleam ivory as Dona's thighs. Tree-knots blur, become petals, openings. Loba's eyes gleam from here, from there. He is suddenly hard. In the valley below, Dona *y* Loba *y* Ria turn in their restless sleep, reach for the warm belly of their lover and find no one.

That night, Joaquin's dreams are haunted by tall pale women. He is a wind among them. When he touches them, they shiver and sigh.

He wakes on fire, thinks of Loba holding him between her dark breasts. He is hard, half-hard, aching and numb. He touches himself, imagines Ria's sweet spine arching below him. His hand is not enough.

He surrenders, gets up and pulls on his boots. He wants to curse some-one, but he remembers his Lola's stories, how curses fly out—and return. Morning light calls him to the creek. He dips his hands into liquid ice, splashes his face and shivers. The sun glints above the mountains. He raises his face, watches aspen leaves twisting in the green dawn. This day, he thinks, will truly be the longest.

"I am lonely," he says. He feels the wind catch his words as though they were prayer. Joaquin is not a violent man. His women have taught him that fierce is never cruel. Yet, as the sun drifts toward the jagged western mountains, Joaquin walks into the aspen, carrying a slender knife. At the first tree, he pauses. For a moment, he believes the tree is trembling.

"It is only the wind," he says. He bows his head.

"*Virgen,*" he whispers, "I do this for passion."

He touches his blade to the tree. This he carves:

this:

and this:

The light begins to cool. He is warm, embers in his belly, shadows on his face tempering—his longing a blade.

"Joaquin," he writes. "Zillet." He could carve for as long as he could make love. "Forever," he whispers. Moves on. More eyes. More women than even he, Joaquin Zillet, could satisfy on this longest day.

The sun hovers orange, his blade a long shadow. He remembers stories of Indians carving magic on animal bone. Once, old Luc found a cache of badger skulls, roared into camp crazy drunk, and threw the moon-white bones into the campfire. Joaquin remembers what he saw before the bones were smoke. Stars. Spirals. Tree, woman, the horns of a great stag.

Joaquin stops, goes to the stream that tumbles over pebbles rosy as flesh. He bathes his face, traces water over his lips, and swallows. He thinks of kisses, of thighs and belly and breath. He is desire, so quiet he can hear his soft heartbeat.

One tree is left, taller than the others, her upper branches singing in the twilight, the song a web, the first star captured, cool blue. There is room on Her pearly bark for all, Dona, Loba, Ria, skin like new snow, a scar like lightning; pillowy thighs, thighs strong as a mare's; young eyes, cat-eyes old and knowing; lips and lips and lips, coral and rose and the sweet killing heat of *habañera chiles*. He bows, touches his heart, looks up, and begins to cut.

By MOONLIGHT he moves his blade, slow as good love, through the last cut. MY TREE His blood sings in his tired flesh, sings of how you can fall asleep loving, wake from dreams into a dream and find the legs wrapped around your waist are real, and you move, you move, with a body heavy as sleep.

He walks back to the sheep-wagon, pulls his shirt over his head. The thick wool takes him into the dark. He smells his body, the scent of long kisses, of how a man can wait, a woman so often not.

"Joaquin." A woman's voice.

"Joaquin."

He pulls the shirt down and takes the knife in his cold hand. Crazy. A knife against a woman. Crazy.

He sees no one.

"Joaquin," the voice says. "My lover. My holy son."

He sets the knife down. Gently.

"Come here."

He walks to the base of the tree. Looks up at Her.

She laughs. "So, I am *your* tree."

She trembles, her leaves sparkling in the moonlight. He remembers a dancer in San Francisco, blue spotlights glittering off sequin, her breasts and belly seen, then hidden, then seen, as though star-struck clouds passed over the body of the New Moon.

"*I* am *yours*." She laughs again.

He steps backward, stumbles, sprawls on his back. Her laughter echoes. He closes his eyes, hears his pulse roaring.

"Open your eyes."

A woman stands at his feet. She is tall, not slender, but supple, her skin the moon's light, her hair silvery-green, her pale eyes lined in black like a gypsy whore's.

"And you," she says, "are mine."

YOU CAN make love with clouds, with foam, with ice shimmering in lava caves. With that which has no heart. No thoughts. No past nor future nor will for anything but making love. You can enter a woman and know what it is to have roots. Lightning scars. Ravens living in your hair.

You can make love in the shortest night more times than even you can imagine. You look up, past Her bone-white shoulder and you see Orion. You know it is winter. The longest night. And, still you will be ready to make love again.

SHE IS GONE. Green light seams the eastern sky. The mountains burn black. Joaquin turns to hold Her, gathers leaves into his arms. She is gone. And not. He lies at Her feet. She is trembling, Her leaves shimmering in the first tendrils of light. *MY TREE,* He rises and traces the cuts with kisses. When he pulls on his shirt, something catches in the hem. A leaf green as dawn.

Only later, bathing in the creek, does he look at himself. He has moved, frightened, through morning, remembering his *lolas'* stories—full moon, men turned into wolves. He thinks he might look at himself in a wagon window and see a tree. He remembers something about magic mirrors, not glass, water, only water to see the truth.

He bends naked over the eddy and sees his face, his dark hair, wet and tangled. All of him ordinary. He smiles and raises his arms in gratitude. He wonders, as we often do, if what passed the night before had been a dream. When he looks down again, he catches his breath. Over his heart lies the outline of an aspen leaf. Brilliant green. Without a flaw.

LOBA EMBROIDERS the leaf on his sleeve, promises to tell no one.

Dona leaves him. "*Brujo,*" she says.

Ria traces the leaf with her tongue. Kisses him. He tastes summer. Remembers roots and lightning and ravens screaming in the dawn.

OCTOBER BURNS in, impossible blue. They wake one morning, he and Loba and Ria, to frost glittering as though the moon has fallen and shattered. Loba brings coffee. Joaquin pulls back the covers to welcome her.

"Joaquin," she whispers. "Ria."

She touches his chest. He looks down. The leaf is no longer green. He wonders if it is a trick of dawn burning silver-gold through the window. Ria smiles. "*Oro,*" she says, "*y plata.*"

BY EARLY November, the leaf is gone. Loba and Ria are not, and there is another. Three women are good. Two can comfort each other, and you can think of that while you are with the third.

By April, there is a fourth and it is she who first sees the pale green leafing out over Joaquin's heart.

Officer Magdalena, White Shell Woman, and Me

I T WASN'T UNTIL they locked Katy and me in the holding tank with the shoplifter and the public intox that I actually had my first spiritual experience. Up 'til then, it had gone pretty much to plan, *It* being the Line Dance Blockade across the Snowbird Ski Resort road. Katy, a.k.a. Sparrow, and I were the only women to link hands in the chain of bloods, bros, whiteguy rastas, and Everett, my best friend. Katy's best friend, Amber, brought a boom-box, so we were more or less kicking in synch to The Butthole Surfers' *Avalanche* when the Feds' caravan dynosaured up the mountain.

"Well," Everett said, "this is it." We all grinned. Up there, in that green-gold Ponderosa pine forest, beneath a late afternoon sun, old Glittering Top mountain shining above us, Katy, Everett, me and the seven other guys squeezed the hands of the people next to us and all thought something like, "If you're gonna get busted, this is the place to do it!"

You might have forgotten how it can be with these things, how affinity circles form, how support people take your valuables and car keys, how everybody starts singing a round or two of inspired and outdated songs which each of us know only parts of, so that our voices waver on the verses, and only on the chorus do they bust loose and soar and send shivers down our linked arms. And, of course, before all that brief and glorious solidarity, there are the meetings with that which Katy calls "terminal consensus," and the frantic phone calls, and the too-long press releases that go out one day short of too late.

And then, at last, there is the stepping out, the half-walk, half-dance to the bend in the winding mountain road. There are the wails of those who have come to mourn for fir and spruce, and for the ravaged meadows and wetlands, for Tuba City and Rio Puerco and Grants, and, if our cries aren't heard and heeded, the holy mountain Herself. That's how we talk, that's how some of us feel, that the earth really is a woman, and She is being killed. I don't know if we're making that up, or if we're finally, like Katy says, just remembering what we once knew.

So there we all are, those of us ready to get busted and our pals, the woman got up as a raven and one as a raccoon. There's always at least one white kid with dreads and Tibetan bells. There're three sharp-looking housewives from Many Farms, a withered, grinning Blue-Green Water People medicine woman in fuzzy bedroom slippers; six determined and appropriately dressed hikers from the birdwatchers' group; and then, almost as an afterthought, there are the sheriffs coming toward us, good old Joe Bob and Carl, the young cop, the one with all the community college human relations courses under his belt, and, smack in between them, Officer Lita Consuela Magdalena, her shining hair caught up neatly under her hat.

They held us awhile next to the road, Katy and me and the eight guys. In the lull, in the nothing much happening, I was suddenly afraid. I could hear our circles singing. I could see banners waving in the fading sun. It didn't help enough. I had a few sprigs of sage tucked in my shirt pocket. That good, green, fierce scent vaporized a little of my fear.

"Thanks," I whispered.

Joe Bob got a message on his radio. He nodded, then he and Carl and Officer Magdalena cuffed us behind our backs.

"Orders from above," Joe Bob said sheepishly.

It took ten minutes for the hurt to start. I went inside myself, away from the pain, away from the steady and unwelcome knowledge of muscles in my shoulders I'd never cared to know about. I'm glad I learned to do that when things get bad, even if that very ability has chased off more than one love in my life.

They loaded the guys into a van and drove down toward the highway. We could see back window catch light, glint and get smaller and smaller, 'til it disappeared. That was a strange feeling. In my stomach. Down in my knees. Officer Magdalena led Katy and me away from road. Katy and I sat on a big Ponderosa stump, resting our aching arms on each other, taking turns, taking comfort 'til the squad car came. We squirmed in. Everybody cheered and waved good-bye. Officer Magdalena sighed, hit the gas, and we were off.

We all rode the first fifteen minutes in silence. I saw where they'd managed the trees along the highway into stumps and I thought about how the Snowbird wanted to clear-cut sixty-six acres of trees so skiers wouldn't have to wait in line. Katy was humming, so it was almost peaceful there in the car, the thin dark scent of high country drifting in through the open windows, the young aspen on the flanks of the Sacred Mountains starting to catch the last rose-gold of sunset. Much later, Katy and I would talk about that time, and we would agree that when you're as scared as we both were, when you're vigilant and surrendered, everything gets magical. The light and rock and sky you've seen for years are sudden miracles. I still hesitate to call that spiritual. It can be ordinary. It can be daily.

Officer Magdalena didn't say a word. Just past the old museum, she turned on the radio and tuned in the anarcho station that beams out of a rusted double-wide trailer on the outskirts of town. We've still got treasures like that out here, little hippie cafes, outdoor blues 'n' barbecue, bars where anybody can dance to good rock 'n' roll, anybody, burned-out, scrawny original Deadheads, nervous college kids in their natural fibers and mock psychedelic tees, even getting-older, built-for-comfort women like myself.

This station Officer M. tuned in plays Ani Di Franco and The Band and Clapton, so, if you looked at it in the right spirit, the drive in, aside from the cuffs, was as good as it could get. Now and then, I'd look up in the rearview mirror and more often than not, I'd catch Officer Magdalena's cool brown eyes catching mine.

Katy fell asleep somewhere in the middle of *Layla*. The feathers she'd woven into her braids shimmered. I watched her eyes rove back and forth under her lids. She loves to dream. She believes we learn more in our dreams than we ever do in our waking life, and she says "Blessed Be," whenever she parts from someone, and she has taught herself about the people out here, about their Grandmothers, White Shell Woman and Spider Grandmother and *Angwusiwuhti,* the Black-Winged, and the old mysteries on the sacred mountain, the places the original residents know is their church.

It was purple dusk by the time Officer Magdalena drove into the narrow alley behind the jail. Katy stretched and winced. Officer Magdalena didn't unlock the squad car doors. She glanced over. You could see the guys in the receiving area looking out at us.

"Listen girls," Officer M. said, "I want to tell you something."

"Sure," Katy said.

"A lot of us are with you in spirit," Officer Magdalena said. She looked down at her hands. "We just have to be careful."

"We know that," Katy said. "Thanks."

Officer Magdalena grinned in the rearview mirror. "For what?" she said. "I didn't say anything."

I heard the doors unlock. Officer M. gently helped us out of the car and led us past a barrage of buzzers and clicking locks. Those clicks are loud as gunshots. They scare you immediately. They, and the fluorescent lights that shed icy green glare down on the receiving area, let you understand in no uncertain terms where you are.

We walked in, past maybe a dozen guys in yellow jumpsuits and rubber flip-flops, sitting on the benches that lined the walls. They were smoking and staring and waiting for something happen. Katy and I were clearly the happening. I got mad and Katy just smiled.

"Assholes," she whispered in my ear.

They didn't catch it and went on conjecturing just loud enough for us to hear about the young broad's butt and the old one's bad attitude 'til Officer Magdalena pointed out quietly that they were walking a mucho narrow line. She took off our cuffs. In that sweet moment of release, I didn't care about the scary green lights, the way my heart was going banzai against my ribs, or even that the guys didn't say anything about my butt.

Officer M. traded papers with the receiving officer, took us in the john one at a time, confiscated our bras so we wouldn't hang ourselves with them, and led us to the ugliest door I've ever seen. It was metal. It was scarred. It held nothing but a tiny barred window and what seemed like a dozen locks. You couldn't look through it. You couldn't see the room you were trapped in until you were in it. I stepped through that door and saw two women, two mattresses, and a toilet smack in the middle.

"This is Liz and Katy," Officer Magdalena said.

"Can you get me a cigarette?" the older lady said. You could tell she was hurting bad. Her brown eyes were red and her dark skin was gray. She shrugged. The younger girl stared at the floor. She was wearing great perfume. She'd set her high-polished cowgirl boots in the corner and her stockinged toes were blue with cold.

"Sallie," Officer M. said, "I'll try." She turned to me and Katy.

"This is Sallie," she said, "and Jessie." The younger woman nodded and stretched out her hand. She didn't look up. I took her icy hand.

"It's past supper," Officer Magdalena said, "but I'll try to get you girls some coffee."

"Oh please," I said. Katy laughed. Coffee's my communion. Officer M. nodded and let herself out. How a door like that closes is a miracle. You learn more in that instant than you could ever imagine.

"She's one of the nice ones," Sallie said. She was still loaded. There was a blue bruise on her cheek. Every now and then she would touch it and she'd shake her head, the way you sometimes think you can shake off pain. She grabbed the toilet and pulled herself up enough to lean over it. When she gagged, nothing came. I could hear the air catch in her throat. I could smell her breath, the sweet wine, the vomit. Jessie looked up.

"I hate doing that," she said. Katy nodded. She was buttoning up her flannel shirt against the chill. I followed suit, found the sage in my pocket. I crushed some between my fingers and passed it around. Sallie sat back down and cupped her hands for the sage. She breathed in deep and smiled.

"Yeah," Katy said, "once when I was fifteen I got messed-up drunk and my mom had me arrested and when they were carrying me to the cell, I puked all over 'em. They wanted to hit me. You could tell, but they didn't do it."

"How come?" Jessie said. "Your daddy rich?"

"Yep. They knew my mom's ex, my good old daddy," Katy said. Jessie nodded. When she moved her head, you could see the black roots of her silvery-gold hair.

"Hey," Sallie said, "that's how it is. You got a smoke?"

Somehow, Katy had smuggled in her makings, so she rolled a couple cigarettes and we settled down for Girls' Night In. I drifted in and out of the talk. I spend a lot of time alone, mostly by choice, and it was new to me, and good, how one woman's voice would rise up, another's chime in, then fade away into a comfortable silence, and then gently moving into the silence, some more words, a little laughter.

"I'm a weaver," Sallie said. "Me and my husband, we got horses, too. We got our own place up Farmington way. He come down here for business. Monkey business. That's how I got *here*. Went lookin' for him. Stopped into Joe's. Next thing you know, fell off the damn bar stool. And *next* thing you know, busted for P.I." She shrugged down into her denim jacket.

"What're you girls in for?"

The question hung there between us. I looked down. White folks' privilege was what I was thinking, getting arrested on purpose, knowing that somewhere outside, forces were moving, calls were being made, bail was being easily arranged. I'd hassled that around in my head before I'd stepped out and I guessed I'd be wrestling it around for the rest of my life. Katy just sucked in a good lung-full of smoke, blew it out, and, as usual, kept it simple

"We blocked the Snowbird Road."

Jessie laughed. "Why'd you do that?"

"So the t.v. people would come," Katy said. "So the ski resort owners and the government would know not everybody goes along with their program."

Sallie stubbed out her cigarette and tucked the butt in her pocket. "My grandma hates that shit," she said, "Uncle Ray, too. Might as well build a Burger King in the middle of one of those Jesus Way churches."

"Well," Jessie said, "I sure wish I could trade places with you girls. I took my little cousin into the Fairmart and he wanted a box of crayons. I didn't have no money, so I just stuck 'em in my purse, no big deal, a buck twenty-nine was all. We get outside and this big old Security comes up behind me and grabs my purse. I thought she was trying to snatch it, so I whacked her." She shook her head.

"Course I was a little drunk." She grinned at me. She'd made her eyes up perfectly, black liner stroked on just so, shadow all shimmery and soft.

"Ooooeee," she said, "my mom's gonna kill me." I grinned back and nodded.

"You got kids?" she said, and right there, right then, I got whomped with my Big Moment of Light. I nodded again. I could hardly talk. I could hardly tell her about my daughter and her daughter, and how my daughter made up her eyes just so and how streaked they were they night she nearly died from booze and I was too loaded to help here. I could hardly tell her about the day my daughter came home clean and sober. And, the day I did.

I could hardly get out the words to name the feelings, the words that could make the knowledge whole. I wasn't seeing things. There was nothing psychedelic, nothing like the visions I hear some people describe. Nobody had colors glowing around her head and there was no big Grandfather God voice speaking. Those Las Vegas moments don't come to me. Blessed Be. I remembered how Katy had taken me to a whiteboy sweat lodge once, and while the guys were singing Navajo songs, hollering Paiute chants, all I'd gotten was drenched and dizzy, a longing for the midnight indigo sky, and the faintest glimmer that my people had done this. Me and my sisters and cousins and aunts had sat in the hot dark, had risen up out of a mountain cave and breathed in the cold diamond stars.

Truth is, I'm grateful to be spared those 3-D visitations. Whatever moves out there, whatever hums and dances in me, She knows I'm scared. She knows I've seen enough, heard enough to last a lifetime. She knows I can only take a little at a time. So, as I knew the way Jessie's big sky eyes were like my daughter's, and my daughter's like Katy's, and Katy's like Sallie's and mine and Officer Magdalena's, and that lady cop's clear tiger's-eye gaze so like my grand-daughter's, I smiled.

"I do have kids," I said. "I've got three sons, a daughter, and three grand-babies. They're the reason I got arrested."

Sallie grinned. "Well, yeah," she said quietly. "That's the way it's supposed to be."

Hag

MARIETTE TELLS ME we still have beautiful legs, both of us, even if our faces have gone to seed. She is fifty-three and doesn't come from this country. I am fifty and the day we have this conversation, which is about discovering that our faces and bodies, in men's eyes, no longer exist, I am heading into town to dye Easter eggs with my best friend, Deena, and her two wild boys. I see a woman walking along the road. She is dressed in brown tights, a cherry-pink top, and turquoise head-band. There is sunlight all around her, clear mountain light, and she looks wonderful. I am jealous.

I pass her and realize it is Mariette and she is walking the five miles into town to do her shopping. She has made herself up beautifully, in that subtle way European women seem to know. I beep. She ignores me. I stop and go back to get her.

"It's you," she says, "you didn't have to turn around to get me."

"True," I say.

"I'm glad you did. There are lots of assholes driving on this road."

"You look wonderful. I am so jealous of your legs."

"Thanks," she says, "about my beautiful legs. Let me tell you a story."

She cracks open the window, lights a cigarette, and aims the smoke delicately out into the slipstream. Not for one second, while she talks, does she turn to look at me.

"I was just become fifty," she says quietly, "in Atlanta. My daughter had given birth to her third daughter and I was helping out. I walked to the big mall to buy some Pampers. A truck came up behind me in the parking lot. The driver going slow, staying behind me. He was saying things that were dirty and they were also said so gentle that they were turning me on. I was wearing tights and one of those big shirts that hides everything but your legs. I kept walking. He finally drove up past me. He was young and cute. Like a carpenter maybe, one of those guys. When he saw my face, he made this ugly, ugly look and he flipped me, you know, that third finger."

I bow my head.

"I wanted to disappear," Mariette says.

"I know," I say.

"Right then," she says, "I was gone. As a woman. Gone 'til the day I die."

Up until now, though we live in a half-acre collection of cabins, trailers and sheds a few miles south of a small Arizona mountain town, we have not talked that much. We are two of three women in the place. The third is Darlene Jackson. She's half-Paiute, half-Chicana. Darlene works at Millie's Cafe and she has some interesting views on men and sex. If she's going to fuck him, he's got to have a car and a job, and, if he doesn't make her come the first time, she doesn't answer the phone for a few days. The guy always disappears.

"I can tell right away," Darlene says. "If they don't have will-power in the sack, they haven't got it anywhere else."

Darlene does manicures on the side, somewhat unlicensed. She has little business cards printed up that say *Darlene Jackson...when it's touch that counts...637-9910*. She weighs two hundred pounds, "two hundred beautiful pounds," she says. "We Jacksons are big scrumptious women," she says and she wears Levi cut-offs, fuschia tank tops, silver cowgirl boots and when you see her heading out in early twilight for a date, you know she's right. All that mocha skin catches the last sweet rose of sunset. She wears eye shadow the same blurred lilac as the mountains. She pauses to wave before she climbs into her truck and you can see how some horny guy would be grateful for all of her, for a woman big and scrumptious, bright and shadowed as the moon.

All our other neighbors are guys, three of them steady tenants, the other four a floating crap-shoot. What we do, Mariette and Darlene and me, in the rare instances when we meet by the community shower-house, is compare notes on the lovelies the fellows bring in. We were going to organize a pool on average age difference between guy and girlfriend, but Darlene said Mariette and I tended toward bitterness and it wouldn't help to see the truth in round figures.

For instance, Amy's twenty-three to Rick's forty; the redhead's thirty to Dale's fifty; and, cruelest cut of all, Tina Rae's twenty-seven to the sober doper's fifty-seven. Thirty fucking years. Damn near Granpa and Granpet.

"Round figures?" Mariette said mildly. "Yes. *Round* figures."

"You bet," Darlene said. "Life on life's terms." She goes to self-esteem meetings where she hears stuff like that. She likes it. It's a small price to pay for no longer waking up next to strangers, looking down at her round dark arms, and counting the bruises that blossomed there.

"You would not believe the way my romance hangovers were," she's told Mariette and me, "just like sitting on your paralyzed butt, looking down a tunnel and the light at the end of the tunnel is the Midnight Express…aiming for you."

"I believe you," Mariette once said. "It sounds a lot like getting fifty to me."

"Don't talk about that!" Darlene says whenever *that* topic comes up. "I'm twenty-eight and I'm not going to think about being fifty 'til I get there."

"You turn around, darling," Mariette will say in her throaty Latvian or Belgian or who-knows-what accent, "and you are there."

Mariette leans back and sets her feet on the dashboard. I open my window. Spring is cooking the pine oil out of the trees. We both take deep breaths.

"So foolish, so sentimental," she says, "when I smell those trees I could be twelve again. We would go to the mountains, to a tiny lake. The summer evenings were so long. We would sit by the lake, my father pretending to fish, my mother doing nothing, just sitting, watching him. Those were the only times I saw her still, not even when she was an old woman. Always something in her hands, always something to keep her occupied. But not there at the lake."

"Do you think she worried about losing her sexiness?" I ask.

Mariette laughs. Cold. An ancient sound.

"The war came," she says. "And then, being refugees. And then…"

I signal, pull into the shopping center and park. I don't know what to say.

"You going to Fairway?" are the words I find.

"I'll get back okay," she says.

"I didn't ask if you'd get back okay," I say, "I asked you if you're going to Fairway."

"I am. I don't need much. Potatoes, some milk. I can carry everything."

I stop, pull in next to a brand-new cherry-red Bronco. Blonde mom swings out of the driver's seat. She's wearing day-glo aerobics gear, her hair pulled back under a visor that says *Lake Pow!ell*. Two cute kids scramble out of the back and they all bounce into the store.

I don't move.

"No," I say. "I'll take you back. I want to talk more."

"You have something to do," she says. "Yes?"

"I'll call Deena," I say. "I hate Easter anyhow."

"Yes," Mariette says quietly, "Easter is for witches, and it got all turned around." She lights another cigarette. "Spring. Fertility. Making love in the fields—that is Easter. That bunny is not about cute. It is about fucking."

I laugh. I watch normal life go on outside the truck. I like that I am in this movie where a gorgeous, silver-haired witch is telling me about holy sex.

"Did you see that mother?" Mariette says. I turn. She is smiling like a '20s German film sorceress. Her green iceberg eyes look straight into mine.

I nod.

"I used to look just like her." Mariette sticks out her chest. "Except my breasts were more beautiful."

Even without a bra, even with what nursing four kids and irresistible gravity have done, she is impressive.

"They still are," I laugh.

She doesn't alter her gaze. She pulls up her shirt. It's eleven in the morning in the middle of the busiest shopping center in West Flagstaff on Wednesday, the day the bonus coupons are in effect. I look at her breasts. Ivory bells. Burgundy nipples. Stretch marks silvery against her pale skin. I think of the moon, half-full, how its surface is scarred and perfect.

"Mariette," I say. "They're beautiful. I mean, you're beautiful. You should see me."

"Go ahead," she says, "show me." Her voice is harsh. She looks down at herself. "No one will bother to notice two old hags." She looks flat into my eyes.

I remember driving the lake-road back from my ex-lover's when he was my lover. A young eagle dropped out of the sky and raced alongside my truck, pure light between me and the dawn dark trees. Somehow, I kept the truck on the road, and studied the bird's cold bright eye for what felt like hours.

Mariette's eyes are the same. I look past her. I don't know what I expect to see. People are schloomphing along, cars and trucks pulling in and out of parking spaces, the bag-boy gathering in a dozen carts. A raven perches on a light pole and screams.

"No," I say. "I can't do that."

She nods. Smiles. "Gone," she says, "both of us. Every woman our age.

Disappeared 'til the day we die."

"Mariette," I say. "Go buy your groceries. I'll wait for you."

"Sure," Mariette says. "Thank you."

She pulls down her shirt and climbs out. I bend to put a tape in the deck. When I straighten, I see that Mariette is waiting. She taps on my window. I open it.

"Hag," she says, "was once a holy woman." The tape starts. Annie Lennox. Mariette smiles.

I watch her walk away, her legs perfect as a dancer's, her back straight, her pewter curls escaping from the knot into which she's gathered them. If I were a man, I would fall down at her feet. I sit alone in the truck. The raven flops down, scavenges what's left of a bag of Fritos. I close my eyes. Mariette's scent lingers. Belgian. Expensive. What's left of the last gift her last lover gave her. Once a day, just before sleep, she puts one drop at the pulse in her throat.

"It is for me," she says. "Otherwise I will forget."

 *Huevos*

Elizabeth drives into town. It's a big mountain day, one of those mornings when the ancient volcanic peaks hovering over the little place seem so huge and brilliant she has to catch her breath. She feels the same way she does when she looks at pictures of outer space, fragile, translucent, her cells barely connected. She thinks anyone would feel that way. Anyone could wonder if they just might disappear into all that vastness, all that clarity. Anyone, that is, except her boyfriend, Grady. Grady never gets it when she tells him about feelings like that.

"Mountains are mountains," he would say. "They change, but it's so slow we can't see it." Still, he would like the part about clarity. It's one of his favorite words.

"Clarity," he says, when the tiger jumps out in *Apocalypse Now.* "Clarity," he says when he scouts a Class 5 Rapid and spots the killer hole. "Clarity," he has said to her countless times, just after he has poured into her and is breathing hard against her shoulder.

She's not having breakfast with Grady this glittering December morning. He's stuck out at the Forest Service garage eighty miles south of town because the Freddie road grader broke down and he's the only one who can fix it. She imagines him, big as a bear, stuffed into the green Freddie work pants, his canvas jacket stretched tight across his shoulders, flat on his back in new snow, hangover fireworks flaring behind his eyes, scraping his knuckles on cold metal and cussing in ways that are so convoluted and vivid it might be poetry.

"Yeah," Grady would say, "a poet, cause my feet show it, they're long-fellows." Goofy grin. Truth be told, he reads Gary Snyder and Charles

Bukowski and thinks Jim Harrison is god, small g, god.

Grady wouldn't like the restaurant she's headed for anyhow. He likes potatoes and eggs and chorizo and beans well enough, but he likes to eat all of that in places where you know they hate the new no-smoking ordinance and there is no decor except a few sequinned sombreros. "Give me honest grease," he says, "no ferns on this boy's plate."

Grady's no boy. Elizabeth's no girl. She sticks a Springsteen tape in the deck. The new one, "Oh yeah," the record store clerk had said, "a golden oldie." Barruce is singing about how you never quite get what it is you dream about and Elizabeth is watching the mountains grow bigger and bigger in front of her. Right in the moment when she thinks they're so huge they're going to swallow everything, she's in town.

SHE PULLS into the parking lot in front of Rita's Fajitas. There is no Rita, just David, cook-owner-p.r. man, ex-ambulance jockey. He is big and blonde and usually red-eyed from the challenging night before. If you ask him why he traded in flashing lights for a short order grill, he'll tell you that if he hadn't, he knows one day he would've been the body in the back of the ambulance. Demerol, amphetamines, uppers, downers, anything that did the trick. Now he drinks Corona, tinkers with *molé* sauce and turns his customers on to the best music south, north, east, and west of the border. The other big draws here are a non-stop salsa bar and the best jalapeño-cheese corn bread Elizabeth ever ate.

Her pal, Joe, is already there. He unfolds his lanky self out of his little eco-dude car and grins.

"You're late," he says. It's a joke. Elizabeth is never late. Joe always is.

"Har," she says, and they go in. David leans up over the glass panel between the cooks and the customers. He's a little gray, wanly cheerful.

"Happy Sunday," Elizabeth says.

"I hate you," he says. "You're just so ambulatory in the mornings."

"Hey," Elizabeth says. "Time was I would've had me a Tequila Sunrise breakfast minus the sun. I still miss it. "

David raises a coffee mug to his lips, stops, and toasts her. She bows. A bunch of ravens flop down on the sidewalk outside the big front window. David scatters all the left-over tortilla chips there for them every morning. He says the birds remind him that women aren't the only ones who are beautiful and voracious at the same time. He usually says that right before he gets to the part about "the planet being nothing but a rock shpinning through spash."

Grady often makes the same celestial observation. He says itsh buddhisht and he locates it somewhere between the ode to the time Ray got shit-faced on the San Juan River, stubbed his toe bloody and ended up gore-glued to his sleeping bag, and the epic trilogy that always goes "How I came home from Laos, turned on my folks' t.v. and saw the president saying we weren't in Laos, and took off next day in my VW bug loaded with a change of clothes and the stereo I'd bought off some Saigon peddler, p.s.: fuck 'em if they can't take a joke."

Elizabeth and Joe sit in the booth near the front window. The pale sun turns the icy parking lot to opal. Elizabeth knows that when she starts making writerly observations to herself she is scared. Joe's call the night before had been strange, his voice tight, his invitation for breakfast less an invitation and more an appeal. For an instant, she thinks about Tequila Sunrises, that ice, those dawns. Bob Marley is wailing over the big speakers about what you got to do for freedom.

"Wish it was that easy," Joe says. "Smoke a little ganja, word up, get the bruddas and seestahs togedduh. Sure." She and Joe have chained themselves to a few bulldozers, thrown a few monkey-wrenches, spent a few thousand hours, for six solid years, writing and meeting and consensusing with people who couldn't agree on anything if it was eroding away in front of their faces. Rivers are their love. Friendship is their river.

The waiter brings them coffee. He's new. He's got dark bushy eyebrows, a buzz-cut, and not one line in his face.

"Hi guys," he says. When you eat in almost any restaurant in this university town you are a guy. What you order is co-ul and you are encouraged to go for it.

"Hey," Elizabeth says. You can also say Yo or Heya or Howdy.

Joe says Howdy. Joe is from Ohio, but he stresses that he's from the hillbilly part, evidence being that one exceptionally frigid winter, his best friend burned the spare bedroom furniture for firewood, and a year later, room by room, the entire second floor. Joe's a writer but he should really be a storyteller. He says Elizabeth is a storyteller who should be getting her stories down on 8½" by 11" pages instead of in the erotic cards she sends Grady every week.

Joe and Elizabeth have been best friends for all the time, minus one month, she has lived near the mountains. The one month represents the time she spent alone, doing nothing but waking, drinking, eating corn chips for fiber, sleeping, and exorcising the ghost of her former one-true-love. Elizabeth and Joe have never been lovers. He is married. Elizabeth has some sense of honor. Plus, she likes his wife, Leah, and, truth be told, Elizabeth and Joe are not attracted to each other. Not in that way. One

Christmas, Joe, who hates Christmas, sent her a card with a mountain lion on the front and inside he wrote, "Thanks for being part of my learning that there is more than one way to love."

"You sure got a lot of *huevos* here," Joe says to the waiter. The kid laughs. *Huevos* are eggs. Out here in the True West, they also refer to manly attributes.

"Har," Elizabeth says. "Ra hah!" Joe and the waiter grin at her.

"*Huevos enchiladas,*" she says, "eggs over easy, jalapeño corn bread... potatoes and tell the cook to burn 'em."

"Co-ul," the kid says. "Go for it."

"The same...*con chorizo,*" Joe says. He gives Elizabeth a guilty look.

"I'm not your wife," she says. "I don't care what you do to your arteries ...or your *huevos*."

"No corn bread," Joe says, "just some fruit."

The kid departs. Joe dumps half and half in his coffee and spreads his big hands out on the table.

"What it is," he says, "why I asked you to meet me is this, Cruz is killing himself. A bunch of his friends want to pull an intervention. You're invited."

"Cruz." Elizabeth says, "What now?"

"Totalled the van, third DUI, his house about to go, and Chapter 13 before the year ends."

"Booze," Elizabeth says brightly. "You can't fool me."

"And just turned forty-three and all his river permits hanging by a slender thread."

Cruz, Elizabeth thinks, *Senor Cruz Control, Senor Cruz de la Rio, the jefe of the river runners, the guy with a big gut, a fat heart, and a skinny wallet. Cruz.*

"Please," she says, "whatever makes you think it'll do any good?"

"We don't," Joe says. The waiter sets two salsa dishes in front of them.

Joe pulls himself up from the booth and ambles over to the salsa bar. He knows what she likes, mild, with lots of cilantro. He dumps "Volcanic" in his dish and comes back. Elizabeth loads a chip with sauce. She loves how the cilantro hits her tongue, how the green, green scent seems to drift up through her brain. She would hold that moment for eternity if she could. Cilantro, good gin, good chocolate, good sex, how a guy's eyes get all moony right before he comes...more is better, too much is best.

"Yes," she says. "Oh yes." The kid sets down their food, pours them more coffee, and is gone.

"All I can do," Elizabeth says, "is my experience, strength, and hope rou-

156   *Huevos*

tine. I can tell you guys that he could be a manic-depressive. And I can tell you to look way deep inside yourselves and see what's behind this neighborly kindness. Come on, Joe, you know that."

Joe grins.

"Speaking of neighborly kindness," he says, "how's good old Grady, how's the King of Miller Lite?" Elizabeth throws a chip at him.

"Cruel, but fair," she says. "No, more to the point, how's Elizabeth? Three fucking you-make-your-own-happiness meetings a week and she still can't tell him she doesn't want to hang out when he's drunk and amorous, or hung-over and dead in the water. Progress, not perfection, that's me."

"Oh, Lizzie," Joe says. "Someday you gotta do what you gotta do. Grace runs out."

The kid reappears. "How's it goin', guys?" he asks.

"Wonderful," Elizabeth says, "Bring me an order of *flan*."

"Awright!" the kid grins. "Way chow down. Do it."

"Me too," Joe says. "Leah will lock me in the closet for three days and shove wallboard and little plates of water under the door, but this is worth it."

"Maybe that's what you guys could do with Cruz." Elizabeth says. "Lure him over to Katz's house. Lock him in the boat-shed. Don't let him out 'til it's commercial boating season. He comes out. He has to row again instead of managing the company. No beer. No dope. No oooo-I-want-to-get-back-to-the-earth river bunnies. No buying sprees. Nothing but the clean, pure life of a Zen river rat."

"Thanks," Joe says. They both sigh. The kid sets the *flan* down in front of them. It's beautiful, golden, shimmering. He's set fresh raspberries around the edge.

"Hey," he says, "what do you think of my restaurant management skills? Cool, huh?"

"I will write references for you," Elizabeth says. "I give great reference." Joe shakes his head. The kid looks a little blank.

"Co-ul," he says. "Catch ya later."

They inhale the *flan*.

"Damn," Elizabeth says, "mother's milk." She looks up. Joe is staring off into the parking lot.

"It's almost 10:15," he says. "They want us there about 10:30. Let's finish up and go. All you've gotta do is tell them about how you've done it, maybe make the point about hitting bottom, I don't know, dim the stars that are shining in their eager eyes. Okay?"

Elizabeth thinks she can live with that. Joe hands her a five. She pulls out her plastic.

"I'll do it," she says. She means the check.

"I knew you would," Joe says. "And, someday, you call me and we'll lock your Sergeant Grady in a room and play *Platoon* over and over until something happens."

"Jeez, Joe," she says, "you don't know squat. You know that? You don't know squat." She thinks of Grady's bedroom, the nine milli and the shotgun right by the bed, the stories he repeats over and over when he's loaded, how he'll tell you that the war made a man of him and that he can't ever forget the stories because then it'll be like it didn't happen, and if that happens then what was the point of Dave and Lou and Xem going home in body bags.

"I'm sorry," Joe says. "It's not that easy. I know that. Cruz, neither. Shit."

"No big thing," Elizabeth says. "No big thing."

WHEN SHE pays the check, she sees the silver band on the kid's arm.

"Why do you wear that?" she says. He holds out his wrist. *Sergeant Eugene Duncan, 1965, MIA.*

"A lot of my buddies in ROTC wear them," he says. "We went to this talk. That war. It was so long ago, you know. 'Nam, Laos, Cambodia. This guy's been missing such a long time."

"My boyfriend was there," she says. "Special Forces medic." She wonders when she'll stop telling people this, when she'll stop waiting for that light in their eyes, for how they say, "Oh yeah, my brother, my boyfriend, my dad, my mom's ex-husband, my kid, my kid."

"Whoa," the waiter says. "Heavy."

She goes to the *Casa des Senoritas*. What she sees in the mirror while she's washing her hands is a middle-aged woman, square-jawed, stubborn-looking, no war bride, no high school sweetheart. Behind her shoulder, right in front of the john, the waitresses put up a poster, a hunk, young, perfect, denim vest and red headband. She thinks about Grady's big face, the wrinkles, the way his eyes can go mean, go soft, can, now and then, go wet and sorrowful. She wonders, as she always does, what he looked like as a young guy, without the beard, without the gray pony-tail, the gut, the softness where once there was lean animal joy. She runs warm water over her wrists. She starts to cry, not for long, a minute maybe. Afterwards, there is that sweet, brief peace, her breath precious in her chest, everything, the mirror, her eyes, even the poster with the hunk and his beer, clear and bright.

When she comes out, the kid is waiting for an order. She leans against the bar.

"If you don't mind," she says, "how old are you? I just wondered."

"Twenty-three," he says.

"My boyfriend," she says, "he was twenty-three when he was running long-range patrols up near Da Nang. Into Laos. Hanging off the skid of some chopper. Holding some three-quarters-dead 'Yard in his arms. Stuff like that."

The kid faces her squarely. His eyes go wet.

"I can't imagine," he says. "What huevos. I can't imagine…" He turns away. For an instant, his shoulders tremble.

"God," he says, "their buddies. You know?"

"I'm sorry," she says. I don't know what got into me." He turns around.

"No," he says. "It's all right. It's right. Somebody's gotta remember."

They shake hands. He hands her a paper napkin with a little red chili printed on it. Elizabeth wipes her eyes and looks out toward the parking lot. Joe is standing there. He is shadowy against the dazzling morning light. His big dark shape could be Grady. He waves. She wonders where he was back then, '65, '67, '70, and she realizes she's never asked him. She thinks of the morning ahead. She thinks of Grady and that it is no longer '69.

Joe shoves his hands in his pockets and looks up toward the mountains. For a minute, Elizabeth watches. The kid touches her elbow.

"You okay?" he asks.

"I'm here," she says. "That's good enough."

 Messin' with the Kid

M Y DAD IS two years, one month, and six days dead—my mom died this morning; and my family is partying in a tasteful corporate-ecru hotel room twenty stories above midnight Rochester, New York—except for me and Max, my youngest, who quit drinking ten years ago, one year before I did. He doesn't need booze, having inherited my Hurricane Hi-Lo nervous system. He's hunched over his guitar. Villa Lobos sings out like a sad wind in dark summer trees. It's a sign of how much I want a drink that I am thinking in those Catalonian images. Max looks up from the guitar.

"I hope Grandma's listening," he says.

"Yepper," says Dave the Suit, my oldest, who is for once disheveled, tie wrapped around his head like a pirate do-rag. His wife, Leni, is asleep across his lap. He smooths her silky black hair.

"I propose," Dave says, "a toast to our grandmother, Lillie Foltz, who made our mother, who made us, expecially Max, who is carrying on the fine family tradition of when the going gets tough, the tough play music. Except, of course, for our mom, who can never be allowed to sing in public, expecially if we, her children, are present."

Leni opens her eyes. "David, you must stop drinking now. You are saying *expecially.* "

"You bet." He grins fondly at her. She is Filipina and is six months pregnant. I like her a lot. Not because she's pregnant, but because she is tough and funny and the only person in the world who tells Dave what to do.

"Yes, David," my daughter, Jen, says as primly as you can when you've had three margaritas and you are five-foot-two and weigh about a hundred pounds. "You know how you get."

Dave tries to look fierce. Max switches into *Pinball Wizard*.

"Excuse me," I say.

Jen's new husband, Charles, raises an eyebrow.

"Your mother," he says, with the dignity conferred by a good education at a good black college and just enough Dos Equis, "wishes to tell us something."

Max sets down the guitar. "Don't be so sure. It's right about now she'll try to sing."

He sits next to me and stares somewhat wistfully at Charles' Dos Eq and lime. I pick up the lime chunk and chew on it.

"Oh no," I say, "it's nothing. Never mind about me."

The kids all groan. Those were my dead mom's favorite two lines, next to "Duke Ellington was God" and "Billie Holliday was an angel."

I find, to my astonishment, that I am crying. "I want to see her right now, in her dark glasses, bent over the piano we would have hauled, courtesy your money, David, into this hotel room, in which we are, courtesy your money, holding a wake of which she would be proud. I want to hear my mom play *Lullaby of Birdland* or *Ain't Misbehavin'* or *Satin Doll.*

Charles pats my hand. "You are the blackest white family I know." He's a jazz musician and I've liked *him* from the minute we met, two days before he and Jen married. Each time we're together I like him even more, because he's the one person who defends me against my kids.

"Only way you guys are different from my family," he says cheerfully, "is it's about time you children gave some respect to your mama."

"Respect is one thing," Dave says somberly, "singing is another."

"Well," I say, and my mother haunts my words, "you, David, are nothing but a fart in a skillet."

Jen stands behind me, wraps her arms around my neck. "Mom, what did Grandma mean when she said that?

"I don't know, but I'd love to hear her say it just one more time."

Jen bursts into tears. Dave sneaks the cuff of his hundred-buck shirt up to his eyes and wipes them. Max looks away.

"It's alright, baby." Charles leans his long face in next to Jen's. She presses her cheek against his. In that moment, even more than I want my dead mom to rise up from the grave playing jazz piano, I want somebody next to me saying, "It's alright, baby."

"Shit," I say. "I'm sick of being alone."

"Alone?" Max and Dave and Jen chorus. "You have us!"

It's an old routine. So is my response.

"Right. In Kyoto. Hong Kong. And Rochester, New York. Plus you, Dave, have a broken wrist, thus preventing you from pushing the button on the fax machine, *send* on your e-mail, or the redial on the phone."

"Oh, little Mom," he says sadly, "you got a point there." He hasn't called me *little Mom* in years.

Leni slaps Dave's wrist. "Bad David. No dessert for you."

"I'm sorry," Dave says, and this time we all join in, *"It's just that I'm so busy."*

Dave puts his big hand over Leni's eyes.

"And," she says sternly, "no more beer."

He pops the Foster can. "Mmmmmm. Evian. Yum yum."

She turns her face into his lean stomach. "I'm ignoring you." We hear her muffled giggle.

"Well, Dave," I say, "my only regret is that you didn't follow your mother's advice when you were young and handsome, and become a model. You could have earned that gazillion you're chasing by the time you were twenty-five, and become a house-husband who writes long, chatty letters to his mother."

"And sister," Jen mutters.

"Regrets," Charles says thoughtfully. "We use to have these truth and consequence sessions in my college fraternity. One night we had to tell our regrets. Actually, rights-ons and regrets. Right-ons for what we were proud of."

"Right-ons?" Max says, "You went to the whitest black college I ever heard of."

Charles rubs a fresh chunk of lime around the rim of his beer. "It wuz 1977 and we wuz not exackly da boyz in da hood."

"Right on." Max hums the opening to Marvin Gaye's *What's Goin' On?*

"Okay," Dave says, "let's play. What are the rules?" He gets a look on his face that I have seen since he was two, eyes narrowed, jaw set, the grin of a shark about to chow down. He loves competition.

"Every person," Charles says, "has to tell one thing they're one hundred percent proud of, that's the right-on, and one thing they truly regret."

"Whoa." Max moves back to his guitar. I look away. I know his secrets and he knows too many of mine; like Judy Collins sings, "I've seen you stumble, you've watched me fall." That song got me through the year Max, wired on cocaine, commuted between Sacramento and South Reno's poker tables and free booze, going home so burnt and suicidal he didn't close his eyes for fear he'd fall asleep and dream himself dead.

"Whoa doubled," I say.

Leni sits up. "Let's do it." She's got fire in her mahogany eyes. Jen nods, takes a deep breath and looks at each of us, her chin stubborn as mine, her back a dancer's.

"I'll start," she says. "I'm most proud I didn't let anybody talk me into an abortion or adoption when I was pregnant with Lashona." Dave, Max, and I flinch.

"And, I regret that I didn't listen to you when you told me how hard it is to be a mom." She takes my hand. "Especially when you've got a 13-year-old who disses her mom's music."

"Do you know what that child said while we were driving up here?" Charles says. "Your daughter had a tape in and Lashona informed her that Roberta Flack was back-dated."

We all shake our heads. Misguided youth.

"I have to speak now," Leni says, "before I lose my nerve." She glances at Dave. What passes between them is, as always, both fond and ironic. "I am most proud my husband is my best friend and, much as I love my family, I'm making my home with Dave." I imagine her family, set tight and intricate as cloisonne. "And I regret that I cannot be in two places at once."

Dave stares past her, his eyes fixed on the yellow-gray city sky outside our window. He sighs, goes to her and kisses her softly on the mouth.

Max looks at each of us. He brushes the guitar strings once.

"I am here," he says, "alive."

I raise my flat seltzer to him. "Right on."

"And my regret?" He shakes his head. "That I don't have one." He plays the opening of James Brown's *I Feel Good*.

Charles walks to the window. "One A.M. Bright lights, not-so-big-city, still, this is the only time this place looks good. Number One right-on: I found Jen. And, I get two *right-ons* because I was fool enough to start this game. Number Two: I'm broke 'cause I won't play Flavor-of-the-Week jazz. My regret? I didn't meet Jen sooner."

Dave slides off the couch onto the carpet. He looks up at me. What lies between us is both loving and uneasy. It holds twenty years of his anger, since he was fifteen and told me he hated the way we lived, my hippie clothes, my weird friends, getting dragged to demonstrations, not knowing which of my twenty million boyfriends he'd find sitting at the breakfast table.

"You know," he says fuzzily, "I was gonna fake this. I hate this touchy-feely stuff." I think he might be passing out, then I realize his eyes are wet. Leni lifts his head onto her lap.

"My right-on," he says, "was when I beat my personal best in the breaststroke in the All-County finals, came in first, and you, Mom, for once were there." He closes his eyes. "My regret…"

I'm not breathing and I have to pee. For once, I don't leave.

"My regret is that I can't slow down." Dave jerks up on one elbow. "You can't use that against me, Mom," he says, "not ever. This is a special night."

"That's fair."

For what seems enough time for dawn to begin shining silver-rose through the window, we are all quiet.

"Well?" Jen says. "It's your turn."

"I have to pee."

Dave shoots a glance at Jen. She shrugs. Here goes Mom, as usual, slipping away.

"I'm coming back."

"And," Dave says, "you can't use that as your right-on."

THE BATHROOM is gorgeous. There is a wedgewood blue phone by the john and one by the tub. I consider calling Room Service and ordering a Tanqueray. A full bottle. I could tell the waiter to pour it into a vase and stick in a silk orchid. I look in the mirror. Ain't much there I haven't seen before. Just another aging hippie anarcho-chick, frizzy hair silvery around the edges, tired eyes that used to be warm, an upper lip gone thin, jaw-line slipping south.

I wonder how long you can legitimately stay in a bathroom under conditions like this. I remember hiding out in the ladies room during a bust at a Southside b-b-q joint. I remember climbing out the little window over the toilet. Here, in the midst of bankers' gray tile and fat ivory towels and two blue telephones, there's nowhere to run. I can't tell these kids that what I'm most proud of is my rage, and my big mouth, and my writing. No mother can say that to her children. I can't tell them my one true regret involves a blues musician, a smoky club in which my boyfriend and I were the only patrons, and an invitation declined.

I stand at one of the two sinks and look into my eyes. The lighting is tricky. I see a woman not brave, not young, but maybe capable of a few gently twisted truths. I wash my hands and dry them on one of the sexy towels. I can hear the kids' voices. I lean against the door and, not making out their words, I still love the sound.

JEN PATS the couch next to her. "You go, girl."

"I get seven right-ons," I say. "One for each of my kids and Lashona, and three more."

"No fair," Dave says. Too many ethics classes in his MBA program.

"Fair," everybody else says.

"One, two, three, and four," I say, "Dave, Jen, Max, and Lashona. Five, my writing, six, my big mouth, seven, my politics."

They applaud. I stand and bow.

"Regrets, three. One, I didn't go be with Grandpa while he was dying. I said it was because he didn't want me there, which was true, but really, I didn't want to be around his meanness. Two, I didn't stay with Grandma the last couple months of her life. I could have. I was *just too busy.*"

"Excuse me?" Dave says.

"Really, where do you think you got it?" Dave wobbles up from the floor and sits at my feet.

"Three?" Charles says.

"Three, that luscious cobalt August night, 1968, when me and my main man, Michael, were at the Bluebow, the only people in the audience for Buddy Guy and his band. Just before they took a break, they played *Messin' with the Kid* and I got up and danced all by myself. Bell-bottoms I'd damn near painted on, ten strings of beads, my hair all Janis Joplined..."

"Oh no," Max says. "Maybe this is a little more than we ought to hear."

"During the break, one of those fine, fine musical gentlemen called me over to his table and invited me to accompany him back to the motel after the show, and that would have been fine with Michael 'cause he was Michael, and—"

Max hits an E-Minor chord.

"I didn't go."

"Have mercy," Charles says.

Jen is doubled over laughing.

Dave shakes his head. "Little Mom, my hopeless little Mom."

"That's it. Everything else, all of it—" I look Dave in the eye. "I wouldn't change a thing."

He takes my hand. "Mom, I promise. I won't hold this against you. Not ever."

I squeeze his hand and I say, "Fair enough."

 Betabank

A BAD HANGOVER has a quadruple heart. There is fear and intolerance in both the chest and brain. Ariel knew this. It was another late afternoon morning and Caliban's wake-up coffee shivered in her cup. When he asked her if she liked it, something called Coconut Mocha, she swallowed intolerance and the stuff itself, and said nothing. She only nodded her head, a head she would have gladly set on the make-up table next to Mr. Coffee, a head often described as elegant, and, at the moment, throbbing.

She was a tiny woman, just turned fifty, with precise features, great mist-blue eyes, and the arms and legs of a slender child. Her nose was long and narrow. In profile, in white paint and white silk costume, her hair covered by a white skull cap, she might have been an egret. One reviewer thought he saw feathers and when she moved, the possibility of flight.

On the wet Georgia night of her conception, her mother, an actress in small-town theatricals, had cried out, "Oh, joy, such dear joy," and they named the baby that. Joie. Joie Cherie Dean. She had played Peter Pan and Puck and Lear's best child, and Ariel a thousand times or more. It was known that Miss Dean brought both charm and fine edginess to her work.

Joie carried her coffee out of the dressing room, through the dim passage way, out onto the beautifully raked sand in the plaza behind the theater and thought, with every step, that this Ariel might be her last. The company was good, the director excellent. The theater was gorgeous, tucked into a corner of an austere building at the edge of a plaza that could have been the set for a witty mystery film. Water trickled through an aluminum channel in the heart of the plaza, in the heart of a desert city. There were frail trees with white globe lamps suspended above their leaves, as though twenty moons hung glowing in the green air. Just above the ramp that curved down to the underground garage, a sculptor planted clusters of burnished steel rods between the paving stones. When the wind was strong they rang against each other. With their chiming, with the water's trill and the unlit lamps orbiting the fountain, Joie, true to her lineage, had vague thoughts about the sad and distant music of the spheres.

She slipped off her huaraches and stirred the sand with her toes. Every day a man in dark clothes and a straw hat came and raked the sand in perfect swirls. Basalt boulders rose from the heart of the spirals, micaceous pebbles glittered at their intersections. Light etched the rake marks with deep shadows. She felt the coffee working on her head. The incandescent wires behind her eyes had gone to ash. Still, the perfect beauty of the garden irritated her. She poured the rest of her coffee onto the sand. It dried instantly, a tattered blotch.

"There," she whispered. "There."

They would play that night to a full house. The couples would pour in with their silver hair and pastel clothes and matte brown skin. They came southwest, in late January, for the muted gold of fool's summer, for imagining that one could stop time. Often, on the sun-bleached streets, in the midst of winter visitors, she wondered if she had *become* Ariel. She wondered, when they looked at her, if they saw anything. Their eyes, especially the eyes of the men, went clear through her, as though she were less than a thermal in their path.

The hangover caught her up, a pulsing reminder that she was, indeed, flesh. She heard Caliban behind her. He was a thudding barrel of a man, furred from head to fat toes. The wardrobe queen had thrown a ragged poncho over him, stuck a few dry leaves in his beard and blessed him for saving her budget. He crouched beside Joie. She could smell his cologne, sweet, expensive, and too much. He held the coffee pot in his great paw.

"Refill, my chick," he asked.

"I think not."

"Why, you spilled some. Not to your taste?"

"A little too sweet."

"Tummy upset?" he said and grinned.

"Hmmmm," she said. She stretched her arm out, just past his nose, and began the fluttering isolation she'd learned years ago in her first dance class, that she brought to every second of her Ariel, that set the silk of her costume trembling as though it were ectoplasm, that persuaded her audience that she was pure spirit, inhabited, inhabiting. Caliban could not watch her. She made him sea sick.

"Very nice," he said. "It's worse at close range."

"Whatever works," she stood, will-o-wisping up from the sand.

"I'm just a little queasy," Caliban said in his Miss Mary voice. "Ooo!"

"Try Dramamine. Wash it down with that lovely coffee." She floated him a kiss and wafted back into the theater.

BY THE TIME Prospero's fingers grazed her in good goodbye, she was exhausted. Her ears rang, the muscles in her shoulders burned. She could barely hear the prize Ariel had earned. She could barely see Prospero's dark green eyes focussed somewhere past her left shoulder.

"*Then to the elements be free,*" he cried, "*and fare thee well!*"

She drew back. The sleek couples watching would believe they saw love made visible between the old magician's eyes and hers. Sighting on the far exit sign, she shimmered up the ramp toward the gauze sky. The audience gasped. A few cried. The critics would commend her: *Ms. Dean transcends flesh and time.* The sweaty silk clung to her body. She backed delicately into the wings, into the cool shadows, and dropped to her knees.

"*Now my charms are all o'erthrown,*" Prospero said sadly. Joie stared down at her hands. The white paint had begun to flake up from her skin. She flexed her fingers. There was a soft ache in them, and in her left side and breast and temple. She pressed her face against her knee. Her skin, through the wet silk, was cold.

Applause washed over the stage. She waited for her call and imagined dandelions, blossomed and gone dead, their plumes bearing them away. When Prospero stretched out his hand to her, she let the fancy carry her towards his touch. The applause held her.

MIRANDA WAS second to leave. The masked sisters, Iris, Ceres, and Juno, had gone off to the cast party. Miranda's babysitter had called right after the curtain and said the three-year-old wouldn't stop coughing. Miranda had bundled up her things, cast a wistful glance at the rest of them, and scurried out the door. One of the *divers spirits* dawdled at the mirror. She was a college girl named Teri, with auburn hair and worried eyes. She had invited Joie to visit her Women in Theater group. Joie had gone, and nearly fled in the face of so much hope and rage and determination. Afterwards, Teri had sent her a spray of pale green orchids and a note that said, "We won't forget." Teri leaned up against the dressing table, her auburn hair doubly luminous in the room and bright mirror.

"Hey," she said. "You are paler than your paint. What happened? With the test?

"Normal. 'You are getting older, Ms. Dean. You are in wonderful condition for a woman your age, but even that cannot change the normal rhythms of the hormones.' I am to drink more milk, less gin, eat more fish and find a hobby."

"Will you?" Teri laughed.

"Would you?"

Teri grinned and pulled a pouch out of her huge patchwork bag. "No." She tossed a handful of M&Ms into her mouth. "What I would do is exactly what you would do."

"Thank you," Joie said. "It appears we have consensus."

Teri trailed a handful of M&Ms along the dressing table top. "Keep your strength up." She kissed Joie's forehead. "Take care," and she was gone.

Joie arranged her supplies along the dressing table, the emerald gin bottle, thermos of ice, tumbler and lime, the little shining knife, and crystal highball glass. She turned off all the lights except the bulbs around the mirror. If she leaned back just right, she saw only the essential planes and shadows of her face, the bones chiseled under the flaking paint. If the lab reports were right, they were going to get a good deal more chiseled. She blessed menopause. It was such a witchy mystery nobody questioned her evasions.

She uncapped the thermos and dropped ice into the tumbler. It was Waterford, perfect in the hand, heavy, a gift from the father of the lover best loved and most thoroughly gone. A blue vapor rose up from the gin.

"Heaven on earth," she whispered.

There was the small reliable pleasure of cutting lime into quarters, the scent, the green against ice and light. She rubbed the rind into her wrist and along her temples. It came away frosted with make up. She leaned back in the chair.

Below the mirrored oval of her face and the glint of ice and crystal, she saw, dim in the table's shadows, the photos of her family, four kids and grandson, Sarah, Daniel, Jenny, Max, Shay, the round and rosy soul that made her a grandmother. She raised her arm and sent a quick ripple of movement from shoulder to fingers. The white silk fluttered. She lifted her arm above her head and saw the silk fall away, saw the shudder of flesh under her upper arm.

Great-Aunt Mary's skin had been like that, fragile as crepe, smelling not of lime, but of eucalyptus oil and mint. She had worn dark silk dresses, with short sleeves and deftly pleated bodices. She had set the needle on the old one-sided records and wound the big mahogany Victrola. They always laughed at the first bay of the music. Great Aunt raised her arms, like a haughty maestra, and Joie danced. Across the linoleum, across the bleached rag rugs, across the gleaming oak floor, she danced. And Great Aunt Mary laughed and clapped and wound the Victrola one more time, her long fingers holding the records as though they were precious black crystal.

During the first steamy days of late spring, one of Joie's mother's suitors had wrestled the machine out to the back porch. It was his last grand gesture in their house. Joie's father reappeared with promises, chocolates, and a basket of hot house grapes. Through the purple evenings, he and her mother settled onto the porch, like a king, a queen, last light gilding them.

"Dance for us," they said.

She leaped and spun on the wet grass. Her white feet and thin white arms shimmering in the shadows, the air awash with the tinny sweetness of Berlioz and Debussy and Saint Saens. The grown-ups applauded and cried out,

"Brava, brava, encore!"

When her great aunt died and her mother became a silent wraith in the closed parlor off the front hall, Joie danced alone on the lawn, winding the Victrola herself and, when the music moaned into silence she went on spinning, slowly in the silent, lilac-scented dusk.

SHAY DID not dance yet. He barely walked. And, as he staggered out into that first giddy and terrified freedom, she would not be there. She considered that for the thousandth time, and freshened her drink. It was a wonderful word. Freshen: to make almost new. She dropped in ice and watched the blue vapor swirl. Shay would walk without her witness, as his mother had given birth; as Daniel had married; as Max had played his first recital and forgot to start the tape machine that would have recorded the music for her. As Jenny had disappeared from all of them, without a word, while Joie, by discipline and fierce ardor, danced alone.

Teri, Miranda, their blithe young women's magazines lied. You couldn't have it all. She added a good splash of gin to her drink and wandered out into the back hallway. Everyone was gone. She pushed open the stage door and stepped down onto the sand. The moon-lights glowed cool in the dark branches. She heard the ice ring in her glass and the sculpture chiming in the midnight wind. At the waterchute she eased off her slippers and stepped in. The water swirled, warm and soft as a cat, around her ankles. She watched the white paint melt from her skin and swirl away. Pale moths skittered in and out of the shadows.

The place was wonderfully quiet. She saw her car in the distant parking lot and imagined driving down the shallow steps into the plaza, parking, opening the doors, slipping Max's unmade tape in the deck, and letting the phantom music weave through the wonderful quiet. In the silence, between the wind's cool fingers, she could dance. She felt translucent. She imagined the gin, clear as good water, trickling through her blood and wished for a man's warm fingers on her wrist, to turn the tumbler out into the waterfall, to hold her fast in the steady current

"Fare me well," she whispered and emptied the glass into the waterfall. It was no libation, only ice. The gin was gone, melting her bones, warming whatever tattered shadow was growing deep in her body. She imagined the dark burned out of it, the cells' translucence restored.

She heard a hum, so faint it was barely sound. It was not a bird. They did not come to those skeletal trees. She thought of the bats that had arrowed out of the black pines bordering the backwoods pond at home. They would skim down over the black water. She was told to be afraid of them and wasn't. The buzz set her cheekbones humming, and was gone.

She walked barefoot to the sculpture, ran her hand over one of the wands, and pushed it. It swayed away, a hair's breadth, and wavered back. She set down her glass and pushed with both hands. It swung forward, connected and set the whole thing chiming. She stepped back and watched the rods, quills of light, swaying, touching, falling away. The unseen thing hummed again, hovered, and was gone. She heard a hoarse whisper.

"Whoa."

Joie looked down. A boy looked up from the ramp. Had she not seen his kind on the sidewalks near the theater, he would have been astonishing. His hair was a mahogany curtain over one eye. He'd shaved the other side. His visible eye was gray, sleepy and hooded, Robert Mitchum at his best. The eye studied her. The kid flipped back his shining hair.

"Co-ul." He moved and something flew up from the sidewalk into his hand, a manta ray surfacing from dark water. A silver skateboard. The boy tucked it firmly under his arm.

"So what are you?" His hair flopped back over his eye.

"Did you know," Joie said, "that with one eye covered, you can only see two dimensions?" The boy stepped into the circle of light. Three silver earrings glittered in his left ear, a tiny fish, a dagger, and a star hanging from a black thread. He raised his hand to push back his hair. There were woven bracelets around his wrist. His arm was mottled with old bruises.

"Yeah," he said, "trippy." He closed one eye. "Whoa, what are you?

Come on." He giggled. "Oh, I am severely fucked up." His voice was high, the words half swallowed.

Joie retrieved the empty tumbler. As she came back erect, she realized she had moved as Ariel. The boy laughed. "Holy shit, too cool. Come on!" he said. "You come into the light." He shivered. Joie studied him. He was near-skeletal. With that red-black hair, she was surprised at the shimmer of blond down on his arms and legs, at the milky sheen of his skin. He had long bony fingers. They were wrapped around the edge of the board, the knuckles dead white, two of the fingernails battered black.

"The worm," he said, "by the girl."

"The *girl*," Joie said.

"I'm a *girl*." She leaned the board against her leg, stretched out her gibbon arms and sent a ripple of movement from one taut hand, up her forearm, across her wiry shoulders, out toward the city's glare, down to her wrist, her palm and the tips of the fingers on her trembling left hand. "That's how we *used* to do it." She cackled. "It's totally not here anymore." She waited, her knees jittering against the skateboard.

"It's not really The Worm," Joie said from the shadows. "It's older than that." She held the glass to her eye and looked up at the lamp. Everything fractured. She considered stepping forward. The gin had loosened the sockets of her bones. "Watch."

She mirrored the girl.

The girl mirrored her.

"I see you, you know," the girl said. "What's in the glass?"

"Light," Joie said. She tossed the girl the tumbler. The kid snagged it out of the air and sniffed the rim.

"Got any more?" she asked.

"I might," Joie eased forward and watched the girl through the leaves. "I don't drink with strangers, especially under-aged." She hooked her arm around one of the branches.

The girl picked up the skateboard and turned it to the light, runes and sea foam and waves and an arched silver flying fish, a great silver moon filling most of the board. "Hey, can you read this?"

"No," Joie said. "It's not English. You can't fool me." She felt woozily righteous.

"Ha!" the girl said. "You only speak English. You're American. You're human." Joie walked out into the light.

"I am that," she said.

The girl looked her up and down. "Co-ul, you're from over at the theater, right?"

"I am."

"So," the girl said. "Look, this language is skate. Skateboard. It's my tag in my own alphabet. It says Grrrl Silver. Grrrl, like grrrl."

She traced the first three letters with her finger. Joie saw them, saw the rest leap out with clarity. A dance could be like that, one second a puzzle, the next, a welcome recognition in her body. "That's your name?"

"My skate tag. For now."

Joie closed the distance between them. She was moving human again, the slate cool and solid under her bare feet. She stopped near the kid. Girl Silver stood a good foot above her. Joie touched the letters.

"Why for now?" she asked.

"Get me some of that Tanqueray, and I'll tell you."

"How do you know it's Tanqueray?"

"My dear old mom drinks it. I'm supposed to be Ala-teen, you know, but whatever. She smells like it in the morning when she's hustling us out to school. I steal it. It's good stuff. You can add a lot of water before she can tell."

"I could go to jail," Joie said. "How old are you?"

"Fifteen," Grrrl said. "I already went. Just a month in Juvie. That's why the tag is only for now."

"Yes?"

"The cops find out, you change it."

"Graffiti?" Joie asked.

"More than that," Grrrl said. "Trespass, scuffing, and art, real art." She tucked the skateboard under her arm. "Come on, I'll tell you. My crew," she pointed to the bottom of the board, "JAM...Just Art Maniacs....we're all into lots of shreddin' stuff. Get me a drink? 'Kay?" She gently took hold of Joie's shoulder and turned her around.

Joie could see the warm glow from the open stage door. Everything else was cool, moonlight, waterfall, damp stones like tortoise shells and the tips of the girl's fingers on her shoulder. Grrrl gave her a gentle push. "C'mon, what's in there? Every night, I wonder what you guys are doing. I'm flying across this ramp, ollie to grind, ollie the rise, whatever, and I imagine what it's like in there."

"I'm supposed to ask you about ollie to grind, right?"

"Whatever," the girl laughed. "C'mon, we'll trade secrets."

Joie moved away from her touch and led her past the sculpture, across the trickle of water in its moon-silver channel and up the shallow steps to the back door. Grrrl stopped.

"Security?" she asked.

"No problem," Joie said, circled her wrist with her fingers and led her in. Grrrl's skin was clammy. There was a scabbed brush burn across the back of her hand.

"You don't wear protection?" Joie asked.

"No. We're like duh. Nobody does. I could be with child as we speak," She giggled.

Joie touched the burn. "I meant this."

Grrrl ducked her head and swung the curtain of hair over her face. "Ooops. Double duh."

"My god," Joie said. "Do you always tell so much so fast?"

"Why not? That's anarchy. Never apologize. Never explain." She sniffed the air.

"Cool smell," Grrrl said. "I went to a play once when I was a kid in Mendocino. It was about this pig and this really excellent spider."

"Charlotte's Web?"

"Yeah. These hippies came out from Willits and put it on. Charlotte was so cool. She died and everything and it didn't matter. My mom cried all the way through." She looked fondly down at Joie. "Did you ever play Charlotte?" she asked.

"No," Joie said. "I mostly do very old plays."

"Like Shakespeare, I bet. I saw this movie with my dad. He likes Japanese flicks and it was called *Throne of Blood* and it was about this outrageous dude who kills everybody and hates himself. My dad said it started out as Shakespeare. Like *Macbeth*. It was scaaary!"

"Like that," Joie said. "I'll show you." She opened the door to backstage.

Grrrl looked up. "I thought you could see all the way to the top, where the lights are and all that great rigging, like at concerts."

"Out front. We can go there."

"Groovy," Grrrl said. She watched Joie's face. "Me and my crew, we say old-fashioned stuff like that, like 'far out' and 'outtasight,' like mock cool, but it's totally cool, too."

"It's called irony."

"Irony. Like, would you say that if you liked something but you didn't want anyone to know?"

Joie laughed. "You'd say it if you wanted somebody to know you thought they'd said something cruel but fair. You'd put this cold look on your face and say, 'Ironic.'"

"Like we say, 'shoofly bail,' when somebody's being a dick." She flopped her hair over her eye and let her face go dead. "Shoofly bail, dude. Like that. Or 'whatever' when something is totally cool and we way love it. Hey?"

"What?"

"Could you paint my face? For when we go on stage? With real make-up? We do it sometimes, me and my crew, with poster paint, but it flakes off. Would you?"

Joie nodded. "Sure." Grrrl smiled and spun in a slow goofy circle, looking up, looking down, looking around at everything.

"There's more," Joie said. "There's a ramp and I go up it."

"No!" Grrrl said. "On stage? You want me to skate it, don't you?"

"Yes."

"Well, let's do it," Grrrl stretched out her arms. "I am ready." Joie looked at her tee shirt. It was new, clean, black as new moon. Over her small breasts, a silver flying fish soared straight towards Joie, its eyes bulging, its wings full-formed, its beaked mouth screaming. She imagined the darkened stage, a blue spot, the creature, shuddering, St. Elmo's fire, flickering down out of the elements, Grrrl gone, no more or less than a carrier, the fish a thing of night and mystery caught, and with a finger on the lightboard, released.

Grrrl Silver leaned back in the make up chair, fists clenched on her jittering knees. She popped M&Ms in her mouth.

"Hold still," Joie said.

"I can't. Hold on." The girl pulled a film canister from her pocket and rolled a thin joint, lit it, and passed it to Joie.

"No thanks. Pot doesn't like me." She dropped the last of the ice in her glass and trickled in some gin. The girl's breathing slowed. The muscles in her lean legs softened. Grrrl checked her pulse with her left hand and caught Joie watching her. "This is heart-stopper shit, but I always live through it." Her hands went limp against her thighs. "Ready," she said and closed her eyes.

Joie brushed back the girl's hair and pinned it close to her head. Then, she painted Grrrl out, black face, black neck and throat, black hands and arms. She fit the black skull cap snug over her hair and ears, outlined her eyes and brows with silver and dropped black tights and leotard in her lap. Grrrl opened her eyes. "Way cool. I be gone. Whoa. I be thirsty."

"Here. Don't smear you." Grrrl took the tumbler from her fingers and drained it carefully. She set the empty glass back on the table and leaned forward.

"You can change behind that screen."

Grrrl Silver emerged, saw herself in the mirror and let out a banshee shriek. "Fish. Fishlaugh. Carries in water." She bent toward the mirror and pointed toward the pictures.

"Hey! Who are they?"

"My kids. My grandson, Shay."

"No!" Grrrl said. "You're too little." She settled into the chair, finished the joint and swallowed the roach. "My mom's maybe gonna' be a grandma. Weird."

Joie rattled the glass to shake up the ice.

Grrrl jumped. "Whoa! Fucked up again." She held out her palm. "May I have some ice, please?" Joie set a cube on her palm. She ran it over her lips, started to pass it over her forehead and stopped.

"No," she said to the mirror, "I'll smear my gone paint. Princess of Darkness, I be. No." She shivered. "Grrrl Midnight, that's cool." She glanced at Joie. "Prince of Darkness. That's Satanic, you know?"

"Not really," Joie said. "I like the dark. It's peaceful."

"Some kids think the Prince of Darkness is cool," Grrrl said. "Not me. I'm anarchy. That's totally opposite."

"How so?"

"Satanic is sick. Anarchy is like right before morning. You know, it's dark but everything is changing. My boyfriend taught me that. He's a wizard." She picked up the black make-up crayon and drew a circled A on the mirror. "There you go. When you see that, you'll know it's anarchy."

"And?"

"It's my ritual," Grrrl said fiercely. "It's 'fuck everything, do what you want.' It's like full moon everywhere and get maniac and don't ever, never apologize."

"You *are* fucked up," Joie said quietly. Grrrl stared at her. Joie grinned.

"Well, what's yours?" Grrrl said. "What's your fucking ritual?"

"I forget." Joie held up her glass. "I think I just finished it." Grrrl's fish-laugh rang out, and Joie remembered how a laugh can be a wall, how a kid could disappear behind it, how a grown-up was left out in the cold.

"Let's go," she said.

She led the girl through the darkened wings, past the hanging flats, the mysterious bulking shapes, the gauzes that fluttered in the small breeze of their passing. Grrrl's hand shook in hers. The board was tucked up under her arm. Joie could see her white teeth in the dark. She was grinning like a baby fiend. Joie led her to the crawl space under the stage, into Caliban's dusty cave.

"Wait here," she whispered. "This is the monster's cave. When you hear my voice from right there, go up these steps and push through that canvas."

"Okay," Grrrl said. She hunched over something.

"No grass," she said. "No fire down here."

"No," she said. "Not that. There's something here." Joie moved away from her. She could hear her quick breathing. Something crinkled.

"Hey!" Grrrl said. "There's a ton of cookie boxes here. Ohmygod, he's the Cookie Monster."

"Have some," Joie said. She imagined Caliban down in this warm dark, wreathed in the miasma of shaving lotion, cheerfully shoving Oreos past his beard with his fat fingers, spilling crumbs among the dry leaves, and she forgave him with her whole heart for the terrible coffee. That was the trouble with booze. Eventually the clean edge of any hangover dulled to muzzy tenderness.

"Hey!" Grrrl said. "I finished off the chippers. The monster will kill me."

"No problem," Joie said. "It's a very generous monster."

She went noiselessly up the steps and crossed over to the light board. She played for a minute and got what she wanted, the ellipsoids on the ramp, the gels cleared, the footlights full on. The sound tech had left the tape in the deck. It was an airy thing: monsoon thunder, then a mix of Pueblo flute and Vivaldi. She set the timer for thirty seconds. The board went dark. She crouched at the edge of the cave. Grrrl was crunching her way through the cookies.

"Okay," Joie hissed. "Get ready." She heard her move. "Wait. Is your hair out of your eyes?"

"Three-D," Grrrl whispered.

"Then, go!" Joie stepped back into the wings.

Grrrl came out into a burst of light, hurricane winds shrieking above. Her eyes glittered. Dark and drugs had done their work, irises nearly gone, pupils silver. The flying fish rose and fell with every breath. Grrrl dropped to her knees. She made the board an air-guitar, keened over it, over the blur of her black fingers on its unseen strings, over the storm pouring out into blinding opal light.

"*Betabank*," she crooned, her voice wailing and breaking on the bass notes. "*On the Betabank*," she screeched, "*you take the first step on the Stairway to Heaven...and...there...is...only...fear.*" She jerked upright and stabbed the skateboard at the footlights.

"*Takin' back the Betabank*," she screamed, and laughed. "Great acoustics."

"Don't turn around," Joie said.

Grrrl nodded. "This is fun!" She picked up the board.

"Now. Turn!"

Grrrl spun, and stopped, facing the darkened stage. Joie threw the switch. The ramp leaped out of the dark, like a comet flowing downstage. The girl hunched her shoulders. She shook her head. "Too fun," she said quietly. "We're gonna skate to annihilate tonight!" She set her foot on the ramp and hesitated. "Can I get up from the back? You'll like it better that way."

"I'll lead you through," Joie said. "Once. Then you're on your own."

"Cool."

Joie couldn't see her. They'd reset the tape, the storm howling anarchy. Joie settled into a first row seat and stretched her aching legs. The carpet was rough and cool under her bare feet. She wished she had something like that for her brain, something abrasive and soothing. The drunk was wearing off. Time went a little odd. She waited, and once waited for Sarah, Sarah at thirteen, late from a cross-country bus trip, arriving home full of relief and defiance. *"Didn't she trust her? Hadn't she known?"* They had sat on the back porch steps in their bathrobes, drinking coffee at 2 A.M., yelling and holding each other tight.

The storm began to fade. Just before the flute soared, Joie heard the hum of the board. Grrrl and fish sailed down out of the swelling light. Joie had been wrong. Grrrl was more than a carrier. Grrrl was full and flawless grace. She floated the shining fish down from the dark, as Joie transported Ariel up, through that false streaming light, effortless and sweating like a fiend.

Joie saw clearly what Grrrl did. It was a matter of nerve and balance and a kind of prayer. The girl called out the names.

"Ollie to grind!"

"Three sixty boneless!"

"To the knee bail!"

"Frontside fuckin' rock 'n' roll!"

She worked the ramp, the riser, the edge of Caliban's cave. Joie found herself leaning forward, braced, hands clenched in her lap. Flute-notes etched the air. The lights threw dawn on the great canvas back drop. Grrrl stood at the top of the ramp, dark against the light that spread, wave after wave, lilac to mauve, lemon to bright, burning gold.

"This is it," Grrrl cried. She kicked off and sailed down. She hit the stage and kept coming.

"No!" Joie cried and the girl sailed off the edge, snatched the board from under her feet and landed, grinning, gasping, paint and sweat streaking her white skin. She tugged off the skull cap and bowed.

"Hail," she said. "That's Shakespeare, right?"

"*All right, Great Mistress. Grave lady, hail! I come to answer thy best pleasure; be't to fly, to swim, to dive into the fire, to ride on the curled cloud!*"

"Cool," Grrrl said. "Now you do it. Your ritual." She flopped into the seat next to Joie and propped the board against the stage

"Look," Joie said. "I'm pretty shaky. I've got M.S. I might make some mistakes. You were perfect."

Grrrl took Joie's hand in hers. "You're dying?"

"Some day. I'm just not as strong as I was." The girl raised Joie's hand to her lips and kissed it. "Ironic."

"Oh yes."

"Go ahead," Grrrl said. "Really."

Joie climbed to the stage, bearing the beginnings of a hangover with every step. She would have sold her waning powers for a cup of Caliban's brew. When she turned and looked, she saw the girl grinning, her arms stretched out along the seat tops. Joie set the lightboard for Ariel's farewell, the ramp washed in soft rose, a circle of white light where Prospero would have stood, his arm outstretched, his cloak a shadow.

Joie stepped into the light. "I am Ariel. I am spirit. A helper. This is *The Tempest* and William Shakespeare wrote it."

The girl started to say something and stopped. She had folded her hands in her lap. She could have been in a classroom or court. The flying fish gleamed in the footlights, leaping with every breath. Ariel drifted downstage, just out of the spotlight. Her muscles burned, and she moved as she knew to move, never still, never rooted, each step, each hesitation calculated and intuitive as flight.

"My Master, Prospero, is an old magician and I am vowed to serve him. He has asked me if I brought a storm upon a ship. I answer." She raised her arm and pointed up to the light. Her fingers were wind, her arms and shoulders rain, lightning caught in her trembling sleeves, flashed, faded, flashed again.

"*I boarded the King's ship, now on the beak, now in the waist, the deck, in every cabin, I flamed amazement; sometime I'd divide and burn in many places; on the top mast, the yards, and borespit would I flame distinctly, them meet and join.*"

"I've seen that," the girl cried out. "My dad had a boat back in California. We'd sail up to Punta Gorda and sleep on deck. I'd wake up and there was that light. It's blue. You can touch it; it touches you, goes round you, but you don't feel anything."

"Yes." Joie turned off the lights. "Close your eyes. You'll like this." She took the flashlight from the lightboard and stepped back on stage. Holding herself steady except for the slightest weaving of her head, she set the flashlight under her chin and flicked the switch.

"Open your eyes." She heard a muffled "whoa."

"Here, some men have betrayed my master. I bewitched them into thinking they saw a tray full of wonderful food. As soon as they went to it, I made it disappear and sat on a rock above them and made myself horrible to see." She moved the light below her breasts and raised one arm like a great contorted wing, the fingers curled, the hand a claw.

"*You are three men of sin,*" she hissed, "*whom destiny—that hath to instrument this lower world and what it isn't—the never surfeited sea hath cause to belch you up, and on this island, where man doth not inhabit, you 'mongst men being most unfit to live; I have made you mad, and even with such like valor men hang and drown their proper selves.*"

"That is cold," the girl whispered.

Joie reset the lights. "Now, the monster has tried to betray my master. He and his pals get drunk and I deal with them."

"Bad monster!" the girl shouted. Joie's arms seemed to lift by themselves. She was so tired she had no will, no words of her own, her thoughts no more than light-motes. She was optical fiber, an invisible messenger, the message, itself. She could have been asleep and her body would have played the part.

"*I told you sir, they were red hot with drinking; so full of valor that they smote the air for breathing in their faces, beat the ground for kissing of their feet; yet always bending toward their project.*" She struck her air tambourine, as the girl had bent over her skateboard. "*Then I beat my tabor; at which like unbacked colts they pricked their ears, advanced their eyelids, lifted up their noses as they smelt music. So I charmed their ears that calf like they my lowing followed through toothed briers, sharp furzes, pricking goss, and thorns, which entered their frail shins. At last I left them I'th filthy mantled pool beyond your cell, there dancing up to th' chins, that the foul o'er stunk their feet.* "

Girl snorted. "More," she cried. She hung her legs over the seat arm. "I'm awake, completely."

"Here," Joie said, "I'm thinking of when I'll be free. My master will let me go after I finish these last tasks." She crouched at the base of the stage, just in the shimmer of the rose light. She rested her chin on her hand and went still.

"*In a cowslip bell I lie, there I couch when owls do cry. On the bat's back I do fly after summer merrily. Merrily, merrily shall I live now under the blossom that hangs on the bough.*"

"Summer is The Best," Grrrl said. "Owls. Bats. Spooky. One of my crew's tag is Blind Bat. You wouldn't believe what he does. He does what I did blindfolded. He's broke one leg three times." She leaned forward. "You know how those summer nights it gets dark and there's all that real mellow light for hours and hours?"

"I do. It's my favorite time."

"It totally rocks," Grrrl said. "Is there more? Please?"

"Just the end. I don't say anything. I'll do my master's part and then, you'll see. You'll have to use your imagination." She walked a few feet up the ramp.

"Imagine I'm a bald-headed guy with a beautiful silver beard. I just dropped my magician's velvet cape on the sand and I'm wearing a fancy captain's uniform." She squared her shoulders and drew in breath. "*My Ariel, chick,*" she said in a deep voice, "*then to the elements be free, and fare thou well!*"

She stepped, it seemed, around herself and began to drift, up and back, up and away, from where her words had sounded. She felt air open out between her fingers and Prospero's, between her and Grrrl's huge gaze. She felt the distance and deepened it, trembling, sure, half-dancing, half-flying, as mortals must, up that curved way. The girl began to applaud. Joie could hear the beat of her hands above the tumult of her own breath.

She reached the opal light at the top of the ramp and stopped. The girl still clapped. She stomped her feet. Joie blew the girl a kiss. Effortlessly, as though the pure light and air of the old playwright's genius lofted her, she drifted back into the dark wings, and stopped. She looked out and saw Grrrl jumping up and down, both fists in the air, screaming. "Ma...gic! Ma...gic!"

Joie grabbed two towels from backstage and walked down to the girl. They dried their hair and wiped the paint from their faces.

"I gotta' go," Grrrl said. "I'm dead. I had a midnight curfew. I'm grounded for the rest of my natural life."

Joie watched her. "Me, too." They laughed.

"We," Grrrl said, "are both in deep shit." She took Joie's elbow and sat her down. "It doesn't stop, does it?" she said quietly. "It doesn't quit just because you grow up."

"I've got a kid," Joie said, "walked right past one of those curfews and kept right on walking. You could be smarter." She watched the girl tense.

"No," Joie said. "It doesn't stop."

"Well, hey," the girl said, "I'm outta' dope. I'm outta' hope. I'm outta' here."

"Wait." The girl drifted back, fading, sure as she stood planted in front of her. Joie waited for the fishlaugh. It didn't come.

"What?"

"One question." Grrrl's face went tight. Joie bet that was what grown-ups always said, how they always ruined it.

"Yeah?"

"What's a Betabank?"

Grrrl flipped back her bangs and laughed, a good, warm, girl laugh. "It's pretty intense. Are you sure you want to know?"

"I can take it."

"Wish I had that flashlight," Grrrl said. "This is really scary!"

"Come on."

"Okay. There's this wall, this long, low, curved wall. It's perfect."

"Yeah? Okay. So what else?"

"Hang on," Grrrl said. Slowly, with a grace beyond calculation, she crouched and looked deep in Joie's eyes.

"You ready?" Joie nodded.

"This wall," Grrrl said. "This completely—rockin'—wall—is behind— the Alpha Beta supermarket in Escondido. That's what it is. It is the *best*! It is The Betabank!"

"Alpha Beta supermarket in Escondido."

"The cops kick us out. We take it back. They kick us out. We take it back. We're roaches."

"Ironic." Joie grinned. "So, was this better?"

Grrrl Silver tucked the skateboard under one arm.

"Spirit," she kissed Joie on the cheek, "you know."

 Delicate

Honey kept getting prettier and prettier. That was what scared Frank the most. He'd heard that people with that sickness, the big C, were supposed to lose everything, their hair, skin color, flesh, almost their humanness. Honey had always been a fine-looking woman, a little on the hefty side, with that combination of heat and dignity that made guys catch their breath. There was bad, beautiful magic in the way the sickness sharpened her cheekbones, the way her lion-gold eyes got bigger and bigger with every pound the sickness ate. It, they had taken to calling the sickness It, made her model-pretty. It scared him to much worse than death.

They were in a little motel in Flagstaff, Arizona, when he knew they were in for the time when death would start to look like a picnic. Honey had slept fine the night before. Earlier, wandering the downtown streets, the two of them playing Fred and Marge Tourist, she'd had to stop a lot to catch her breath, but Flag was a mountain town, seven thousand feet up, so it hadn't been a big deal. They had no plans, that was part of the plan—no plans.

Frank bought beer and hoagies and chocolate cake and they rambled up to the pine-shadowed park for lunch. He watched her swinging on the kids' swing, her thin dry hair glistening in the sunlight. He remembered when he might have swung beside her. They'd walked slowly back downtown and that was when she'd started leaning on him, laughing breathlessly, hugging his thick arm. They had stopped for coffee in a hippie cafe and listened to the chug of Creedence Clearwater over the CD speakers.

"I was a mom then," she'd said wistfully.

"I was a grunt," he said, "like you didn't know."

Later, she wanted to make love, moving slowly and delicately above him. Looking up at her face, he'd puzzled again at her growing beauty. It nearly drove him numb and useless, 'til he made himself think of someone else's lush body, that woman's plain face and, betraying, had moved up into Honey's loving flesh.

In early morning, she crept from their bed. Frank heard her. He always heard her. She closed the bathroom door, as she had each time, and turned the shower on full force. She hadn't even bothered to turn on the light. He hated that. The idea of her in that blackness, like a wounded creature curled up into the coolest, darkest corner of its lair. In all his life, he'd never felt as bad and mean and helpless as he did at those times, lying there minute after endless minute, while the shower ran and ran, not quite muffling her desperate noises, and he couldn't knock on the door. It was thirty minutes before the pills took and she turned off the water. He'd watched the thin green second hand on the travel clock creep around.

It was barely dawn when they woke. Honey stretched and sat up, leaning against the pillows piled along the velour headboard.

"Frank," she whispered, "get me a cigarette."

He looked up at her glittering eyes, faded gold around the pin-prick of iris. He started to remind her of the doc's orders, then stopped himself and lit cigarettes for both of them. The blinds were drawn, but a good, strong, early-morning light came up fast in the window. There were few sounds, just the purr of the big trucks, moving through, not stopping. Honey smiled at him.

"There's nothing like that first smoke," she said. "Isn't it nice here, so quiet, such a sweet little town? I'd like to stay here forever."

He nodded. It seemed he had lost the way to speak to her. He lifted a pale curl away from her face. She laughed.

"Glad one of us can do that…"

She pulled his head down to her breast and rubbed his bald patch. He was a short man, furry-chested, solid as a keg above his thick, strong legs. "Built for comfort, not for speed," Honey liked to say. Tight against her cool skin, he wanted somebody, something to finish it for them right there, in the peach light, with the sweat and smell of love still on their bodies, her fingers slipping through his hair. She had made him promise he'd go on—find somebody, love again.

"My kids are grown," she'd said. "You're just a young punk. There's lots of good women out there."

She had tried to tell him that, pissed off and scared as she was, she had gradually started to see things different. She'd found a new beauty in things. He couldn't see it. They'd been divided before, her jealousy, his bad temper, but they'd always found their way back to each other, to "seeing with the same eyes," she called it. The time was different. He pressed his face into her, but without the cover of her rich flesh, he felt only bones.

FIVE YEARS together. He'd heard people say that time went faster in your forties. He hadn't noticed that 'til he met her. She'd been forty-four, him forty-two when they met, both of them drinking a little too much, both of them fed up with romance. She'd said she'd been juke-boxed half to death. It was no surprise they met in a bar. It was a shock that it worked.

He'd gotten used to stopping in at The Cordial on Friday nights. It was one of those places with no windows and a doorway that had been kicked in and rebuilt so many times it looked like most of the customers' faces. They were largely younger guys, carpenters, cops, roofers, small-time hustlers. He'd met a few of them on the jobs. They didn't mind that he was a little older. Young as they were, most everybody was divorced or in lousy marriages. Sandy, the chunky barmaid poured a fair shot and kept the beer ice cold. And, there were dancers. Young broads, mostly lezzies, tough enough to keep the occasional frat party in line, smart enough to make you think you wanted them.

He'd been sitting next to Tiger, a fierce little butch who was in love with Miss Sheila, a tall, delicious, sweet-faced dancer, the first time he saw Honey. Tiger was staring off into space. She said she couldn't stand to watch men watch Miss Sheila, and she couldn't stand to not watch. Suddenly, she straightened and stared over his shoulder to the front door. "Toss you for this one."

He swivelled on his stool and watched the woman walk toward them. She had a plain face except for the eyes. Her pale hair was pulled back into a bun. He couldn't figure out why he kept watching her. Nobody else paid any attention. She might have been somebody's wife. Or mother. She wore Levis, high-heeled boots, and a turquoise fake fur jacket that was a little too snug across the tits. She glanced at the bar, saw him, and stared straight into his eyes, like some big, proud alley cat.

"Lady lion," he thought. And, surprised himself. He was no poet. He'd hated words since he'd found out in Laos they changed nothing.

She walked to the far end of the bar and sat down between two guys. Sandy pulled a face. She hated women, swore they couldn't drink and never tipped. The woman ordered a draft, left the change in front of her and turned to watch Miss Sheila, who had just planted her high-heeled foot square in the middle of some college punk's chest and sent him flying off the stage. Tiger bought Frank a beer. The woman grinned.

"Make your move, asshole," Tiger hissed.

"Thank you so much for sharing," Frank said and made his move.

He got up, walked over to the woman, stood behind her, his heart ricocheting off his ribs, and watched her in the cracked mirror, 'til she looked up, saw him and smiled. It was easy. She turned around, told him her name was Honey and told him to not make a joke about it. She said she was hungry. Surprise, he was too. It was Friday. They both loved shrimp. He named a place down by the lake and that was fine. He would follow her to her place, she would drop off her car and they would drive out together.

On the way, she talked a lot. He liked that. She told him about her four kids, three gone, one still in the house, driving her crazy. He especially liked it when he said, "Bad marriage?" and she looked him straight in the face and said, "What else? We'll just leave it at that."

She let him buy her meal. The Sandbar was crowded, full of locals, drinking hard under the fish nets hung with starfish and erratic Christmas lights. She ordered another beer. Frank was nervous so he switched to J.D. It would ease him up a little faster, put a blur on it so it wouldn't really matter what happened. It troubled him that he already liked so much about this woman, her solid body, how she didn't wear much make-up, the strange silver rings on her thin hands, the way she held her shoulders when she walked, that she wore two earrings in her right ear, like a teenage girl, but didn't say a word about her age. He guessed her to be in her mid-forties and it seemed to him that all the forty-year-old women he met had to slip in an apology, a slap in their own face somewhere along the way. He liked that she laughed, really laughed, a lot. She said you had to, the way things rolled most times. He knew what she meant.

He even liked the way she ate. They got their table and she ordered a big dinner, no apologies, no cute bullshit about calories. When the rolls came, she piled in. He was having trouble swallowing, so he just kept drinking.

"Aren't you hungry?" she said.

He set down his glass. "Yeah, I'm just taking my time here. I haven't been to dinner with a lady in a while."

She grinned. "Good."

His throat got tight like it had when he was sixteen and he had suddenly known that the girl was actually going to get in the back seat of the car—with him!—and he realized what's more he liked her and he'd never undone a bra before. Honey reached across the table and touched his hand.

"Hey," she said, "you talk. I've yakked your ear off. You tell me your story and I'll shut up and eat."

He told her his story, more than he remembered telling anybody. He knew it wasn't just the booze. It was something about the way she watched him, so steady and calm.

"There's now," he said. "I wire houses, old ones, new ones, I live alone, I like it. That's about it."

She was quiet.

"And," he said, "There was then—my folks up from Missouri when I was eight, so poor I had to start school late, hooray, because there wasn't enough money for decent shoes, dropping out of high school, looking five years older than I was, enlisting and going to Nam." He didn't tell her about Nam and he liked that she didn't ask. He told her about coming back to nothing, no welcome, no job, not even recognition that he'd been there. "No American personnel in Laos," government officials had said.

"There may have been no personnel," he said to Honey, "but there sure as shit was me."

He told her about going home and finding out that the girl in the back seat, Sherry, was already divorced and only too ready to give him something, a marriage, a kid. He didn't have to tell her about how that marriage had gone and, again, she didn't ask.

"I just got restless," he said. "I'm not proud of that, but that's the truth. Since then, some good ladies, some not so good." They were both getting loaded. She sighed.

"I should have known better," she grinned. "These beers are getting to me. I'd like to get out of here—maybe a drive along the lake."

"Sure," he said. "But I better get a little coffee under my belt."

They both slowed down. She ordered pie. Blackberry with ice cream. He drank his coffee. They didn't say much. A band, two middle-aged guys with slick haircuts and cowboy shirts and a couple of punks in flannels and big shorts, set up at one end of the room. They were truly terrible.

"Let's get out of here," Honey said. "I been juke-boxed half to death."

Booze and coffee danced sweetly in his blood. He felt he could drive along that inky lakeshore for a lifetime. They rolled down the windows and the wet late-summer air streamed by their faces. He turned off the headlights. She yelped. And then, out of the blackness, as always, as it had done since he'd been a kid driving the same road, beer between his knees, his hand in somebody's crotch, her young hands on the steering wheel, the bright white glare of the old amusement park leaped up. Frank swerved. Honey grabbed the dashboard and laughed.

Delicate

"Damn!" she said. "That always gets me. I've driven here every summer since I was a teenager and it scares me every time." She leaned over and kissed his cheek. Looking back, he figured it was at that moment that he fell in love with her.

She said it was different for her, that the minute she'd seen the square back of him, in the Cordial, the fine set of his head, she'd felt something was going to happen. She'd never had any trouble attracting men but she had felt a little shy. It had been hard for her to look at him in that come-get-me way, but she'd done it. Harder still for her to walk right by and sit at the end of the bar and wait, but she'd done that, too. They were walking on the narrow beach out at the Point, under hovering stars, when she told him that she didn't think she'd taken a breath between the time she saw him and he'd walked up behind her.

"That's something," he laughed, "sat down, ordered a beer, looking like a lady, seduced me, looking like a lady, made me buy you dinner, looking like a lady and all the time not breathing. You sure are something."

He kissed her; She kissed him back, all solid and warm in his arms. Her mouth tasted like coffee and brandy. He didn't want to stop to breathe, but he felt shy and pulled away from the kiss, his legs shaking, his heart doing the caged bird imitation again. Holding her, he looked out and saw the moon shivering silver in the water. She burrowed into his shoulder and held him close to her by the lightest pressure on the nape of his neck. He felt it right down to his balls.

"Please," she whispered, "we've got to slow down. I don't know why but I'm scared to death," and he felt it was no tease or come-on. He pulled her to his side.

A ragged stone wall stretched about knee high between the swaying beach grass and the sand. He folded his jacket for them to sit on and pulled out two cigarettes.

"What'd we do without smoke?" Honey said. Her voice shook and faded into the lakewind. He ducked his head. She looked down at his clasped hands.

"Nothin's gonna' make this any easier," Frank said, "but I might as well get it over with. I been no virgin since my marriage. If you've been around the Cordial, you probably heard some stories." She put her cool hand over his mouth.

"Ditto. You know I'm the nervous type. I sort of got the habit, after Eddie left, of going out, getting a little loaded, getting laid, and going home. That way, I didn't have to think about it. I had four teenagers, computers eating up my job and all my friends half crazy, without my having to think about what I was doing with who."

He put his arm around her shoulder and pulled her close. They sat a while in silence, then, without a word, got in the car and drove in more silence to her place. Somewhere, on the road, something went strange. They moved silent through her door, up the stairs, out of their clothes, and into her big bed. And then, her all silk and wet and gleaming, he panicked. He wanted her so much, wanted to give her so much, he couldn't feel a thing.

She touched him. She moved her breath, her mouth, all over his body. She whispered words. Nothing. He crushed himself against her, wrapped his hands in her hair, bit her tan shoulders. Nothing. She pulled away, rolled on her belly on the far side of the bed and made herself rigid and gone from him. He touched her. She shrugged away his touch. He got up, pulled on his clothes, stumbled for the door, and closed it softly behind him. He was dead sober.

Making it down the dark stairs was like a nightmare, where you know you're dreaming, you hope you're dreaming and you suddenly know you're not. There was a crash against her bedroom door. He stopped.

"What?" he said under his breath. He took the stairs two steps at a time.

He went back in, saw her sitting in the bed lamp's rose glare, huddled against the wall, naked, the sheet tangled around her.

"I threw the ash tray, you son-of-a-bitch," she said. "Who do you think you are? What was all that heavy breathing at the lake? Haven't you been with a grown woman before? Okay, I'm no Britney Spice, whatever, but what the hell are you?"

He stared at her. He had never wanted a woman as much in his life.

"We could have talked, you know," she said. "We could have said something. I'm not just some dumb, bar pick-up piece of pussy," she started to cry and grabbed the sheet-edge, wiping furiously at her face.

"Talk?" Frank yelled. "You want to talk?"

"The kid!" she snapped. "Keep it down."

"You want to talk?" Frank said. "You turned away. You could have given me some time, you stupid broad. What the fuck! You clam up. You roll away. What was I supposed to do?"

She grabbed his cigarettes off the night stand and threw them at his belly.

"You don't ever use that language with me. You haven't known me, you will never know me, long enough to talk that way. You. Men. Make. Me. Sick. You're all the same!"

They glared at each other. "Cats," he thought. "In heat. Or something."

He could hear the clock ticking, the faint sounds of the kid down the hall, trying to sound like he was asleep. Honey lit a cigarette and exhaled fiercely. She looked about fifteen, the three earrings, her shadowed golden eyes, her hair like cotton candy around her face.

Slowly, cautiously he sat down on the edge of the bed. He was fully alert, deeply tired. She flounced away.

"Stop that," he said. He looked down at his hands. They seemed ugly and thick.

"Well," he said slowly. "Well, listen or not, I'm gonna' try to say something." She pulled her knees up under her chest and stared at him. "I don't know what the hell is going on here," he said flatly.

"We should have kept drinking," she said dully. "I knew I shouldn't have gone into this half-sober."

He pulled off one boot, then the other. She did nothing to stop him, except those icy, teenage looks.

"I'd like to lie back down next to you," he said. She nodded. He lay down and rolled on his stomach. She looked down at him.

"I think the trouble is," he said, "is that this is no one-night stand. I'm gonna' kiss you and we're gonna' go to sleep. I don't know much right now, but I know I want to wake up next to you in the morning." She nodded again. She giggled.

"Prom queen," she said. "I said you were no prom queen."

"Don't tell Tiger," he said.

He leaned up on his elbows. She bent down to him. He kissed her smoky mouth, closed her eyes gently with his fingertips and kissed her lids. She slid down into his arms. He held her through the night, wide awake and with the most stubborn hard-on he'd ever had. He just held her, stroking her thick hair, murmuring to her when she woke. He didn't know how he knew to do that. He just did.

HE MOVED IN three weeks later. They found out the important things, he couldn't talk until he'd had his coffee, she faded by 9 P.M., they both woke up horny, he hated apologies, she hated explanations. They kept fighting. Suddenly out of nowhere, like those ferris wheel lights, a fight would blaze up, fast, hot and incandescent. They survived them. Frank saw them as weather, North country weather. He'd never liked the year he'd lived in southern California, where each day's air and sky were exactly like the day's before.

That fall, the kid moved out and they were alone. They liked it. About once a month, with semisarcastic nostalgia, they'd hit the Cordial for a few beers, spar with Tiger, make a show of tipping Sandy, and drive out to the Sandbar. The old lady owner had died and her daughter, a huge, gaudy woman, was cooking. She'd lean out of the kitchen, leer at Frank and send them the best of the scallops. The band was just as awful, but they'd gotten to almost like the jam-sweet ballads and the thudding stuff the band called "country metal." Honey said that her life didn't feel like one of those damn songs anymore. That made the difference.

ONE THING that surprised Frank was that he still liked to kiss her. He'd always been like most guys, once he got to the real thing, the kissing sort of faded away. But with Honey, he felt like a teenager. They'd finish off a Friday summer night with a drive to the stretch of sand below the rock wall. They'd sit and watch the slow stars, and maybe neck a little, or a lot. One thick summer night when the apartment was a swamp, they'd stayed all night, spotting meteors, drinking Irish coffee out of a thermos, kissing the whiskey off each others lips. Four A.M., they'd driven back to an all-night diner for breakfast, a little hungover and wired, gentle from lack of sleep, their faces tender and far from young.

They didn't see people much. It was easier just being together. They bought a VCR and watched all the movies they wanted.

"No more cooking," Honey said, so they'd pick up ribs or fried rice or Italian to go and sit in the blue light of those old and new movies, drinking beer or maybe not. Honey would doze off, her blonde head in Frank's lap.

They got their vacations at the same time and discovered that they loved to drive and drive in Frank's maroon-and-black Monte Carlo, with the stereo blasting—Seger, Springsteen, Sinatra. Tiger taught Honey to love k.d. laing. Frank put up with it. She'd lay her head back on the seat and close her eyes, her fists tapping out the music on her thighs. It always got him hot. They ate breakfast three times a day. She collected bumper stickers. Back home, she plastered the refrigerator with them. They talked about getting a camper. Frank taught her how to fish. Weekends, they'd go up to the marina, rent a boat and motor and fish all day Sunday, hauling iridescent lake bass from the gray water. She hated to see their colors fade. They'd give the fish away and go to the Sandbar. It was a lot of happiness, nothing but happiness.

"There's never been a time like this," Honey said, and for as often as she'd said that old, old line, this time it was true.

SO OF COURSE, Honey got sick. She was tired, too tired. There was a month or six of thinking that it was change of season or middle-age woman's troubles or a little too much beer. Frank nagged her to see a doctor. When she did, it was too late to stop anything but the pain.

She took the treatments, the radiation, the pills, the poison, and hated them. She told Frank she could stand the pain better than feeling so sick to her stomach that her blood ached. She said she could forget pain if she was having a good time, but the nausea cut through everything. He begged her to continue. He took sick days to drive her to the clinic. He stood by her through the knife-keen minutes of retching and the hours, somehow worse, that she sat on the edge of the couch, not able to bear his touch, fighting off the nausea. As much as he hated seeing the no-color of her face, he believed the nausea was a sign she was fighting back, a sign that the treatment was working. He talked a lot about them licking It together. Together. Closer because of It. He'd heard that could happen.

On a late summer afternoon, in the thick, wet heat outside the icy ozone air of the clinic, she told him she wasn't having any more treatments. She was done. It seemed to him that her words ripped his gut. As they sat in the front seat of the car, with all the raggedness inside both of them, he could hardly look at her.

"I got up last night," she said. "I sat out on the back stoop. The treatment had worn off. I was a little hungry. Boy, did that feel good! It made me brave. I watched the stars move across the sky. There were Northern Lights. Pink and green. So pretty. No big deal, but all of a sudden I could feel my body. I felt peaceful. I felt horny. I got up and walked through the wet grass." She paused. "I wanted a peanut butter sandwich and I knew for sure that I was going to die."

Frank grabbed her hands.

"Don't say that, babe," he said.

"Don't you say *that*. If you love me, just listen. I realized I am going to die. I'm going to die soon and I know just how I want to live until then. I want your help."

In that moment, he saw her become movie-star beautiful and it scared the piss out of him. He felt dizzy.

"I want your help," she said again. "Frank." And it was as if Honey was already a million, million miles away, her voice coming to him from outer space. That was when they planned the unplanned trip. That was when he started faking.

"Hey, you," Honey said softly, "you okay?"

"I'm great," he said against her slack breasts. "Let's get cleaned up and hit the road."

They ate breakfast in a cute cafe she had picked out the day before. The owner was trying. There were checked cotton tablecloths, the home fries were thick with onions, the biscuits fat. But while Honey picked at her fruit and yoghurt, Frank watched a puddle of grease seep out of his "country omelet" and he remembered with numb longing, breakfast at his grandma's table: the hunks of apple pie, the home-made sausage, the way she served that meal morning after morning, harvest after harvest. Honey smiled at him. He winked and shoved a forkful of the slick eggs into his mouth.

On their way out, she stopped to read the posters taped to the front door.

"It'd be fun to live here," she said. "Look, dances, pot lucks, all kinds of stuff."

Middle-aged rich-hippie shit! he thought, but kept his mouth shut. He just watched her eyes glitter while that new, mysterious smile played over her lips, and he was surprised that pick-ups didn't careen onto the sidewalk, their drivers struck stupid by her beauty. He took her arm, a bundle of bones under her quilted cotton jacket and he moved her gently away from the door, out into the street. She clung to him, chattering happily.

"Babe," she said, "let's go get a map, stick a pin in it, and go there. Okay?" He nodded.

Holding her close, he covered her eyes while she leaned over the map on the car hood and stabbed it, somewhere in southern Utah, near a town called Moab, a park called Arches. She turned in his arms and kissed his cheek.

"Let's do it," she laughed. "No guidebooks, no motel reservations, no nothing. We'll be gypsies!"

They bought film for his old battered camera, two jugs of water, a bag of apples, a pound of sharp cheddar, a six-pack, and a carton of cigarettes. Heading north on a strip of highway that could have been anywhere in the States, Frank glared straight ahead.

"I thought this was frontier," he snapped. "I never saw so many muffler franchises in my life…must be rough roads out here."

"Rough drivers," Honey said. A rusting, primer-blotched Chevy cut dead in front of them.

"Assholes," Frank said. Honey slapped his arm.

"Hey, they're just kids," she said.

"What they need," he said, "is a good war."

They were quiet for a long time. He thought he ought to say something, but he felt too tight, too mean. Honey opened her window and lit a cigarette. He glanced over at her profile, the sweet, pared line of her jaw. She closed her eyes. The lids were like the petals of some bruised flower. He wanted to kiss them and he wanted never to see them again. He wanted to tell her how he felt, but as she exhaled blue smoke into the window's slipstream, he felt himself choke on the wanting.

"Look!" she cried and pointed to an ancient Dodge truck, draped with blankets and shawls, bright as electronic rainbows. A hard breeze jerked some of them up and away from the tailgate. They trembled in the air like wings. Frank thought of a trained falcon one of the guys had brought into the Cordial, its eyes blinded by a leather hood, its talons digging into its owner's studded wrist band. It had sat there motionless and silent. Under its feathered belly, there had been some awful quiver of muscle, as though deep inside, it leapt and was yanked back and leapt again.

"Let's stop," she cried. "It says they sell real Indian jewelry."

"On the way back," he said shortly. She nodded.

A hundred or so miles up the road at Tsegi, Frank saw the smooth burnt-orange folds of sandstone flowing back into the hidden canyons and he wanted to stop the car, get out and run until his breath was gone. He wanted to disappear back into those shadowed clefts. He would just lie down on that warm stone that must have been the belly of the earth, and rest there until it was all over. In that peace. Then he saw the shards of broken beer bottles, the metal trailers between him and the canyons. Something, a used diaper, a torn potato chip bag, blew up off the road and flapped past the windshield.

Drive on, he said to himself. Don't mean nothin', drive on.

Monument Valley, Honey made him pull over to the side of the road, so she could take pictures. She posed him against the shadowed base of a towering wedge of black rock. He didn't know what to do with his arms and hands. He felt like a twelve-year old kid. He suddenly wanted to punch somebody. She folded his arms over his chest and backed away, the mid-afternoon sun glinting in her hair.

Like a fuckin' angel, he thought.

"You're beautiful," she said. "You look like a real cowboy."

He forced himself to grin. The muscles in his face felt strange, like when he smoked reefer. He looked down at his feet. The sand sparkled with broken glass.

"Babe," he said, "how can people do this?" Honey pulled his arm around her.

"Hey," she said, "lighten up. This is somebody else's home. I've had to pick up your beer cans more than once." She kissed him. "Cease-fire, Sarge, okay?"

"Yeah," he said. "I think the altitude got to me. I'm tired. Could you drive?"

She patted his butt. "Sure."

They swung down over the narrow bridge in Mexican Hat, past cottonwoods in Bluff, stopped for chili and corn bread in Blanding, and drove through sunset and black pine into Monticello.

"I'm ready to stop," Honey said, "let's stop, get up early, and drive through this in daylight. I don't want to miss anything."

"It's just rocks," he started to say, then stopped himself.

She made it through the night okay and woke before dawn. He'd been watching her sleep, terrified by the cool beauty of her face in the blue motel light. She looked like a perfect ice sculpture.

They reached Moab by early morning and stopped for breakfast at a cutesy cafe on the main drag. The Genuine Home-style hashed browns were crisp and perfectly oval. He'd seen the package in super market freezers more than once. There was no real coffee, just espresso that they soaked you three bucks for. He listened to a big guy in a cream Stetson bitch about the E.P.A. screwing with his development. The waitress was all wide-eyed attention. When the big guy left, she snarled something to the cashier that Frank couldn't quite hear. She caught him listening and flashed a fluorescent smile. Honey ate a stack of pancakes.

"I can't tell you how good it is to have food taste good," she said, "and stay down. I feel like a new woman."

He was relieved when they were back on the road. They crossed the Colorado. It wasn't what he'd expected. He'd thought it would be clear and green. It was silty, a drab olive. You could hear it constantly. Honey asked him to turn around. She wanted to drive a ways up river and stop and touch the water.

They drove into a little side canyon on the other side of the highway. Even there, he could hear the river. He closed his eyes, heard Honey run ahead. He found her crouched by the side of a pool fed by a mineral-stained seep in the canyon wall. The sandy lip of the puddle was obliterated by trash and pop cans. Ferns and some kind of hanging flower, purple and delicate, grew out of the wet rock face. Honey looked up at him, the magic smile on her face.

"Isn't it wonderful?" she said. "They're growing right out of the rock."

He saw the burger box next to her right foot and he wanted to hit her. He stood above her, his arms heavy as rock, his big hands clenched. He wanted to smash her face into the trashed sand and leave her there. He reached down and stroked her hair.

"I wonder how they do that?" he said and knelt down beside her. He knew, in that moment, how it was one afternoon that Big Dave had left the Cordial, climbed into his red Bronco, driven to the lake and blown out his brains. He wanted to tell her that and he knew that if he did, he might as well kill her, right there, right then.

They crossed the highway and walked down to the pebble beach. A feathery plant spilled down from the highway, its blossoms catching light and holding it. Honey took off her sneakers and waded into the water.

"Damn!" she said. "This'll kill the pain!" Frank dipped his hand into the water and splashed his face. It was rock-cold, bone-cold, a cold he'd once held in his arms. "Sarge," the kid had said, "not yet."

Pebbles glinted at shoreline. He picked one up, a tiny thing, gray and white and mica-flecked, and slipped it into her jacket pocket.

"Thanks," she smiled. Slowly, she walked across the wet sand and stopped. She looked down at her wet foot prints. Frank thought he saw something in her face, something that touched the beauty, then was gone. She leaned on him and slid into her sneakers.

"Let's go see the arches," she said. "I've had the canyon. I've had the river. I'm ready for the rocks."

He patted her butt. She pressed against him and kissed him. Her mouth felt greedy, her lips too full, her teeth sharp against his mouth. He pushed away the feeling that she was feeding on him. She took hold of him.

"I'm ready for *you*," she said.

"Later," he tried to sound lusty. "First, the arches."

DRIVING UP the switchbacks into the park, he couldn't figure out his feelings. He was as tired as if he'd worked a full day in drenched August heat. He was tense, as wired and racy as he'd been in Nam, buzzed out on Army speed, seeing everything, hearing every sound.

Honey was quiet. They came out into a landscape that seemed both alien and more of the earth than any place he'd ever seen,.

"It makes me want to cry," she whispered. If earth was flesh, this was earth both male and female, vulnerable and eternal, new-born and ancient. He didn't know the names of any of the formations and he was glad.

"Look," Honey pointed. "Delicate Arch. Let's go there."

Frank drove down the washboard road, the car shuddering and fish-tailing, plumes of gritty dust rising behind them. His stomach lurched.

"Look at those cliffs," Honey said.

"Jesus!" he said. The gray cliffs were scored with bands of arsenic green.

Poison, he thought, *the color of the taste of a hangover.* He pressed his foot on the gas pedal, hard, because all he wanted to do was turn around, tear-ass out of that park and drive her past that damn smile, past her protests, past her fucking joy-in-life, to some clinic where doctors would, somehow, wrench the cancer from her body.

He pulled into the empty parking lot, into silence and heat and air so dry he could feel his eyeballs ache. She tucked apples and beer into a backpack and slid it over his shoulders. He remembered when they had both carried packs. She moved out ahead of him, her trim butt swaying. He knew she did it on purpose and he hated her for it. They walked past an empty corral and a sod dug-out, its walls green and sickly with some mineral seep.

She led him across a suspension bridge over a clear black creek. He couldn't get the rhythm of the bridge's bounce. He was clumsy and red-faced and baffled. He wondered about the creek. Had they used it for animals? Was it safe to drink? He saw the gray shoreline blurred by chalky green residue. What few flowers grew there were pale and shrivelled.

The switchbacks rose abruptly before them. Honey started out with her wild woman's stride but, after a few steps, she stopped.

"Whew," she said. "Took me by surprise." Frank set his hand in the middle of her back and pushed her gently ahead. She smiled back over her shoulder. "You'll never let me hear the end of this."

At the top of the switchbacks, they paused. Frank looked out across the barren valley. Everywhere, the rock was harsh and broken, the ledges and mesas looked burnt. He found himself remembering gouged earth, great teak trees shattered, the once-wet earth beneath his boots black and steaming, and, later when it cooled and you picked it up, crumbling in your hands.

It occurred to him that he might be having a flashback. But, Honey was next to him and there was nothing lush or green about this place. This air was as dry as the air in Nam had been wet. Nothing was veiled. What you saw was what you got. In the cliffs along the trail, the rocks looked like rough opals. They climbed slowly up onto the bare pink slickrock, past a pothole choked with larvae, slowly, more slowly up over the rock edge onto soft sand. Honey motioned him to stop.

"Can't breathe," she whispered. He put his arm around her and braced her against his side. She trembled. He heard the air moving harshly in and out of her throat. In front of them, the hills and mesas had shrunk to striped ribbons, wine and gray-green and distant purple.

"I'm okay," she said. They hiked on into a four-foot-high amphitheater.

The rosy stone curved down to clean sand, damp where the shadows fell, delicate claw prints tracing into the wetness and out. Honey sat down and looked up at him. He stepped aside and let the sun fall full on her face.

"Thanks," she said softly. "That feels so good. Come sit by me, babe. Please."

They sat in that good strong light, eating apples and drinking warm beer. Below them, the seep dried. The tracks remained. Honey brushed her hair away from her face. She was golden. The climb had reddened her cheeks, trail dust shimmered on her skin. He brushed it away gently. He couldn't look away. He wondered what she would see in his face, if she turned to look at him, if he couldn't look away. They climbed to their feet and moved on.

The trail twisted to the right, past a deep red valley and a shadowed arch. Someone had set cairns to mark the way. They seemed ancient. Solid rock rose to the south. Only air fell away to their left. A ledge curved up along the rock. Honey came to its edge and disappeared around the corner. Frank followed.

She was gone. Below him, balanced on sloping slickrock, Delicate Arch curved up and over the horizon. It could have been floating there, buoyed by the air currents, anchored by sunlight. He heard footsteps. He held his breath. Honey reappeared from between two huge boulders and began to walk out toward the arch. Frank sat down on a low shelf. Through the arch's heart, he could see distant mountains, a wedge of pure blue sky and rock, indigo, burnt orange, ashen. He let his hands dangle between his knees. His pulse beat strong and steady in his wrists.

Maybe I'll feel something, he thought.

What he saw could have been a postcard, a tourist come-on, a miracle. Then, Honey was at the far curve of the arch. She waved. He took the camera from his neck and fitted the telephoto lens. Honey moved slowly into the opening of the arch and he saw how big it really was. Honey waved again. Numb as stone, harder than the rock beneath him, he moved the camera up to his eye.

Space narrowed. Through that tunnel, he saw the flat blue sky and he thought about the way her death had already narrowed time, as though the two of them, each moment together, moved alone toward the end of a dark passageway.

As he lowered the camera, slowly, more slowly, his pulse quickening in his throat, the keystone of the arch floated into sight, the stone framed mountains, a blur of bird, the purple mesas; down through the air and light he seemed to drift, to come to see clearly the shape of Honey's skull, her ragged hair, her ravaged face, her jaundiced skin stretched tight and dry as parchment over her sharp bones; then her taut smile, her withered neck and shrunken body. She swung out one hip, arched her back and raised her head, vamping him, fluttering her lashes over her pained and glittering eyes. It was hideous. She was hideous. He saw that.

Her face. Her body. He took them in as flesh takes shrapnel, and snapped the picture, his finger moving automatically, his sight obliterated by a rush of tears.

"Thank you," he whispered, set down the camera and stepped out across the bright, bare rock.

photo by Badger, 1995

M ARY SOJOURNER writes short stories, essays, novels—*Sisters of the Dream*, 1989 and *Going Through Ghosts*, in progress—and commentaries for National Public Radio. She came west in 1985 to fight for the Earth and write. She is bewitched by the Mojave and makes her home in Flagstaff, Arizona.

Ten percent of the profits from *Delicate* will go to hard-core environmental groups.

Any tool is a weapon if you hold it right. —ANI DIFRANCO